POINT OPTION

POINT OPTION

A Time-Travel Military Thriller

IAN A. O'CONNOR

Pegasus Publishing & Entertainment Group

LIBRARY OF CONGRESS CATALOGUING-IN-PUBLICATION DATA
Library of Congress Control Number: 2021912135

O'Connor, Ian A., 1944-

Point Option
Fiction - -Novel
Thriller – Military – Mystery - Action – Adventure – Sci-Fi (Softcover)

ISBN-13: 978-1-7374229-0-7 – Trade Paperback
ISBN-13: 978-1-7374229-4-0 – Kindle e-book
©2021 Ian A. O'Connor. All rights reserved

Pegasus Publishing & Entertainment Group - USA
First Printing, October 29, 2021

Cover artist: Kim D. Lyman
Jacket design: Muhammad Hassaan
Interior design: Accuracy4sure (*fiverr*)

Visit the author at: www.ianaoconnor.com
Contact the author at: ianaoconnor@ianaoconnor.com

This is a work of fiction.

Printed in the United States of America
LSC-C
1 3 5 7 9 10 8 6 4 2

Pegasus Publishing & Entertainment Group

Acknowledgement

In the Pacific Theater during WWII … "In order to allow pilots to navigate back to their aircraft carriers after a long search, or strike mission, they had to know where the carrier would be after the mission was completed. This was known as "Point Option."…Point Option was given as a course and speed the carrier would follow while the aircraft were away, allowing each pilot to calculate where his carrier would be, depending on the length of the mission."

SCRATCH ONE FLATTOP: THE FIRST CARRIER AIR CAMPAIGN AND THE BATTLE OF THE CORAL SEA
By Robert C. Stern
Indiana University Press, Kindle Edition, May 14, 2019

*Carrier Air Wing Twelve (RCVW-12) is portrayed as being aboard the *USS Lyndon Baines Johnson*. In reality, it was a Reserve Wing which was disestablished on 30 June 1970. In this story it is portrayed as the active Carrier Air Wing Twelve based at NAS Oceana, VA. (See Chapter 2)

I owe an extra special thanks to Margaret Datzman O'Connor who again undertook the unenviable task of editing my manuscript

Dedication

This book is dedicated to my wife, Candice Myers O'Connor, still my forever very best friend.

Fiction Titles by Ian A. O'Connor

- ❖ *The Twilight of the Day*
- ❖ *The Seventh Seal*
- ❖ *The Barbarossa Covenant*
- ❖ *The Wrong Road Home*
- ❖ *Point Option*

Nonfiction Titles by Ian A. O'Connor
With Howard C. "Scrappy" Johnson
SCRAPPY: Memoir of a U. S. Fighter Pilot in Korea and   Vietnam

Short Story Title by Ian A. O'Connor
"The Last Grandmaster"

Contents

PROLOGUE

The Eastern Atlantic - Off the Spanish Coast

June 16th – June 20th

The Russian nuclear-powered, multi-purpose submarine *Yakutsk* was cruising at a depth of 200 meters and on a heading of 170 degrees. She was twenty miles off the coast of Southern Spain, moving quietly at sixteen knots which was less than half of her thirty-five-knot capability.

Yakutsk was the pride of the Northern Fleet. The Laika-class, fifth generation submarine was built at a cost of 180 billion rubles (USD three billion) and had taken nine years to complete. Her ten officers and one hundred twenty-four submariners were the best of the best.

"Captain, here it comes again," the sonar operator called out in an excited voice. Captain First Rank Dimitri Gasparin quickly moved to a position behind the seated sailor, donned a set of headphones and listened intently while studying the acoustical "waterfall" display on the sizeable flatscreens before them. Until an hour ago, this sound was unlike anything he had ever heard. His puzzled frown spoke volumes. Activity in the control room had now ceased, all eyes on their captain and the passive sonar operator.

"You're saying this thing is surrounding us again, but it's closing faster than before?"

"Yes, Captain, and it's pulsating as it moves towards us. At the present speed we will collide in thirty seconds, maybe less."

"And you still insist the *thing* has no mass, yet it's painting this return on your screen?" The captain removed his earphones. What the man was telling him was a physical impossibility.

The sailor clamped both hands all the tighter over his headphones. "This is not a false return, Captain, I'm certain. Fifteen seconds to impact, and this time it will be bad."

"Prepare for impact," Gasparin called out, and his executive officer immediately repeated the command on the boat's intercom to all compartments.

The *Yakutsk* and the unknown object collided with such force that it caused the twelve thousand ton vessel to be tossed to starboard, creating a violent rolling motion which pitched it ninety degrees off vertical. For a horror-filled moment, Gasparin thought his boat would roll over completely. A thunderous, external explosion erupted somewhere close to the hull, causing a series of undulating shudders up and down the entire structure.

As the *Yakutsk* struggled to right itself by activating its computer-assisted trim tanks, a huge globe of emerald green ball lightning appeared out of nowhere, raced the length of the boat, careening from deck to ceiling and back down again, passing through the watertight steel bulkheads, and leaving dozens of flashing and arcing electrical panels in its wake. Several men screamed as the hellish sphere bounced off them, but not before setting two sailors' heads afire. The fiery mass exited the hull, a lingering smell of burning sulphur a testament to its unholy presence. The boat's lights flickered once, went out, then came back on a few seconds later. And above all the noise in the control room, everyone heard the sonar operator's terrified scream as he tore off his headphones, blood pouring from both ears.

Pandemonium reigned.

This cannot be happening, Gasparin thought, his heart pounding and mind racing, refusing to believe what he was seeing. *Ball lightning only occurs during a severe thunderstorm; it can't enter a submarine five hundred feet down in the ocean!* He heard his crew calling out to one another, the fear in their voices a confirmation they realized their deaths were imminent.

A minute passed … another … a third … then silence and answered prayers. They were still alive, and the *Yakutsk* was intact.

"Stop engine," Gasparin commanded. Charging ahead without knowing the damage done to the *Yakutsk* would be foolhardy. Plus, he had no idea how his mainframe computer and inertial navigation system had fared under the power surge. He flicked on the intercom. "This is the Captain. I need damage reports from all departments. Nuclear Engineering, report immediately."

It took a minute for him to hear back. "Captain, this is nuclear, Serdyukov reporting. The reactor is intact, it seems to be functioning normally, there are no radiation leaks, but the ship's computer is telling me the reactor shut itself down for several seconds. I know that's impossible, Sir," he added quickly, "but that's apparently what's happened."

"Very well, Lieutenant, give me a full report once everything else is under control."

One hour later, Gasparin sat huddled with his executive officer, Captain Second Rank (Commander) Ivan Medvedev to summarize what they knew. No one was dead, but four sailors were severely injured: the passive sonar operator, two with severe burns to their heads and faces, and one with a broken leg. However, the hull was undamaged, and no water leaks were found. But the best news was the reactor. Captain-Lieutenant (Lieutenant) Alexander Serdyukov, the head of Nuclear Engineering declared it completely safe, a finding supported by the civilian technical representative aboard from the reactor's prime contractor, Afrikantov OKBM.

But the report from the communications department was not good. Nearly all the *Yakutsk's* electronics were inoperable, destroyed by the electrical power surge.

* * * * *

Thursday Morning - June 17th

"Captain to the control room." Medvedev was unable to hide the worry in his voice. It was midnight, and he had the conn. Gasparin arrived in less than a minute.

"Captain, Alex is now reporting problems with the reactor," he said in a low voice. "It started acting up about five minutes ago, but he says things are deteriorating. He might have to initiate an emergency shutdown. Also, more men are complaining they're feeling ill."

"Tell Alex to update us every ten minutes, and I want you to monitor the men. Now, do we have any of our onboard navigation and communications capabilities back online yet?"

"Very few, Sir. My recommendation is we take the boat up to deploy the photonics mast and look around. That will also let us call Severomorsk on the external satellite link. They need to be informed of our condition. And, if something happens to the reactor, well, at least we'll be close to the surface."

Gasparin had full confidence in his second-in-command. He nodded his agreement. "Very well, take us up to periscope depth." The word *periscope* was a misnomer, a throwback to a bygone era. Modern submarines had ceased using periscopes decades earlier in favor of the less obtrusive, but highly effective digital photo scanning devices.

Ten minutes later Gasparin had his eyes glued to the photonics, flat-panel display screen showing a 360 degree collection of real-time, color photographs of the ocean's surface. For some inexplicable reason, the photonics mast was one of the few electronic instruments still working. Using a joystick, he turned the camera around for a second sweep, this time moving it more slowly, having switched to an infrared lens. Nothing but empty ocean. He made a decision. "Rig for surfacing," he called out, loud enough for everyone to hear and spring into action.

Five minutes later Gasparin was up in the sail with two lookouts and a communications officer. He was surprised to find the weather considerably colder than he had expected. "Plug in the satellite phone, Stephen, and we'll talk with our friends at Northern Fleet Submarine Command. It's likely they'll order us home."

Fifteen minutes later, a visibly exasperated Gasparin had given up. He had been unable to make a connection with any secure Russian Navy satellite. At the same time, below in the control room, the senior communications officer had attempted to contact any Russian vessels on the portable UHF and HF radios, and then as a last resort, any ship at all. Nothing. Because they were on the surface with multiple antennas up, he had tried picking up FM stations in Spain on his personal Apple iPhone. Again, nothing but static. He assured the captain that the two radios he had used were undamaged simply because they had not been connected to the ship's communications suite when the power had surged. But he couldn't understand why he had failed to receive any signal from the many FM stations, or even make a phone call.

As Gasparin was readying to dive the *Yakutsk*, Medvedev made another suggestion. "Captain let's stay on the surface but move closer to the coast. It'll still be dark for three more hours; we know there are no ships out there, which means we'll be safe from prying eyes."

Two hours later the *Yakutsk* was sailing just below the surface on a southeasterly heading, making five knots. Captain First Rank Dimitri Gasparin was now a very worried submarine commander. He had sailed to within three miles of the Spanish coast and, from his vantage point high up in the sail, neither he, nor the two lookouts, had seen a thing. No lights from any towns lit up the night sky. There was not a single sign of civilization along the entire coastline.

"My best guess is there's been a widespread electrical power blackout in Spain," he said to Medvedev. "It could also be affecting Portugal, possibly parts of Southern France as well. We know this has been an unusually hot June in Southern Europe, which means their electric grid couldn't keep up with the high demand. But that's nothing new; it's happened in the past."

"You must be right, Captain, there can't be any other explanation. But that doesn't explain the bad satellite link." He shrugged. "Maybe things will be better after the sun comes up."

At six A. M., Nuclear Engineering reported that the reactor was now operating normally, and the problems of the past few hours had completely disappeared. The computer confirmed this finding, causing Gasparin to smile for the first time in hours. Forty-five minutes later, he ordered the *Yakutsk* back down to 200 meters, but instructed the helmsman to idle-in-place, using only enough power to compensate for the moving current. There was much work to be done before getting fully underway again.

* * * * *

Friday Morning - June 18th

Twenty-four hours later, Captain Gasparin knew the *Yakutsk* was doomed. The entire crew was now suffering from the unknown ailment, some close to death. Without warning, the reactor had ceased functioning entirely and was undergoing a time-consuming emergency shutdown to prevent the core from melting. The final blow had come when he had given the order to surface the boat. Nothing happened. Unbeknown to him, the air flasks had been damaged in the collision, so much so that they could no longer pump the compressed air necessary to displace the water in the ballast tanks, a task crucial for raising the boat. And even the emergency manual surfacing procedures had failed. The heating, ventilation, and air conditioning system (HVAC) had also been inoperable for the last seven hours, and the temperature inside the hull was showing 40 degrees Fahrenheit and falling. Water droplets had formed on all metal surfaces, and the glass screens on the monitors were obscured under a haze. The Banks of Lithium ion batteries were now the lone fragile lifeline powering the oxygen generators and the carbon dioxide scrubbers, the latter critical for removing that deadly gas from the air. The men had been ordered to their bunks to conserve precious oxygen, and the lighting had been reduced to only a few bulbs throughout the boat. Captain Gasparin and his crew were all aware they had just enough battery life to maybe last another forty hours if lucky then after that …

All aboard the *Yakutsk* prayed for the miracle they knew would never happen.

PART ONE

CHAPTER I

It wouldn't be correct to say she heard it first because he never heard it at all. Bolting upright, she covered her ears to shut out the offending clamor. After what seemed like an eternity, she reached across his sleeping figure and brought a hand down on top of the alarm clock. She found the light switch and snapped it on. What noise couldn't accomplish; light did. His breathing stopped, and an arm reached up in reflex action to guard his eyes against the enemy.

"Five o'clock, Dave," she whispered. "Are you sure you've got to go?" A long moment passed and she added, her voice wheedling, "Couldn't you call in sick or something?"

Dave Fleming laughed, then yawned. "Fat chance, but nice try."

"Just a thought," she mumbled, then threw her arms around her husband's neck and buried her head in his throat.

Fleming held her close for a long moment, stroking her hair, saying nothing. Finally, he glanced at the clock. Time to move.

Fifteen minutes later, both were seated at the kitchen table sipping coffee, she dressed in a flowered housecoat, he in an Air Force flightsuit.

"How long will you be gone?" she asked for the umpteenth time since being told of this assignment in February. It was now June, and both knew the answer.

"Honey, I'm not going to war," he said, reaching over and tweaking her nose. "This deployment is still considered part of the *Lyndon*

2

Baines Johnson's shakedown cruise. The carrier will be joining up with the rest of its strike group which is already in the Med. Its official name is *The Lyndon Baines Johnson Carrier Strike Group*, but I'm told all her sailors just refer to the carrier as the *LBJ*. Anyway, my guess is we'll be out there for about six weeks, maybe eight, tops. Then I'm taking leave, and we'll have a whole month to ourselves." He drained his cup then added softly, "I'm really looking forward to this assignment, Susan; it's a dream come true. A lot of guys I know would kill to be in my shoes."

Her answer was drowned out by the honking of a car horn.

"*Ohhh*, shit, that's going to piss off the entire block," Fleming said, jumping up from the table. In three short steps he had the kitchen door opened and began signaling frantically for silence. He turned and hugged his wife. "I'm going to miss you, honey, but I'll be back before you know it. Promise." They kissed for a long moment, then slowly separated.

She smiled bravely. "I know you'll have fun even though it'll be a lot of hard work. And I'm so proud of you, Dave, I really am."

"Remember, eight weeks at the most. I'll text you as soon as we land in Italy." He picked up two large duffel bags and went out to the waiting car. She stood in the doorway and waved until it disappeared up the street.

* * * * *

David Fleming, Major, United States Air Force, turned to face his friend, Bud Hamilton. Like Fleming, he too was dressed in a flightsuit, but his was Navy issue. He wore the insignia of a full lieutenant on his shoulders.

"We're finally rolling, old buddy," said Hamilton. "And I still can't believe my Navy is actually going to allow an Air Force "zoomie" to fly our jets off of our biggest, badass, newest aircraft carrier." He shook his head in mock disbelief, then with a quick, sideways glance, deadpanned, "Straight skinny, Major, are you really a carrier-qualified pilot?"

Fleming guffawed, then answered. "*Noooo*, but I can fake it. Look, if mentally challenged guys like you can do it, then it's got to be a no-brainer for a hotshot pilot like me. I promise not to let you down, *Percy*," he added, emphasizing his friend's hated first name.

Fleming knew he was wholly accepted by the Tiger Sharks, his new squadron, and by the entire carrier air wing. He was proud of his accomplishments. At thirty-two, he was a newly promoted major, but more importantly, one of only three from a pool of ninety Air Force pilot-applicants selected to serve a two-year tour with their sister service. And somewhere out there, three Navy exchange pilots had been selected to fill similar billets in the Air Force for the same two-year period. Traditionally, such assignments meant those chosen to serve in other branches were earmarked for bigger things, and David Fleming certainly saw himself as a man going places. Projecting ahead a few years, he would apply for a command slot within one of the other NATO air forces, but that was still a way off. This gig was going to be great; he could feel it all the way down to his toes.

They passed through the gates of Oceana Naval Air Station and drove towards the flightline, spotting the huge grey T-tail of the Air Force C-17 Globemaster parked on the ramp beside a cluster of hangers. This giant would fly fifty-eight men and women to Italy to join up with the *LBJ*, already in the Mediterranean. Most of the five-thousand-man crew, including the air wing was already aboard but, for one reason or another, this last group of stragglers had not been there when the carrier had sailed from Norfolk, Virginia, ten days earlier.

Hamilton parked the car in the lot next to the operations building, shut off the motor, and placed the keys under the front seat. "One of the wives will drive Marsha here later," he said. "No way that girl was getting up in the middle of the night just to see her old man off. She's been doing this goodbye stuff for far too long now. She's all too glad to have the house to herself and the kids for a spell."

4

They walked into the building and up to a counter swarming with people. They were checked in, their names confirmed on the manifest, and their bags tagged and placed on a cart. This was an Air Mobility Command (AMC) plane, the Air Force's answer to the scores of civilian airlines. It would be a no-frills flight with uncomfortable seating.

"No pretty faces and no hot meal this trip," Hamilton noted as they walked toward the plane. Each carried a box lunch under his arm, a meal for a journey that would last twelve hours, with a stop in the Azores before going on to Italy. Then, after an eight-hour rest stop, it would be down to the port and out to the waiting aircraft carrier.

They found seats toward the back of the plane. As the loadmaster closed the huge tail ramp, a first lieutenant called for attention.

"Listen up!" he shouted. Some ignored him completely. "Give me your attention!" he roared, and instantly there was silence. "That's better! OK, my name is Lieutenant Sirola, and I'm the aircraft commander. What I say goes for as long as you are on this plane. We want to make the flight as pleasant as possible, but there are some words I've got to say about safety." He spoke for five minutes, pointing out certain items peculiar to the C-17, explaining how the floatation equipment worked, where the emergency exits were located, and what to do in the event of a ditching at sea or a crash on land.

"That's it, folks. Also, once we're in the air, if some of you would like to come up to the flight deck and see how we fly this big boy, that'll be fine with me. Just clear it with Sergeant Enwright, the loadmaster. We don't follow the same strict rules our friends in the airlines do about visiting the cockpit, but just don't tell anybody, OK?"

The four large engines were started, and the Globemaster taxied out to the end of the runway. After the runup check and clearance for takeoff was given, the two hundred eighty-thousand pound aircraft raced down the tarmac and lifted gracefully into the morning sky. In no time it was cruising at its assigned altitude for the first leg of the long journey.

"Ever fly one of these?" Hamilton asked.

"Never, thank God," replied Fleming "These guys put in some godawful long hours, and Air Mobility Command flying is about as tough as it gets. But it's a great steppingstone for pilots wanting to build up a lot of heavy-jet time to get hired with the airlines."

"So, your whole time has been in fighters?"

"Yeah. Out of flight school it was right into fast movers. First, as an F16 driver, then into F-15s, and now the Navy's F/A-18 Super Hornet. I'm still learning how to crash-land a good airplane onto a little piece of metal floating in the big bad sea."

"Man, we're going to make a real pilot out of you yet. Any candyass can land on a ten-thousand-foot runway, but only Navy jocks *really* know how to fly. OK, I'll include a couple of jarheads in that group," Hamilton allowed, begrudgingly, "and 1 say a couple, only because so very few of them are trainable."

This was a rude reference to Marine pilots who were trained by the Navy to Navy standards. All pilots in the Corps completed a series of carrier landings before earning their wings of gold, but their mission was close air support, and so they were usually not found in a carrier-based squadron.

"Shall I tell those two Marine pilots up front what you just said?" Fleming asked, a look of pure innocence on his face.

"You want to see me get whacked?" Hamilton replied, in mock terror. "I'll deny the whole thing, unless of course, you outrank them both and promise to protect me."

"Nope. You'd be on your own, pal." Both men laughed at the thought of tangling with the Marines.

Hamilton faced his friend, "Let me be serious for a minute, Dave. How does your wife really feel about this whole Navy assignment? Poor gal thought she had married a guy who would live his life on *terra firma*, but now, she finds her bunkmate has become an anchor clanker."

Fleming rearranged himself in the narrow, uncomfortable seat and waited a few seconds before replying. His face showed his concern, and he sighed. "Deep down, Bud, I really don't know. Ever since I checked in to Jax Naval Air for carrier qualifications school, she's been, well, different."

"Different, like how?"

"Several times since February I've had to waken her from what she said were recurring nightmares, but really it was always the same nightmare. They've obviously upset her, and when I ask her to tell me more about them, she talks about seeing my plane being hijacked by some unexplainable force, and I become lost forever at sea. She says the image is as real as can be, but then she gets embarrassed and changes the subject. So, yeah, I sometimes get the feeling she isn't thrilled about me flying with you guys, but I write it off to the fact that she doesn't know much about the Navy way of life. And the only thing she knows about aircraft carriers is what she has seen in old World War II flicks with newsreel footage showing planes crashing right and left onto their decks before skidding off into the ocean."

"I hear you," Hamilton replied, "and we do have our fair share of accidents the public never hears about. I guess a couple of the wives have told her some hair-raising stories. But she's become pretty close with Arlene Fitzpatrick from what I hear, right?" It was more a question than a statement of fact. "Arlene's a no-nonsense gal, so you know at least she'll get the straight skinny at all times from that lady."

Arlene Fitzpatrick was the squadron executive officer's wife. She had been a young Navy nurse who had met her husband while they were both stationed together during the early days of the resurgent ISIS War in Iraq. Now, ten years later, Arlene was the mother of three girls, and the wife of a well-respected full commander. All the wives seemed to gravitate toward Arlene for comfort and advice when their men were at sea.

"My Susan is hiding a strong lady behind that gorgeous face of hers. She'll do fine." The tone in Fleming's voice told his friend that subject was now closed.

* * * * *

Six hours after takeoff, they touched down in the Azores, where the aircraft commander announced a two-hour layover. Everyone was glad to deplane, walk around, and stretch cramped muscles. It was late afternoon, and all found the weather invigorating with a stiff breeze blowing from the north. An hour and forty-five minutes later, the flight was reboarded for the final leg to Naples.

Two hours in they encountered severe turbulence, causing many of the passengers to turn green and start reaching for air-sickness bags.

Even Fleming admitted to feeling a bit ragged, but Hamilton was no worse for the wear. However, he was able to empathize enough with Fleming who wanted no part of eating, so he excused himself and went up to the flight deck, taking his box lunch with him.

Touchdown came at a few minutes past one o'clock in the morning with most passengers now feeling fine, but tired. They had landed at Naples International Airport, three miles from the center of the city, and as everyone deplaned, they were boarded onto buses and driven to the Naval Support Activity Base located on the same property, which also housed the headquarters of the US Navy 6th Fleet.

Within forty minutes both pilots were sound asleep, but before drifting off, Fleming had found his thoughts harkening back to his wife's recurring nightmare of him disappearing forever while flying with the Navy. He shuddered involuntarily at the thought of such a thing ever happening.

CHAPTER 2

Friday morning – Friday afternoon June 18ᵗʰ

M ind if I join you, gentlemen?" The request came from a Navy lieutenant commander.

"Please, help yourself," said Fleming, nodding at the vacant chair to his right. He glanced at the man's nametag. HIRSHBERGER.

"Morning, Sir." This from Hamilton between sips of coffee.

Hirshberger seated himself, and as he arranged his breakfast, surreptitiously studied Fleming. "You must be the Air Force officer assigned to the *LBJ*. Allow me to welcome you on behalf of the meteorological department. The name's Joel."

"Dave Fleming. And this is Bud Hamilton."

Hirshberger was tall, rail-thin, with a neck full of chords and an Adam's apple that danced as he spoke. "You guys notice anything strange about the weather this morning?" he asked, slathering his toast with butter.

"Heavy fog," said Hamilton. "Of course, I've been up all of a half hour and it's already, let me see, oh, almost seven-fifteen. Why do you ask, Sir?"

"Well, I called base weather to get a rundown, and after what they told me, I'm thinking someone's flying on uppers over there."

"What do you mean?" Fleming asked.

Hirshberger filled his mouth and swallowed before replying. "This is my third tour in the Med, and the main reason I keep bouncing back is I speak Spanish and Italian fluently. Anyway, when I spoke

9

with the Italian meteorologist this morning, he tells me that things are totally messed up, and that he can't give me an accurate forecast. So, I ask why? He says his information is all screwy and I wouldn't buy it. I tell him to try me, and boy, does he ever," Hirshberger said, and followed up with a loud harrumph. "He then proceeds to give me a weather report that is nothing short of nonsense. It did absolutely nothing to explain the heavy ground-hugging fog we had earlier, you know, stuff such as the basic meteorological correlation between dewpoint and temperature. And the rest of his briefing was worse. But just as I was beginning to think he had a thing against Americans, he apologizes, and says there must be something wrong with his instruments. Then he tells me his readings are totally at odds with what he's receiving from other weather stations, some as close as fifteen miles away."

Hirshberger obviously thought this a good time to finish eating because he hunched over his plate and began scooping up food as if his breakfast companions were about to steal it.

"This ever happen before?" Fleming asked after a few minutes of silence.

Hirshberger shook his head. "Nope. The man said it started at five A.M., and without warning. Before that, everything was normal. Then the fog came. It rolled in really fast and totally unexpected, because none of the meteorological conditions at the time were conducive to fog. Then he volunteered this little nugget: All radio communications for the past couple of hours have been spotty and broken at best, that the airport's radar has become so unreliable that the tower has closed the field to all landings and departures, civilian and military, even though the field is technically not below minimums. They're diverting all incoming traffic to alternates until further notice. It's one helluva a mess."

"So, what do you make of it?" Fleming asked. "You think they're maybe trying to cover for someone's screwup?"

"Don't know, but I intend to check it out as soon as I get aboard the *LBJ*. Those folks are the best anywhere, bar none. Not only does the entire Sixth Fleet look to us for accurate weather reports, but even the Russkies pay attention when we broadcast weather updates in the open. Come visit us when you get squared away, Major, guaranteed you'll be impressed."

"The name's Dave, and, yes, I'll take you up on your offer, Joel. Thanks."

* * * * *

At ten minutes to nine they boarded a waiting bus. The fog had lifted, and all indications pointed towards a beautiful, clear day. The three officers sat on the large bench-seat at the rear, with Fleming in the middle. His face took on a puzzled look, and he turned to Hirshberger.

"You know, just before breakfast I called my wife on my cell, and the connection was as clear as if she was right next door. We spoke for about twenty seconds, then just as abruptly as that," he said, snapping his fingers, "the signal was dropped. I tried redialing her a couple of times, but no luck. I wonder if that had anything to do with the weather anomaly?"

"My hunch would be yes," said Hirshberger. "It makes sense. Most of your international calls from Europe to America are bounced off satellites nowadays, and not routed through undersea cables. But as to the how and the why it happened, well, I can't answer that one, but I'll definitely find out more once we're aboard. My curiosity's now up, to say the least."

* * * * *

"Gentlemen, may I draw your attention to the *United States Ship, Lyndon Baines Johnson,* the greatest fighting machine ever built," Hamilton said, as if conducting a navy yard tour for a group of civilians. "Technically speaking, she's a *Ford Class* carrier, although she is slightly larger than her two sister ships, the *Ford* and the *Kennedy.* She measures one thousand two hundred feet from bow to stern and

11

displaces just over one hundred two thousand long tons. But unlike the old *Enterprise*, which had eight nuclear reactors, the *LBJ* has only two for her four shafts, and they can propel her at speeds which, although are still classified, are generally believed to be in excess of thirty knots. When she ..."

"We surrender! We surrender!" Hirshberger said, with hands held high.

"And I thought I was going to impress you with all my knowledge," Hamilton replied.

Fleming followed his Navy friends off the tender now tied to the Stern Dock and climbed up a metal accommodation ladder. He stole a quick glance back down to the water, and the several launches shuttling back and forth to the pier. He stepped aboard the *LBJ* via the aft 'officers brow' leading to the Quarterdeck, and after saluting the flag, turned to the officer of the deck, and saluted again.

"Permission to come aboard?" he asked the duty officer, a lieutenant commander.

His salute was returned with a "Permission granted." A hand reached out. "Welcome to the *LBJ*, Major. It's a pleasure to have you aboard. If there's anything we can do to help you in your transition from Air Force to Navy, just ask."

"Thank you, I'm sure I'll feel at home in no time." He followed Hamilton under cover, where they were met by a lieutenant j.g., in a flightsuit, who introduced himself and volunteered to show them to their quarters.

The two officers followed the young officer from the hangar deck, up the ladderwell to the deck above. They walked down a well-lit, but cramped and narrow companionway smelling of new paint and deck cleaner. Fleming found it hard to believe he was on a ship. There was no motion at all, and after a few more turns down a maze of other companionways, their guide paused at a door and nodded to Hamilton. Fleming remembered that to all sailors, doors were called hatches, stairs were ladders, and walls were bulkheads, the language of the sea.

"This will be your quarters, Mr. Hamilton. Major, you will be three down on the right."

"Dave, I'll meet you in about fifteen minutes, then we can go check in at operations."

"Sounds good," replied Fleming, heading towards his own cabin. He was handed a key.

"You weren't aboard for the air wing shakedown cruise were you, Sir?"

"No, why do you ask?"

"I can give you some help with directions for getting about, that is until you have a better idea where everything is. This is a mighty big ship."

"Appreciate the thought," said Fleming. "Lieutenant Hamilton was aboard for the shakedown, so he'll have to be my nursemaid for a while. Thanks for the help, and I'll see you in ops." As he was about to enter his cabin, he stopped. "Any idea when we get under way?"

"We're scheduled to weigh anchor at twelve hundred hours, Sir. That's about forty minutes from now," the lieutenant replied, glancing at his watch. "The admiral will be moving his flag back onto the *LBJ* sometime around eleven-thirty, and once that's complete, then we're off."

"Thanks again." Fleming returned the salute and entered his small stateroom. There were two bunks, and he noticed that the lower berth was already made up while the upper had blankets and linens lying on top of the bare mattress. That would be his. He walked to his bed and pressed down on the mattress. It was brand new, made from a firm foam material, and ample in length and width. A small reading lamp was affixed to the headboard which he tested by snapping it on and off a couple of times in rapid succession.

There were two of everything in the room: lockers, desks, and chairs, except for a single hand basin with hot and cold faucets wedged in a corner. Above it was a mirror with lights and electrical outlets conveniently nearby.

He turned his attention to the desks. Both were metal with Formica tops, and equipped with bolted-down reading lamps. His eyes drifted toward a framed photograph on the closest one. He studied the picture. The color photo showed a woman and two children standing in front of a church. He shuddered. Without a doubt they were the homeliest threesome he had ever seen.

"Oh, lordy me!" he whispered, eyes transfixed to the photograph. He blinked and looked again. It hadn't changed. He walked over to the lockers. One had a paper nameplate: Lt. Commander Joseph E. Caldwell, USN.

At least he now knew his companion's name. Just as he opened his empty locker there was a sharp knock at the door. A slick-sleeved seaman stood at attention with his two duffel bags.

The seaman gave a puzzled look as he saw the Air Force uniform. "Your gear, Sir," he mumbled while saluting.

"Thank you, sailor, I'll take them in." For the next ten minutes he stowed away his gear and finished by placing Susan's photograph on his desk. He was debating whether or not to change into a flightsuit when a knock on the door interrupted him.

Hamilton strolled in and looked around. He stared at the photo of Caldwell's wife and children. "I see you've already met the princess. Cute, huh? And how about the little darlings?"

"Lovely!" was Fleming's one word whispered reply.

"You know, I've met her a couple of times, " Hamilton continued, holding the photograph up for closer scrutiny, "and I've got to admit, this photographer is really good. In real life she's not nearly as pretty."

"Say no more," commanded Fleming. "Let's get out of here."

* * * * *

14

As they entered the main wing ready room, a loudspeaker came to life, and the bosun's mate announced the arrival of the Strike Group Commander, Rear Admiral Stanford Taylor.

Nobody seemed to pay the slightest attention. Hamilton introduced Fleming to various members of the air arm. They were mostly junior grade officers: ensigns, and lieutenants, all exuding a similar air of superiority. Not an obtrusive in-your-face kind of cockiness, Fleming thought, but rather theirs was an attitude of men who were confident in their unique skills.

Someone called the room to attention. Everyone froze, and stood silent and erect.

"Carry on," said a silver-haired captain striding into the room followed by another captain.

"That's the Carrier Air Wing Commander (CAG) and his executive officer," Hamilton said out of the side of his mouth.

The captain spotted the Air Force blue uniform and came over to Fleming. "Welcome aboard, Fleming," he said, glancing at the name tag while offering his hand. "My name's Gowdy, and I'm the CAG. It's good to have you with us. I know it was a last-minute change of air wings for you, but I hope you'll enjoy your tour flying with us."

"Thank you, Captain, and I'm sure I will," Fleming replied. The change that Gowdy referred to was that Fleming's orders had been re-cut, literally at the last minute. The new ones assigned him to the *LBJ* rather than to the Carrier Air Wing (CVW) that was currently serving aboard the *Gerald R. Ford*. No explanation had been given. He had received the new set of orders less than a week earlier, thus the reason he had not been aboard for the shakedown cruise with the four strike fighter squadrons in Carrier Air Wing-12* assigned to the *LBJ*. "I'll want to speak with you later, Fleming, once we're under way."

Gowdy turned to face the assembled flyers. "Gentlemen, and ... ladies," he began, nodding his acknowledgment in the direction of two female pilots. "I want a meeting in the wardroom with all of the wing's flying officers at sixteen hundred hours. Pass the word along to your buddies who aren't here now, even though the info will be piped

15

later to all areas of the ship. My plan is to get to flight quarters as quickly as possible, so we've got a lot of hard work and long days ahead of us. I expect everyone to do his or her part in ironing out any bugs, and I speak for the admiral when I say that this air wing must be in A-one fighting condition in no time." He paused and looked around. "I want to see the strike squadron commanders and executive officers in Charlie Tate's ready room in ten minutes."

He turned to the group closest, and along with them studied a TV monitor which showed a freeze-frame photo of the *LBJ*'s port side anchor along with a digital clock ticking off the hours, minutes, and seconds.

"You have a number, Sir?" asked a freckle-faced ensign. He was referring to the age-old Navy tradition of betting among a crew as to the exact moment the ship they were serving aboard would either drop anchor coming into a port, or weigh anchor upon leaving. Among the thousands of sailors on the *LBJ*, there would have been a hundred various pools, and probably as much as a total of fifty thousand dollars riding on such an insignificant event as to when the ship would weigh anchor. But to all hands on the *LBJ*, this event was far from insignificant.

"I do indeed." No sooner than Gowdy had spoken, the chain began to move, and as the anchor broke the surface, the numbers on the digital clock froze on the screen.

The loudspeakers in the wardroom came to life.

"All hands, now hear this. The *LBJ* is under way having weighed anchor at twelve hundred hours, four minutes, and seventeen seconds." Throughout the ship some men cursed while others cheered. This officers' wardroom was no exception. There had been four pools among the nine squadrons, and all four were won by lieutenants. Some older hands grumbled that this was a bad omen, but all the junior officers thought it was great, especially the winners!

* * * * *

Friday Afternoon

After lunch, Fleming walked onto the flight deck for some fresh air and a stretch of his legs. He was with his new roommate, Lieutenant Commander Joseph Caldwell, a man nothing like Fleming had imagined. He was tall and muscular, built like the football player he had been in college, yet surprisingly reticent. Anyone would have classified him as good looking, which begged the question: Why had he wooed and married his oh-so-plain wife? He was thirty-six years old, and had just received word earlier in the week that his name was on the promotion list to full commander.

The sea was smooth as glass, and as the two made their way towards the stern, they could see that the *LBJ* and the accompanying Nimitz-class carrier *Harry S. Truman* had already taken up their protected positions as the *raison d'être* for the strike group's existence. Within the hour, the *Truman* would break away and rejoin its own Carrier Strike Group 8 (CSG) positioned two hundred miles to the north. At the end of June, the *Truman* was scheduled to return to Norfolk.

In the immediate vicinity of the *LBJ* was the *Tacoma*, one of two surface warfare destroyer escorts, while steaming five hundred yards astern on the carrier's starboard side was a frigate. Well behind the *Tacoma* was a guided-missile cruiser in the shadow of the *Truman*, and ahead of that cruiser was the other destroyer-escort, which itself was accompanied by two anti-submarine frigates. And at the tip of the spear of this very lethal surface force, an Improved Los Angeles Class fast attack submarine was sailing below, ensuring no enemy lurked beneath.

From where the two officers stood, they could not see all of the other ships in the group, but took comfort knowing that both the carriers were very well protected.

"Did you get your gear squared away OK?" Caldwell asked. "I remember how lost I felt on my first carrier tour, so I kinda know how you might be feeling. Especially on this baby. She's beyond incredible.'"

He paused to savor all he could see. "It's my not-so-secret ambition to skipper one of these beauties someday. It's the ultimate command for any Navy flyer."

"Well, you just continue what you're doing, son. Finish high school, go to college, and your dream will come true. Got to, it's the American way," said Fleming, in his best pontifical voice.

Caldwell laughed. "Good advice, dad." He glanced at his watch. "I'm off to write a couple of letters, and maybe grab a little shuteye."

Twenty minutes later, Fleming rode an elevator up to Vulture's Row, a balcony area high up on the island with a bird's-eye view of the flight deck where pilots and non-flyers alike could watch the planes takeoff and land. It was a popular spot with sailors who wanted to snap photos, and a favorite of family and friends when the carrier was in port, and visitors were allowed to come aboard.

A sailor, standing behind one of several binocular stations anchored to the railing glanced up, saw Fleming beside him, and pointed toward a cruise ship coming abreast on their port side. She was less than a quarter mile away, her safety-glass parapets lined with passengers waving at the American carrier.

The *LBJ's* 1 Main Circuit PA system came to life.

"All hands, this is the Captain. For those on the flight deck, I direct your attention port side to where we have a visitor wanting to say hello. And for crewmembers below, you can see it on the TV monitors throughout the ship. She is the British liner *Princess Royal* on her maiden voyage, and her captain, crew, and passengers wish to salute us."

"Go ahead, take a look, Sir," the sailor said, offering his binoculars to Fleming. "She's really something to see up close!"

Fleming adjusted the focus and zoomed in on the hundreds of happy passengers who had begun cheering loudly, the sound easily carrying across the water to Vulture's Row.

"Hip, hip, hooray," the crowd cheered three times, then followed up with an enthusiastic round of applause and whistling.

The *LBJ* answered with three long blasts of her horn, causing the British audience to break out in a second spontaneous wave of clapping and cheering.

A few minutes passed while both vessels sailed in concert, then Captain Blizzard again keyed his mike. "On behalf of us all, I have extended your thanks and appreciation to the crew and passengers of the *Princess Royal,* and to say we wish them the best of luck and a *bon voyage.* Her captain has informed me that he will slow his ship to allow the rest of our strike group to sail past her unimpeded. That is all."

Fleming turned and thanked the sailor and, after one last, appreciative look at the British liner, headed for the elevator thinking, *now that's a ship I won't soon forget.*

He made his way back to the main wardroom, and still feeling restless, headed off down the companionway. He passed various strike fighter squadrons' briefing rooms and ready rooms, all part of the air wing's quarters, then trekked along narrow passageways jampacked with pipes and electrical conduits snaking their way along the ceiling and bulkheads, taking him further into foreign territory as he got closer to the center of the ship. Here were housed most of the ship's shops, the cacophony emanating from within, a testament to the seriousness of the work being done. He heard the screeching of a dozen drills, the rhythmic poundings of presses and the crunching of metal cutters, along with other noises, some barely audible, others ear piercing in their shrillness.

He descended a ladderwell to another deck, then continued his exploring as he made his way toward the bow. Here the bulkheads were painted a pale beige, and the decks were covered in a non-slip blue material sprinkled with white flecks. He wandered into the pharmacy only to be asked by a sailor if he needed help.

"No, just getting acquainted with the ship," he replied with a wave of his hand. He passed clusters of corpsmen entering and exiting various doors, all seemingly preoccupied with the seriousness of their calling.

19

"Allow me to show you around." The voice from behind startled him. Fleming turned to face a full commander. "I'm Father Caffarone. I'd heard we have an Air Force officer assigned to one of the strike squadrons. Welcome aboard, Major."

"David Fleming, Father," Fleming replied, shaking the proffered hand. "I'm just looking."

"I know what you mean. I've been in the Navy eighteen years now, most of that time on flat-tops, and I'm still left speechless at their sheer size. I'm just finishing checking the hospital for patients, so let me show you around our medical facilities." He opened a large set of two-way swinging doors and entered the hospital with Fleming a half-step behind. "My first carrier was the old *Enterprise*," he continued, "and I thought at the time her sick bay was the finest; but I must confess, the *LBJ* makes hers look downright prehistoric. *LBJ* has a complement of five medical officers, all of them specialists, but that excludes the flight surgeons who are assigned directly to the squadrons. Our Chief Medical Officer, or CMO, as he's called, is Captain Potter. He's a cardiologist by trade, and a darned good one. He's also a rated naval flight surgeon. Clarence can be cantankerous at times, but those of us who know him well, know that his bite is non-existent, and that he's really all bark. Anyway, the other doctors range through the specialties: surgery, internal medicine, radiology, psychiatry, and EENT. And backing up these doctors are the other professionals: Nurse Practitioners, Physician Assistants, nurses, and about thirty-five corpsmen. Then there's the pharmacy, one of the best you'll find anywhere in the world I might add, and finally, the dental department with two dentists, plus staff."

They entered the hospital with beds for forty-one patients. All were empty. "There are enough beds to handle about ninety total cases if we had to surge," continued Caffarone. "Severe injuries in the rest of the fleet will be choppered over to us or to the *Truman* from the escorts. The worst are the burn cases, really horrible to see, but the *LBJ* has a sterile burn center which I fervently hope we won't have to use for a long time."

Passing through a series of wards, the priest greeted everyone with a smile and often a pat on the shoulder. It was obvious to Fleming that the man was genuinely liked and respected by officers and enlisted alike.

"And here are our operating theatres," Caffarone said, opening a double set of swinging doors and entering the observation room. From this vantage point one could look in on either of the two complete operating theatres that gleamed, all stainless and ceramic. "We can handle anything from a simple tonsillectomy to a heart transplant. It's something to see when those fellows are at work. A theatre ballet troupe couldn't put on a more riveting performance."

You spend much time in the hospital, Father?" Fleming asked, as the tour continued.

"Yeah, quite a bit. But I do have an office, a cubicle really, next to the officers' wardroom. I'm fortunate to have two other excellent chaplains assisting me. In addition to taking care of the spiritual needs of the crew, I also run the ship's library, which is the chief chaplain's responsibility. Oftentimes, that translates simply as seeing that the fellows get checked for VD after each liberty. *C'est la vie!*"

"Amen!" replied Fleming, thinking this is a real stand-up guy. By the time he got back to his own quarters, he had a far better understanding of his new home. But along with the understanding came a sudden and indescribable feeling of aloneness, something he had never experienced before. It unsettled him.

He would later reflect back on the feeling, and after comparing it to Susan's recurring nightmare, he would come to wish that had been the full extent of his troubles.

CHAPTER 3

Saturday morning – June 19th

First light found Miles Austin Blizzard, USN, Captain of the *LBJ*, preparing for another busy day at sea. It was six o'clock, midway through the morning watch, and the captain of the world's most lethal fighting ship had already been up for over an hour. He had not slept more than five hours a night since leaving Norfolk two weeks earlier, yet he felt not the least bit tired. This command, coveted by every captain in the Navy was his alone, and he was not ashamed to admit that he was damn proud of himself. He had been the skipper of the *Carl Vinson* for only eight months when he had received orders to take command of the *LBJ*. Those officers passed over for the assignment consoled themselves with such thoughts as *What else would you expect? Hell, if my daddy-in-law just happened to be the Chief of Naval Operations … well …*

The chimes of the red phone on his desk brought Blizzard out of his reverie.

"Captain, this is Lieutenant Glasser, Admiral Taylor's aide," a voice announced. "The admiral asks if you could join him for breakfast in ten minutes?" It was a command, no matter how polite the message.

"My regards to the admiral and, yes, I'll be there. Oh, in his quarters or on the flag bridge?"

"The flag bridge, Captain."

Blizzard rang up the command bridge and asked for his executive officer (XO). Alan Paige was a first-class XO, and like Blizzard, he

22

too was a four striper and fully qualified to command the *LBJ* in his own right.

"Al, I'm joining the admiral for breakfast on his bridge. I imagine he wants to go over some last-minute details before we go to flight quarters. I don't expect to be there for long, but if I'm not back on my bridge by oh seven hundred, bail me out, OK?"

"Roger that, enjoy your prune juice!"

"Up yours, Al."

Stepping onto the flag bridge, one level below his command bridge, Blizzard paused to survey his kingdom. He took note of the activity far below. A crew was hosing down a section of the fight deck, and from sixty feet above, he could hear the petty officer in charge of the work detail telling the men "to get the lead out." His gaze turned skyward to the maze of antennae and radar dishes that seemed to sprout everywhere. The radio and navigational aids on board were cutting edge, giving Blizzard the ability to talk to anyone, anytime, anywhere. The navigational aids were state of the art, equal to those found in any control tower in any international airport. The major difference was that his airport could roam the seven seas for the next two decades without having to stop to refuel.

The bridge Blizzard was standing upon was an integral part of the whole, and the whole was technically known as the ship's island. It is the operations center for all carriers, the place where the captain and his staff call home. The island on the *LBJ* was situated on the starboard side, smaller, and more than one-hundred forty-feet further astern than those found on previous classes of carriers.

Blizzard glanced once more at the deck party then turned back under cover. The flag bridge was the one area where he exercised no functional control whatsoever. It housed the Fleet Combat Control Center and the admiral's quarters, from where Taylor ran the day-to-day operations of the entire strike group. True, he had a staff of forty to help him, but the admiral was known at times to be a hands-on perfectionist.

The marine guard came to attention and saluted smartly. He opened the door after knocking once and beckoned Blizzard to enter.

"Good morning, Miles, hope you're hungry." The greeting came from a table set up in the middle of the room. Seated next to the admiral was his chief-of-staff, Manfred Eisenhauer, an unflappable captain known to his friends as Manny.

Blizzard saluted the admiral, nodded to the chief-of-staff, and pulled out the only vacant chair and spread a pristine napkin on his lap. A steward stood ready to take his order.

"Two eggs, over easy, bacon, toast, coffee. And, oh yes, orange juice," he added quickly, warily eyeing the beaker of prune juice in the middle of the table.

"Don't know why you insist on eating that garbage, Miles, or you too for that matter, Manny," the Admiral said. "All that cholesterol and fat will clog your pipes and screw up your pumps. It's only a matter of when."

"You're being redundant, Sir," said Manny, deliberately smearing a slice of toast with enough butter to feed an army.

"What's redundant?"

"Cholesterol and fat. They're one and the same," Eisenhauer replied, then immediately popped a huge pieces of toast into his mouth. "Mmmm, but that's good," he managed with a full mouth, knowing he was aggravating the admiral to no end. Any lesser mortal would have been banished to Wake Island, or some other godforsaken backwater hellhole for such impudence.

The admiral glowered at Eisenhauer for a second, then turned to Blizzard. "How soon are you planning on going to flight quarters?" The admiral was asking when Blizzard would start launching aircraft from the four strike fighter (VFA) squadrons assigned to the *LBJ*, knowing that once a carrier goes to flight quarters, all essential services on board begin operating on a twenty-four-hour schedule, and the tempo of life increases accordingly. Planes will be launched and recovered day and night for as long as the carrier is at fight quarters, a condition that can last for as long as a week during peacetime.

"Sean Gowdy and I planned for seven o'clock, an hour from now," replied Blizzard. "The squadrons were briefed yesterday afternoon, and the flight crews are itching to go. Same holds for the air wing on the *Truman*. Unless you have any other plans for us, Admiral?"

"Nope. Told you yesterday that I would be flexible. The damn Russians will try to screw with us with their phony fishing fleet trawlers cutting in and out of our formation, but I want them to see that the *LBJ* is fully capable of knocking them out of the water at a moment's notice. I'll string the strike group out to make the Russians work for their pay, but I want you and the *Truman* to remain farther apart for the next few days. But I'm willing to change my plans to suit your needs."

Blizzard knew this was a significant departure from the admiral's usual dictatorial stance. He found himself pleasantly surprised. "Thanks, George, I appreciate that." It was not often that he addressed the admiral by his first name, but there were few flag officers who awed him. He had personally known many for years because his wife, Anita, was the eldest daughter of Admiral Wayne Turnbull Christensen, the four-star Chief of Naval Operations.

For the next twenty minutes, they spoke of other things until Eisenhauer reminded the admiral that he had a string of meetings starting at seven o'clock. Blizzard took the hint, excused himself, and returned to the command bridge. He glanced at his watch. Twenty minutes until the carrier would go to flight quarters.

* * * * *

Alan Paige sneezed for the third time in as many seconds and silently cursed his sinuses. He was in the Combat Direction Center (CDC) running through a checklist with his department chiefs. The ship's navigation officer, Lieutenant Commander Reece Birdwell was present, along with Joel Hirshberger, the meteorological officer. All were aware of the pending order for the two carriers and the strike group to go to flight quarters.

25

"Keeping an eye on the Russians?" Paige asked the navigation officer. Birdwell was an Annapolis graduate who also held a Ph.D. in engineering from Purdue. He had helped design the new generation of inertial navigation systems now found on most surface ships, submarines, and larger planes.

This constellation of satellites was built around an IBM supercomputer platform that continuously updated any ship's position relative to a given spot on earth at any given time. The forty-five satellites were in orbits twelve thousand plus miles above the earth, and even America's submarines could use the system while submerged to a still-classified depth, enabling them to plot their true positions to within ten meters.

"We're tracking all Russian surface vessels in a large area relative to our position, Sir. We also have fixes on two bogey submarines within fifty nautical mile radius."

"And no problems reported from the rest of the strike group?"

"None, Sir. Everyone has the track that's been plotted."

Paige nodded his approval and turned to Hirshberger. "How about weather, Joel? What's the outlook for the next week?"

"For the sake of your sinuses, Sir, I wish I could say rain to clean up the air, but unfortunately it looks like a continued dry spell with unlimited visibility for at least the next seventy-two hours. Sorry about that, " added Hirshberger, his Adam's apple bouncing vigorously.

"So am I, Joel. I'm going to have to see if anyone in Doc Potter's gang can prescribe something for me." No sooner were the words spoken than he began to sneeze. With a silent wave, he stepped out of the CDC for a tour through the *LBJ* to listen to and solve problems.

Hirshberger returned to the weather department. He had almost stopped the XO to mention the weather anomaly that had occurred in port yesterday morning, but at the last moment decided to say nothing. *What are the facts?* he thought. *There are none.* However, he made a silent vow that if something similar occurred in the future, he would inform the XO immediately.

"Heads up, here comes Sick Sally," a sailor called out as Hirshberger entered the room.

"So, that's what I'm known as behind my back," said Hirshberger.

"Oh no, Sir!" answered the red-faced culprit. "I meant the mail plane." He pointed to a television monitor showing a view of the flight deck and an approaching plane flying low off the *LBJ's* stern, now only moments from touchdown.

Everyone watched. It was the MV-22 Osprey used to transport men and mail out to the fleet from the headquarters back in Naples. The beauty of this plane lay not in its physical appearance, but rather in its ability to land on a carrier no matter whether or not the ship was sailing into the wind. The same held true for take-offs, in that it could raise and lower itself like a helicopter.

The pilot flew the tilt-wing plane gracefully onto the deck, and as Hirshberger watched, he silently prayed the plane was bringing a letter from his daughter, his only living relative.

CHAPTER 4

Saturday morning – later -June 19th

All squadron ready rooms of Carrier Air Wing-12 were electric with tension. The ship had gone to flight quarters at seven hundred hours, starting the initial day and night cyclic flight operations schedule. The deck was spotted for the first launch.

There had been outward grumbling when CAG informed the junior members of the squadrons that they would have the duty of spotting the deck for launches, as well as taxiing planes back to the elevators for removal down to the hangar deck. This calls for a pilot being in each cockpit when a plane is moved about on the flight deck. Sometimes the planes are pulled by tugs, but just as often they are positioned operating under their own power. Once a plane is spotted, it is then securely tied down to the deck with heavy cables and is freed only when time comes to move it to the catapults. On many carriers the deck crew has the authority to spot the planes, but Blizzard and Gowdy had co-signed a directive that until further notice the job would be done by pilots.

"There will be a roster typed up giving you your assignments," Gowdy said, "and all ensigns and JGs will pull the duty."

"For how long, CAG?" asked a lieutenant, junior grade. "It's been years since I've heard of something like this." He double-popped a wad of gum to show his displeasure.

"*Stand up when talking to me!*"

The lieutenant jumped to his feet and stood at attention, a look of total fear spreading like wildfire across his face.

Everyone in the room could see the CAG was furious. "Let me answer your question by making a statement that goes for you, mister, and everyone else in the air wing. I've never been in the habit of giving reasons for my orders, and I sure as hell don't plan to start now. Junior pilots will spot the deck, and that's final. Now, for this next item, and I'm only going to say it once. God help any man who talks to me with gum in his mouth, unless he happens to be an admiral. This is a disciplined US Navy fighting air wing, and if any of you think the operation is going to be run like a country club, you're mistaken. When you address either me or the Deputy CAG, you'll get off your asses and onto your feet. If anyone feels he should be the exception, well, he can come to my office and explain his position."

A dozen hands reached into mouths and extracted wads of gum which they secreted somewhere in their flightsuits.

'Now let's get down to the business of flying,'" Gowdy said, and with a nod, turned the meeting over to his deputy, Captain Thomas Dowling.

Dowling positioned his six-foot-four frame behind the podium and studied his audience. He was a force to be reckoned with in his own right. His flightsuit did little to hide his physique, but the focal point of attention was his head. It was completely bald. That fact was further accentuated by a scar running from one ear all the way across the top of the scalp to end less than an inch from the ear on the other side. Eyebrows too were non-existent, and his eyes were the closest thing to being colorless that Fleming had ever seen. The man was an absolutely fearless pilot, and those who had flown with him during the Iraq and Afghanistan War years spoke in awe of his exploits. He had been shot down twice, both times being rescued mere minutes before being captured. His injuries the second time were so severe it took a year for him to heal and return to flight status.

Dowling now ran down the order of launch for the three strike squadrons which would be participating and, after he finished, fielded questions. Within minutes the room was again silent. "OK. I show the time to be exactly eight ten, so everyone hack on me." As he spoke, all the pilots readjusted their watches to the time the deputy CAG had called out. He wrapped with a final comment.

"CAG will fly in the first launch with Alpha-Romeo flight, and I'll be flying with Bravo-Foxtrot on the second launch. Let's make this look professional so the skipper and the Admiral will know they have the best pilots in the world assigned to the best damn ship in the world! I don't need to remind you, that as great as the *LBJ* is, she's only as good as her air arm. Let's not let anyone down, and now I'll turn you over to your individual squadron commanders."

The men rose and stood at attention as CAG and the deputy left the room.

Fleming walked towards his ready room with his roommate. Caldwell had been restless and had talked until well after midnight. When Fleming finally said "goodnight," Caldwell, still unable to sleep, read until almost three. When he finally snapped off his light, it was not because he was tired, but because he knew he should rest.

They were soon joined by Hamilton. Their flight was Bravo-Foxtrot, and the schedule called for them to be launched at ten.

"CAG sure let us all know where we stand," said Hamilton, stirring his coffee. "You know, he was also spring-loaded during the shakedown cruise. I remember when we were about two hundred miles north of Oceana, and I was down in the hangar deck with a couple of the guys. We were standing about three yards away from CAG, the deputy, and a technical rep from Northrup Grumman. The three of them were working on a problem with one of the F-18 Super Hornets when suddenly, Gowdy gets all pissed-off, yells at the tech-rep, and shoves the man. I mean, he *really* shoved the guy hard! Well, within a microsecond that tech rep had CAG pinned to the side of the Hornet with a death-grip on his throat. Then the dude says, 'If you ever touch me again, I'll frigging punch your lights out and heave your ass over the damn side. I'm a civilian, pal, not one of your blue-suited weenies you can piss all over at will.' Well, we all shagged our asses out of there lickety-split before the old man could see us. CAG went storming off in the other direction, but I can tell you, I thought there was going to be some really bad shit there for a moment."

"That same tech rep still aboard?" Fleming asked.

"Oh, yeah," Hamilton replied. "I've seen him several times since. I've even spotted him with CAG. They're super polite to each other now but stay out of the other's way unless it's for business reasons."

"I bet most folks have no idea there are a couple of hundred civilians on board an aircraft carrier," said Fleming. "I know I sure didn't. I always thought that when a ship left port it was one hundred percent Navy aboard."

"And now you know," said Caldwell. "The civilian technical representative, or tech-rep as he's called, has been an integral part of the seagoing Navy since World War II."

"But don't the civilian tech reps in the air wing come under Gowdy's control?"

"Yes, technically speaking, they sure do, Dave, no pun intended," Caldwell replied, "but these guys are highly paid specialists, and a bunch of them are drawing much fatter salaries than even the admiral. They're *prima-donnas*, and most don't take shit from anyone. However, in all fairness, I must admit that they are a hard-working group, and ninety-nine percent are the average Joe if you treat them right."

At the moment Caldwell finished, the announcement they had all been waiting to hear came over the 1MC loudspeaker system.

'Now, hear this. Now, hear this. Stand by to bring the carrier into the wind for launch operations, and the smoking lamp is out." The message was repeated by the bosun's mate.

Everyone in the ready room was silent as they watched the TV monitors relay a closed-circuit picture from the flight deck. For the next few minutes, they saw the huge fighter jets being placed on all four Electromagnetic Aircraft Launch Systems (EMALS) catapults, two on the angle deck and two on straight deck. They sat spellbound as the planes spooled up to full military power. The "Go" hand-signal was given by the catapult officer, and the first Hornet roared off its catapult, but without the signature cloud of steam seen in all prior generations of US carriers.

* * * * *

Saturday mid-morning

Fleming sat in the cockpit of his two-seat F/A-18F Super Hornet making last minute adjustments to his shoulder harness. He had started his engines fifteen minutes earlier and was now number two in line to be launched off the port side catapult on the straight deck. He smiled, remembering the first time he had heard the voice of "Bitchin' Betty" in his earphones admonishing him, *flight controls, flight controls*, her authoritative, digitalized voice and Tennessee twang grabbing his full attention.

F-18 Pilots all over the world are familiar with "Bitchin' Betty" and listen when she speaks. Glancing in his mirror he could see that his backseater, Lieutenant J.G. Charles Lafayette was adjusting his oxygen mask, trying to make it fit more snugly.

"Everything OK back there, Chuck?"

Lafayette keyed his mike. "Everything's green. Should be a good mission: we've sure got the weather for it."

"You can say that again," said Fleming, looking around. Not a cloud in the sky, barely any swells on the water. He glanced down at the clipboard strapped to his thigh and quickly reviewed the notes he'd jotted down.

The squadron commander, the weather officer, the intelligence officer, and the navigation officer had each taken turns briefing the squadron flyers prior to launch, and all had written the pertinent information on their mission data clipboards, including the codename for the carrier, *Bigfoot*, the codename for the operation, *Thunderball*, and the codename for the squadron, *Sundancer*. Also included were radio frequencies, bearings, and distance to the nearest land bases should it become necessary for any or all of the planes to divert away from the strike group.

The officer of the deck ordered Fleming forward. It was his turn to launch. He brought his engines up to taxi power and was guided to the catapult. He gave the signal to Lafayette he was lowering and locking the canopy. Keeping his eye on the yellow-shirted plane director, Fleming moved his thirty-two-thousand-pound fighter into position on the EMALS until the director gave him the 'stop' signal. The director then pointed downward towards the deck at a forty-five-degree angle, the signal for Fleming to bring his power up. Satisfied, the man turned control over to the green-shirted catapult officer. The air officer gave the "go" signal to launch, and the catapult officer dropped to one knee and thrust his arm forward with forefinger extended.

Even though securely strapped in, Fleming felt the immediate strain as he was shoved back into his seat while the Super Hornet raced toward the leading edge of the deck. He held the twin throttles firmly in his gloved left hand while holding the stick steady with his right, and all the while keeping his eyes glued forward. In an instant there was nothing but blue sky and water in front of the Hornet, and he felt the plane dip before it recovered and rapidly gained altitude.

Glancing down at the vertical velocity indicator on his glass cockpit display screen, he noted the positive indication that he was climbing, then smartly moved the gear handle to the up position. The ensuing rumble told him the wheels were cycling properly into their individual wells. He reset the huge flaps and, all the while, his plane climbed higher to its rendezvous with the rest of the flight. The entire procedure had taken less than a minute.

"Beats flying off a two-mile runway, right?" Lafayette said, speaking for the first time since launch.

"That's affirmative. Hope I didn't scare you too badly."

"Nope," came the one word reply, followed by, "Anyway, what could I do about it?"

Fleming laughed. "OK, let's settle in for the mission. Give me a rundown on your system back there." They had joined up with the rest of their flight, all four jets flying in echelon at fourteen thousand feet but still climbing as they had been briefed during the mission planning. There were five flights of four aircraft each, and the mission today was an easy milk run. It called for an intercept on the *John L. Lewis*, a Fleet Replenishment Oiler sailing on a northerly course two hundred and seventy miles west of the strike group. Each Hornet would make a simulated bombing pass on the vessel, climb, and regroup, then head back to the carrier. The purpose of the mission was simply to dust off any cobwebs and sharpen up reflexes which had not seen a workout in two weeks.

Because of the unlimited visibility, there was no talk of sneaking up on the oiler. Also, none of the planes were carrying external stores other than air-to-air missiles for defense should they be attacked by truly hostile aircraft. Their sister carrier, the *Truman*, was operational, which meant her aircraft were fully armed on all missions.

From a height of twenty-four thousand feet, Fleming easily saw the ships far below looking like so many dots, but because of the perfect weather conditions, there were no shadows cast on the near-smooth sea by clouds which can hide a vessel from even the most experienced eye. Luckily, they did not have to depend on their eyes for contact confirmation. Lafayette was busy monitoring his surveillance radar, and with his experience in differentiating between various classes of ships by their silhouettes, knew they were not yet over their target.

Their earphones came alive. "*Sundancers*, this is lead. Target bearing zero-five-zero moving north, northeast, at twelve. We have a positive identification. Standby to attack on my command. Flight leaders acknowledge."

Three terse "rogers" were heard, then silence.

"This is *Sundancer* lead, commence attack! Maintain five thousand feet separation between flights." Dowling heeled his Super Hornet over sharply and proceeded to dive on the target that was still no larger than a dot.

'Hang on back there, Chuck, we're heading for the deck," said Fleming, flying the number three position of the four-ship formation. The huge plane responded easily to his touch, the hydraulic elevators sending the fighter down at a constant speed of just under point seven mach. He went through the motion of setting arming switches on non-existent weapons systems, knowing his squadron mates were all doing the same. Down he went, the oiler taking on a distinct shape as they got closer to the surface. He zoomed within two hundred feet of the ship, flying from stem to stern and, as he roared by, easily saw sailors and officers standing on deck, holding their ears, while they followed the wave after wave of aircraft passing close overhead.

"Man, this is what I call overkill," came an unknown voice over the radio causing Dowling to reply immediately, "Cut the chatter! *Sundancer* flight regroup, and head for the boat." It was an uneventful ride until some twenty minutes out from the carrier, Lafayette came on the intercom.

"Dave, how's your air conditioning up there?"

Fleming put a gloved hand up to one of the ducts expecting a cold draft to hit him between where his glove ended and his flightsuit sleeve began. There was air moving all right, but it wasn't cold. He checked the circuit breaker, tripping and resetting it several times, all to no avail. "Looks like it's crapped out on us, Chuck," he answered, then silently cursed as the heat began to build up. He reached over and moved the selector from automatic to manual and held it. The temperature started to come down immediately.

"You on manual?" asked Lafayette.

"Yeah, no big deal. I'll write it up when we land."

"Probably just a short in the DC bus."

Twenty minutes later they were going through their landing check list. The planes were now spaced at sixty second intervals for landing. The *LBJ* had been brought around into the wind only minutes before, and the carrier-controlled approach controllers, (CCA) were monitoring fuel levels in each aircraft by means of computers and were busy keeping an eye on which planes might need to be brought

35

in first. In addition to the two airborne rescue helicopters which were hovering about a half mile from the carrier's port side, there were two Super Hornet tankers aloft in case some of the returning planes needed to take on fuel fast.

Each of the planes in the stack ahead of Fleming made solid approaches and touched down on their initial attempts. His own landing was uneventful as he followed instructions from the landing signal officer, who in turn was following his progress on a special TV monitor equipped with cross hairs. It was Fleming's job to listen to instructions from the Landing Signal Officer, and for the two of them working in concert to bring the fighter firmly down onto the angle deck, where the Super Hornet's tail hook would snag one of three arresting cables.

Fleming was now fully concentrating on the task at hand, unaware that his heart rate had climbed to 160 beats per minute. He instinctively knew that any mistake made in the next few moments could prove fatal. His eyes darted back and forth in rapid succession from the "meatball" to the deck, and back to the "meatball" for affirmation that he was on the proper glideslope. As soon as he felt the head-snapping jolt of the hook catching the cable, he immediately brought his engines to full military power in case he had to bolt off the carrier. The cable held. He pulled his throttles back to idle, and seconds later his hook was manually disengaged by a color-shirted deck crewmember. He taxied off the angle deck and followed the signals of the deck crew where to park. More sailors then scurried underneath his plane and tied it down securely. He cut off the engines and completed his shut-down check list. Finally, he opened the canopy and took in deep gulps of fresh air. He was pleased with himself and with Lafayette. Theirs had been a good flight.

Shortly after nine o'clock that evening, he returned to his cabin to find Caldwell and Hamilton reliving the day's mission. Like pilots everywhere, both were gesticulating wildly to press home their points.

"Hey, man, have you heard the latest?" Hamilton asked, sitting on Fleming's desk with an unlit cigar hanging out the corner of his mouth.

"No," replied Fleming, "but I'm thinking I won't be kept in suspense for long."

"Absolutely right, good buddy!" Taking the cigar out, Hamilton waved the foul looking thing inches from Fleming's face and said, "Scuttlebutt has it confirmed that CVW-12, that's us, boy, will be converting to the F-35C in December, and we'll be operational this time next year."

Fleming glanced at Caldwell for confirmation, and his roommate nodded, then said, "We can expect to be relieved off the *LBJ* sometime in late November to begin ground school training in the Lightning III, we'll be replaced by Carrier Air Wing 3, already operational in the bird."

"It's puzzled me from the git-go why they didn't just put an F-35C air wing onboard to begin with," said Fleming. "Strange how the newest carrier in the Navy didn't have the newest aircraft, but who are we peons to question the powers that be?"

"That's it in a nutshell, '' said Hamilton sliding off his perch. He froze momentarily, turned, and reached over to Caldwell's desk and scooped up the photograph of Caldwell's wife and kids.

Holding it close to his chest, he turned to Fleming and said in a serious voice, "Major, I think you owe an apology to Commander Caldwell for calling his wife and kids godawful ugly yesterday. Not only is that flat-out untrue, but it was totally uncalled for."

Fleming felt a flash of anger followed by a rush of acute embarrassment. *Why has Hamilton turned on me so suddenly?* he wondered.

Hamilton was not about to let it die. He continued to escalate the conflict. Pressing his point home while now holding the photo aloft for Fleming to openly see, he asked, "How could you have possibly called this woman and these two fine children uglier than dirt?" He shook his head sadly. "What's the matter with you, Major Fleming, the cat got your tongue?"

Fleming just stared at the picture in a fish-out-of-water moment. *The photo had changed!* The woman and her children were still standing in front of the same church, but she had transformed to an incredible beauty, and the children to miniature reflections of their mother!

Hamilton and Caldwell could not stifle their silence any longer. Both doubled over in fits of laughter, and only then did Fleming realize that he had been the unwitting mark who had just fallen for the ultimate practical joke.

"You pricks. You lousy pricks," he repeated in a whisper. It took him a long moment to allow the luxurious feeling of pure relief to wash over him, then he too began to laugh. Soon he was laughing as hard as the jokesters. "How many guys have you fooled with that?" he managed.

"Many," was Caldwell's one word reply. He continued to laugh, savoring the memory of the pained expression seen on Fleming's face moments before.

CHAPTER 5

Saturday – Early afternoon – June 19th

"Miles, have you seen the noon weather report?" the admiral asked Captain Blizzard who had joined him on the flag bridge. Three other officers were present. The afternoon's Hornet launchings had commenced twenty minutes earlier.

"I have, and I'm also aware there were problems with some of our meteorological instruments, and that was the cause for the bad information we passed along to the rest of the strike group. Commander Hirshberger will have a full report for me shortly."

The phone rang on Taylor's workstation. "Admiral Taylor," he said. Several moments passed, then he handed the instrument to Blizzard. "It's Alan Paige," he said.

Blizzard listened for a minute, a frown forming. "Hold on a second, Al. I want you to repeat this. I'm putting you on the speaker so that Admiral Taylor can hear as well." He pressed the speaker button.

"OK, Al, you're on speaker. Go ahead."

"Captain," came the XO's voice for everyone to hear, "I'm in the Carrier Air Traffic Control Center (CATCC), and we have a problem."

"What kind of problem?" interrupted the admiral.

"It's one of the Hornets, Admiral, a two-seater. They're in trouble, yet the pilot can't define what the problem is. He's one hundred twenty miles west of our position, and his radio communications are garbled at best. But on top of that, we're having a hard time getting a solid fix on him."

"Is he down low on the deck?" asked Blizzard, wanting to know if the plane was flying so low that it was not being seen on the ship's radar screens.

"Negative, Captain, " came the reply. "We tentatively have him painted at flight level three one zero, but for some reason none of us can explain, we can't seem to lock on. We'll have him for a second or two, lose him, have him again, lose him, and so on. I know that sounds asinine, Boss, but that's what's happening down here."

"Is Gowdy there?" the admiral wanted to know.

"I'm here, Admiral," replied CAG, "and I'm at just as much a loss as Al Paige. All our equipment is functioning normally. We're having no problem tracking and communicating with any other aircraft, including his wingman. I can't explain it, Admiral."

Taylor absently drummed his fingers on the desk. He glanced at his chief of staff who shrugged his shoulders. He paused for a few more seconds, then asked, "Where are the Russians?"

"Nowhere near that Hornet, Admiral. We have them all accounted for, and there's no jamming coming from any of their ships."

"OK, let's go over what we do know. One. We can't get a good fix on one of our F-model Super Hornets flying at thirty-one thousand feet some one hundred plus miles west of our position. Two. The communications link back to us is patchy at best, so we should assume he's having the same problem on his end. And, three, we don't have a clue as to the real nature of his trouble. That an accurate summary?"

"That's about right, Admiral."

"CAG, who's flying? Some green kid?"

"No, Admiral. The pilot is a man named Robinson. He's a full lieutenant, ten years of service, and has thirteen hundred hours in the Hornet. The backseater is equally experienced."

"So, if he says they're in trouble, you know they're in real trouble, right?" Blizzard asked.

"Absolutely, Skipper," CAG replied. "Hold on a second, we're getting a transmission from him now. Let me pipe it up to you." The assembled officers heard static, then a faint voice.

"*Bigfoot* this is *Sabre six*, do you read?"

The men had to strain to hear the words. There was no hint of panic in the voice.

"This is *Bigfoot*, *Sabre six*. We're trying to get a fix on your position. Say again altitude, heading, and airspeed."

"*Bigfoot, this ...*" was followed by heavy static for fifteen seconds. Then, a very weak ...*"magnetic ... heavy fog, radar jamming ... fuel eight thousand ...*" and more static. Then nothing.

Gowdy came on the speaker. "We've lost him again, but we now have a firm fix. We have just sent a two-ship to intercept and guide him home. As soon as we hear something, we'll let you know, Admiral."

"Roger," replied Taylor, then flipped the switch to the off position. "I have a feeling this is going to be one of those days," he murmured to no one in particular, then dismissed the group.

The admiral is right on one thing thought Blizzard as he made his way below. This sure was going to be one of those days.

* * * * *

Saturday – late evening, into night

It was close to midnight before Blizzard was able to call it a day. Al Paige was to take command of the night launches scheduled for oh two hundred hours, and Blizzard was glad for the relief. Doctor Potter had left his stateroom minutes earlier, leaving behind a preliminary medical report on the condition of the pilot and his backseat systems operator.

"What have you got, Clarence?" Blizzard had asked.

"I briefed the admiral before coming to see you and told him I'm confused and alarmed."

"It's that bad?"

"Miles, let me put it to you this way. Both of those fellows are extremely ill, and I don't know why. Something happened to them

41

up there today, something that I have never seen happen to any other human being in my over twenty-five years as a physician. We'll be running tests on them for days, but as sure as I'm standing here, we're not going to find any answers."

"Clarence, are you telling me they encountered some sort of *Andromeda Strain* of an alien bug, kind of like in that old sci-fi flick from thirty years ago or maybe some other such nonsense of a thing from outer space? Something we have no cure for here on earth?" Blizzard asked, his voice carrying more than just a hint of sarcasm.

"Nothing of the sort," replied Potter, ignoring Blizzard's caustic tone. "Do you remember what those lads looked like when we got them out of their cockpits?"

Blizzard shuddered at the memory.

* * * * *

The two-ship flight of Hornets had rendezvoused with the cripple eighty-six miles due west of the carrier. Both planes were flying at thirty-two thousand feet in an echelon formation, both radars scanning out to a distance of two hundred miles. They were painting normal returns, identifying all of the commercial airline traffic in the area, and had just updated the *LBJ* Combat Direction Center when the missing Hornet popped into view at their nine o'clock position, two miles away, and slightly below them.

Both back-seat operators reported the sighting at the same time, and *LBJ* came on the air to acknowledge that they too were now showing all three aircraft. The Hornets wheeled into protective positions on each side of their squadron mate. Flight Lead radioed the carrier after repeated attempts to raise Robinson.

"*Bigfoot*, this is *Dasher one*. Do you read?"

"Roger. What have you got *Dasher one?*"

"Problems. We have a bird that can't talk, and from my visual, I don't even know how it can still fly. The skin is a mass of wrinkles, all the paint, markings, and decals are gone; both canopies look like they've been sand blasted, heck, the whole thing looks like it's been sand blasted! It's freaking unbelievable! I can't begin to imagine what they might have tangled with."

"Any bogies in the area, *Dasher one?*"

"Negative, *Bigfoot.*"

"*Dasher one,* this is *Ajax,* do you read?" Ajax was CAG's call sign.

"Roger, *Ajax,* go ahead."

"Can you raise *Sabre six* visually?"

"Give me a second." Dasher one slowly inched closer until both canopies were only feet from each other. It was impossible to see into the cockpit.

"Negative, *Bigfoot.* I can't get a visual. They could be dead in there, flying on autopilot."

As he spoke, his backseater alerted him to the fact that the damaged Hornet had just powered back its engines and had extended the speed brake. For some reason Robinson was slowing down. But at least they had proof he was alive.

Dasher one and *Dasher two* backed away from the cripple, waiting to see what would happen next. Robinson kept bleeding off airspeed until he was down to one hundred and eighty knots. His next move caught both pilots by surprise. He blew away the canopy. The semi-cylinder of plexiglass began turning end over end as it began a long, graceful tumble down to the Mediterranean. The expected ejection of the crewmembers never materialized.

"*Bigfoot, Dasher one. Sabre six* has just blown his canopy. He has his speed board out and he's down to one eight zero knots. I'm going in for a closer look."

Dasher one again inched into a position beside the damaged airplane and was greeted by Robinson trying to wave a feeble recognition. He then held his hand to his helmeted ear indicating that his radios were gone. *Dasher one* rocked his wings to acknowledge that he understood.

"*Bigfoot,* this is *Dasher one.* I'm in visual contact now with *Sabre six.* We'll guide him back to the boat. Recommend you be prepared for a hard landing. He's in bad shape and will not be able to do a go-around. Frankly, at this point I don't know if he'll be able to get his gear down. Also, I have no way to determine the condition of the backseater, he's slumped low."

"*Dasher one*, this is *Bigfoot*. Understood. Be advised that *Rocking Chair* is your alternate in the event of a problem here."

"Roger." *Rocking Chair* was the *Truman*, and the Combat Direction Center was telling them that if *Saber six* crashed on the *LBJ's* deck while attempting to land, then *Dasher one* and *Dasher two* would fly to the *Truman* for recovery.

It took twenty minutes to get back to the carrier, the damaged Hornet flying slightly below and aft of *Dasher one*, so that he could always keep it in sight. *Dasher two* had pulled in as Tail End Charlie.

Dasher one had planned the return trip for the three planes to descend rapidly to twelve hundred feet while maintaining a constant one-eighty airspeed. *Dasher one* wanted *Saber six* down from the freezing temperatures aloft. He knew that Robinson and his backseater would not last long in open cockpits at that higher altitude.

They overflew the carrier for Robinson to get his bearings and set up his approach.

Dasher one stayed with him all the way, realizing that Robinson was having a hard time just trying to see. Two rescue helicopters hovered nearby, and the destroyer escorts had been alerted to the very real possibility of the plane going into the ocean.

The landing gear had come down only after Robinson had manually blown it down. It was an incredible feat of flying skill. He was high coming over the carrier's lip, but must have realized there would be no go-around because he forced the huge jet onto the deck, and as the tail hook caught the number 3 wire, the impact tore off his left main landing gear. The plane sank to one side while the wheel assembly skidded crazily along the remaining length of the angle deck, and disappeared over the side. Before Robinson could shut down the engines, several asbestos-suited figures were already busy covering his plane with foam, while others had climbed up to the cockpits and were feverishly working on getting the crew out. Within moments, both men were on stretchers and being rushed down to the hospital. Damage to the angle deck had been negligible, and *Dasher one* and *Dasher two* landed ten minutes later without incident.

Blizzard had gone down to the hangar deck, accompanied by Gowdy and Commander Ted Seymour, the chief maintenance officer. The plane had been cleaned of foam, and was now propped up on jacks, but basically looked as it had after landing an hour earlier.

They spent several minutes carefully examining the aircraft, saying nothing, but seeing everything. The hangar deck crew kept a respectful distance; the department chief, a lieutenant commander, hovered nearby, making himself available for questions.

Their inspection was interrupted by the arrival of Admiral Taylor and Captain Eisenhauer. The three officers were so preoccupied, that their first indication of the admiral's presence was Eisenhauer clearing his throat and saying, "Gentlemen." All came to attention and saluted.

"Tried calling you, Miles, but Al Paige said you had already gone below, so I took the liberty of coming down for a look-see myself." Taylor pointed to the plane. "What in the blazes could have done this?"

Blizzard shook his head. "I'm at a loss, Admiral," he said; then quickly added, "we all are. Never seen anything like it. This plane was being torn apart, literally from the inside out, and we have no idea how or why." As he spoke, he began a slow walking around the plane, pointing out various things for the admiral to take note of. The skin was so badly buckled and wrinkled that it resembled a prune. The paint had been stripped from all of its surfaces, and the now-bare metal and all of the advanced composite materials were dulled and pitted. The Hornet was a total loss.

"Come look in the cockpits, Admiral," Blizzard said as he climbed a ladder on one side, Taylor on the other. "For some reason, the electrical system was blown out, burning everything. You can see some of the wiring harnesses are completely fused together, telling me that one hell of an electrical charge went through them." He gestured with his right hand to encompass the entire instrument panel. "All the static pressure instruments are kaput, and the only things the pilot had left to navigate by was his standby compass and Attitude Reference Indicator."

"Speculate for me, Miles. Say anything that comes to mind, no matter how wild. What do you think happened?"

Blizzard shrugged his shoulders. "I can't even do that, Admiral. CAG and I both saw the two aviators as they were being taken to the hospital. They looked as if they should have already been dead. The back-seater was unconscious, but the pilot was in-and-out of it. Doctor Potter and his folks are working on them now and should have a preliminary report ready by early evening. Something bad happened to those two up there, Admiral, and I intend to find out what it was."

"I sure hope you do. Appreciate the walk-around tour, Miles."

Blizzard, Gowdy, and Commander Seymour spent another half hour studying the plane.

"I'm going to have my metallurgical engineers go over it also, Captain," Seymour said, "and I'll make sure you get a complete report when the admiral and Captain Gowdy get theirs."

Later, before Blizzard fell asleep, he kept thinking of something the injured pilot had managed to tell him and Gowdy. Robinson had whispered that he had flown into a heavy fog which had come out of nowhere in the blink of an eye and said that's when their troubles had started. But that critical piece of information was totally at odds with what the meteorological officer had told him later. There had been no fog anywhere over the entire Mediterranean Sea at the time.

Something is very, very wrong, Blizzard thought wearily as his mind harkened back to the admiral's prophetic, earlier warning. *"I have a feeling this is going to be one of those days."*

"No, Admiral," he now whispered aloud, *"I have a feeling we're about to go where no mortal should ever dare to tread."*

CHAPTER 6

Sunday morning -Daybreak – June 20th

Blizzard joined his XO on the bridge at oh six hundred hours. Less than a day had passed since the incident. They took their mugs of steaming coffee outside to the catwalk.

"Looks like rain," said Blizzard, turning a full 360 degrees. After days of seemingly endless blue skies, he noted that the horizon was now blotted with low scudding cumulus, and the seas had turned a sickly grey color.

"Joel Hirshberger says it's just a small front, Boss, and that we should be back to clear weather long before nightfall."

As he spoke, a sailor came out onto the catwalk carrying a portable phone in his left hand.

"Doctor Potter conveys his compliments, Sir, and would like to speak with you."

Good morning, Doctor, what's on your mind?" His face turned solemn as he listened. "I'll want you with me when I see the admiral. Plan on it within the hour." He hung up and waited for the sailor to withdraw.

"The back-seater died ten minutes ago. Doctor Potter said the heart just stopped. The man never regained consciousness. Of course, they're going to do an autopsy to determine the exact cause of death. The pilot is still listed in guarded condition, but he appears to be getting stronger. I guess you heard me tell Potter I want him with me when we speak to the admiral."

Paige shook his head. "I don't understand it. They weren't injured, at least not anything that we could see, yet their plane was nearly destroyed by who-knows-what. Now that young fellow is dead because something killed him. We've got to find out what that something was."

Blizzard cradled his steaming mug with both hands. "After looking at that banged up plane yesterday, I went to see Joel Hirshberger and kicked over some ideas with him." Blizzard paused to regroup his thoughts, then continued. "I suggested that just maybe those guys had flown into one hell of a freakish, highly localized sandstorm. That maybe there had been a disturbance deep in the Sahara which caused thousands of tons of sand to be swept up into a jetstream, that Robinson tangled with this huge cloud of sand which would be whirling every which way, and before he could fly out, his plane was damn near torn apart." He paused, then added, "Of course, Joel confirmed that everything was calm in the Sahara, and quite correctly pointed out that such a huge sandstorm would have painted a picture like some great mythical monster on every radarscope from here to hell and back." He harrumphed. "So much for that idea."

Twenty minutes later as Blizzard stepped into the admiral's sea cabin, he heard Taylor say to someone, "Miles has just walked in." The admiral waved him over to the desk. On the flatscreen monitor was the image of his father-in-law, Chief of Naval Operations, Admiral Wayne Turnbull Christensen. He was seated behind his desk in the Pentagon.

"That about cover everything?" asked Christensen.

"Yes, Admiral, I think it does," replied Taylor.

"If you'd be so kind, Stanford, I'd like a word with Miles alone for a moment."

"Of course, Admiral."

"Hello, Miles," came the familiar voice from the other side of the Atlantic. "I hear you're having some problems."

"Nothing I can't handle, Chris," he replied, addressing his father-in-law by the nickname everyone in the family used. "Did Admiral

Taylor brief you on what's happened here, or did the news reach your desk via the daily rundown?"

"Both, but I've got to admit, it sure sounds strange."

"Well, it's now gone beyond strange, Admiral," said Blizzard. "The young back-seater died within the hour. My medical folk are doing an autopsy now to determine the cause of death."

Admiral Christensen rubbed his jaw and eyes. It was three o'clock in the morning in Washington.

"You been there all night?" Blizzard asked.

"Yeah. The Secretary of Defense has to go up on the Hill later this morning to defend our new ship-building program, so my staff's been busy getting him prepared for a grilling."

"Try to get a couple of hours shuteye between now and then. You look like hell, Admiral."

Christianson smiled. "Thanks for the compliment, Son. I'll let Anita know we spoke."

Blizzard saluted the image of his father-in-law, and Christensen returned the salute. As the picture faded, there was a light popping sound, and the screen went black.

Taylor returned with Doctor Potter fast on his heels. "Clarence told me about the bad news outside while you were talking with your father-in-law," he said, a not too subtle reminder that Christensen was family, and not just the Chief of Naval Operations. "When will the autopsy report be ready, Doctor?"

"Late this afternoon, Admiral."

"You plan on keeping the body on board until we get back to the fleet anchorage at Naples?" Again, Taylor swiveled to address Blizzard.

"Hadn't really given it any thought," replied Blizzard. 'But now that you mention it, unless Clarence objects, I would just as soon notify the next of kin and have the body escorted home as soon as possible."

"I see no conflict with that," interjected Potter. 'Once the autopsy is completed, we'll have no reason to keep the remains. If any of the organs reveal something out of the ordinary, then of course, we'd hold onto them for further study."

"OK, do what has to be done. Try to pick an escort who is familiar with the boy's family. Was he married?"

The admiral's question caught both men unprepared. |Blizzard and Potter exchanged glances. Neither knew.

"Well, take care of it," Taylor said, not wanting to press the issue. "We still have a lot of flying to do before returning to Naples. Sadly, accidents happen aboard carriers. It's part of our way of life, something we've learned to accept."

* * * * *

Fleming heard of the systems operator's death while sitting in a barber's chair. The news made him dwell for a long moment on the dangers of his chosen profession. His thoughts then turned to Susan.

They had been married almost one year, each day better than the one before. He hoped that he would never lose that feeling. He had almost gotten married on two prior occasions: once, soon after graduating from the Air Force Academy, and again, a few years later while stationed in Europe. After his second *almost* misstep, as he referred to it, he had resigned himself to the fact that he probably was not the marrying kind. He enjoyed his bachelor's lifestyle and knew he was the envy of more than just a few of his married friends.

Two months after reporting to the 412th Test Wing at Edwards Air Force Base, California, he was at Club Muroc having dinner with another pilot in the squadron when he spotted a young woman seated at a table nearby. She was with Colonel Tanner, the base commander, his wife, and another young woman about her own age. Fleming could not take his eyes off her.

She appeared to be in her mid-twenties, with long blonde hair and a face that was perfection. And when she spoke, her large eyes sparkled. The other girl was certainly pretty in her own right, but to Fleming, she didn't hold a candle to the blonde.

His dining companion had no idea who she was when asked, suggesting that maybe both girls were the colonel's daughters. Before Fleming's main course arrived, the blonde and the other members of her party rose and departed, amid a phalanx of appreciative stares from the men in the room.

She faded from his mind. He spent his days flying special test missions and enjoying every minute. His social life remained active as there were no shortage of good-looking women in Southern California.

He was driving off base one Saturday morning when he spotted her. She had just stepped off a curb while he was waiting for the light to change, then disappeared into a crowd. He knew it was ridiculous to park to try to find her, but that quixotic notion did not deter him. It was a wasted hour. She was nowhere to be found.

Later that week, he decided to track down the base commander's daughter and ask about her friend. That too failed. Jenny Tanner had gone to San Francisco for a couple of weeks to visit her brother. Fleming was crestfallen: it was just not meant to be.

But the third time was the charm, and it came from a totally unexpected source. Lieutenant Colonel John Dillon, his squadron commander, had asked Fleming to join him, his wife, and a few others for an informal barbecue for a Sunday afternoon two weeks later. The boss offhandedly suggested that Fleming not bring a date. He didn't elaborate and certainly didn't make it sound like an order. Fleming was assured there would be other singles present. He said yes.

And there she was, dressed in skinny jeans with a shirt knotted at her waist, sipping a tall drink and chatting with two pilots from his squadron.

Before Fleming could move, Marjorie Dillon, his boss's wife, linked arms and guided him toward a portable bar on the other side of the patio. "What will you have, Dave, I mean, besides Susan?" she said, with a know-it-all smirk.

"Excuse me, what? I didn't quite hear you." He was flustered and couldn't remember having had a similar feeling in years.

"Oh, a little bee told me that you've been trying to meet Susan Renninger, so, hearing how all else has failed, I felt I had a duty to step in and at least introduce you. After that, my boy, you're on your own, so follow me."

She dazzled him with a smile upon introduction and did something he had not expected: She took the lead and reached out her hand to shake his. The group continued to chat, but now included Fleming in the conversation. To a keen observer, it would have been readily apparent the three young men were each silently wishing the other two would simply vanish.

Fleming finally managed to steer Susan Renninger away and found a quiet corner to talk.

She volunteered that she taught fifth grade in the elementary school in Lancaster and had been there since the beginning of the school year. It was now early May. By evening's end he had asked her out for the following Wednesday, and she had said yes.

Late that night, lying alone in his bed, he realized he had fallen madly in love. *'This is the woman I've been searching for all my life,'* his pragmatic ego crowed to the darkness, only to be immediately challenged by his superego. *So, what do you plan on doing about it, David?*

* * * * *

"That should hold you, Major," came the barber's voice from behind Fleming, snapping him out of his reverie and back to the present. "By the way, Sir, you never answered the commander in the chair beside you."

"Huh? What was that?" Fleming asked, looking quizzically at the chair beside him. It was empty, the last occupant long gone.

"He asked you if you knew the backseater from the accident yesterday? You know, Sir, the one from the plane that got all tore up on landing." There were very few secrets on a carrier.

"No, no, I didn't know him," said Fleming. He paid and returned to the Tiger Sharks squadron ready room. He was scheduled to fly in three hours and had a lot to do to prepare.

CHAPTER 7

Sunday morning – early - June 20th

Dr. Potter stood before Admiral Taylor, Manny Eisenhauer, Captain Blizzard, and CAG, the autopsy report down by his side. His face told the story. He was not bringing good news.

"Rather than read it, Doctor, why don't you just give us a summary. We can read it later."

"Yes, Admiral." Potter let loose a small sigh. "How do you explain that a healthy, twenty-six-year-old man has just died of old age?" He held his right hand aloft, a signal for more to come. "It's absolutely preposterous, I know, but that's what we have here. There was total degeneration throughout the body. The heart was one you would expect to find in a man in his late eighties, and the same can be said of his cardiovascular system. The musculature had atrophied to reflect what you would see in an octogenarian, and the bones were brittle and dry. I could rattle on with the medical mumbo jumbo, but the end result would remain. The lieutenant died of a malady known to us *medicos* as simply old age. It's all here in my report."

Taylor pursed his lips and glanced at Manny Eisenhauer with a look that said, you go first.

The chief of staff took the cue. "Clarence, tell me, did he actually look like an old man? I mean, externally. Was he all wrinkled and bald-headed, … you know?"

"Yes and no, Manny, and I'm not being a smartass. The tissue had degenerated, and this was very apparent microscopically when we

54

examined the epidermis, the dermis, and the subcutaneous fat layer. His hair was also in bad shape. Much of it fell out between the time we recovered him and the time he died, and I venture to say, had he lived another couple of days he would have been completely bald. So, yeah, you could certainly say he looked old."

"And the pilot?" asked the admiral. "What kind of shape is he in?"

"Not good, Admiral, and I don't know why. He was progressing nicely, then this morning he started going sour. He's now lapsed into unconsciousness, and it's the medical staff's considered opinion the man will die shortly."

"The same thing?"

"Yes, I'm afraid so."

"This is just impossible," the admiral said, as he began to pace. "OK, I'll buy into the idea that one's dead and the other's dying from shock brought on by only God knows what, but I refuse to believe they suddenly turned into little old men. Doctor, your colleagues back home would laugh you out of the profession if you presented them with the same findings you're foisting on us right now." The admiral went quiet for a long moment, then said in a low voice, "Aw, hell, Clarence, of course we believe you. It's just all so preposterous. Anyway, please keep it to yourselves in the medical department. I don't want this word spreading among the crew or getting out to the rest of the ships in my strike group."

Potter nodded his agreement, then left. Five minutes later, Commander Seymour, and two civilian technical representatives presented an equally disturbing report on the condition of the plane. The four officers spent the next few minutes reading the findings.

"You're all in agreement on this?" the admiral finally asked, looking to each man in turn.

"Yes, Sir," the three replied in unison,

"Let me summarize for my own benefit what I've just read," continued Taylor, "because I want to be absolutely sure I have it right. Commander Seymour, you write here that the Hornet did not fly into a sandstorm, but rather, it is now falling apart due to old age. The pitting and the wrinkling of the structural metal parts, and on the composites which we all inspected yesterday, was caused by fatigue; that the molecular structures of the metals, alloys, and other materials are showing all the classic signs of wear associated with aging, and if sophisticated Carbon-14 dating tests are performed in a stateside lab, they will confirm those findings. So, tell me, gentlemen, based on what you have been able to establish so far, how old do you claim this airplane to be?"

"I can't give you a hard and fast answer on that, Admiral," said Seymour. "Certain parts of the plane have aged faster than others. There's no rhyme or reason to it that we can tell, but that's what's happened."

"Explain."

"The vertical stabilizers and tail assembly were all in fairly good shape, only minor fatigue found there. However, both cockpits were another matter, especially the backseater's. Somehow, the metals in that part of the plane aged well over two hundred years, yet a mere few feet away the aging process was less than a hundred years. Admiral, we've checked and rechecked our equipment thoroughly for malfunctions; everything tests normal. I'm at a loss to give you an explanation. There's got to be a scientific answer, and when we find it, we'll report back to you."

"I'm sure there is a reason, Commander. Meanwhile, who else knows these findings?"

"Only those who worked on the aircraft."

"And how many is that?"

"Less than a dozen."

"As of right now your report is classified Top Secret. Tell the rest of the people working on the plane to keep this to themselves. I don't want the information spreading throughout the ship and to the rest of the fleet. Clear?"

All three acknowledged that they understood.

One minute later klaxon bells sounded throughout the *LBJ* calling the crew to general quarters, and five thousand sailors immediately shared the same thought: *Is it a drill ... or could this really be war?*

CHAPTER 8

Sunday morning – Late night – June 20ᵗʰ

Father Caffarone was celebrating mass on the hangar deck for almost three hundred sailors when the klaxon sounded and a voice commanded: *"General quarters, general quarters, all hands man your battle stations, this is not a drill."*

Men dashed to their battle stations; all thoughts of the Lord forgotten in the scramble to get to their assigned positions. Pilots not on duty rushed to squadron ready rooms, while those on alert raced for the special escalators that would whisk them topside in seconds. At the moment of the first sounding of the alarm, the *LBJ* began turning into the wind, her escorting destroyers dancing nimbly out of her way. Her foaming wake was a seething cauldron as hundreds of tons of water were churned by her four huge screws turning at maximum revs, allowing the one hundred-thousand-ton behemoth to come about. Three minutes after the first note of the alarm had sounded, four jets roared off the maglev catapults and headed away from the ship. The *LBJ* had not needed to come about more than twenty-five degrees to starboard in order to have the wind coming directly down the angle deck, and now, for the first time, she was reacting to the end for which she had been created: To attack the enemy.

Two hours later Blizzard addressed the ship's company to explain what had happened. "All hands, this is the Captain," he began, his metallic voice being piped from the bridge to the far ends of the ship. "This morning at oh eight hundred hours a Russian submarine made an emergency surfacing approximately one nautical mile from our position. She was a nuclear Laika-class boat and gave no warning of her intentions."

Blizzards paused for a moment, then continued. "Long before she surfaced, we were aware of her presence and, of course, knew that she was not one of our own. Four of our escorts surrounded her as soon as she broke the surface, and before the Russians had their hatches opened and could put observers up into the sail, we had four Hornets flying overhead. I want to stress that at no time did she present the slightest threat either to us or any other vessel in the strike group."

Again, he allowed a few moments for the crew to digest his words, then added, "I can further inform you that her surfacing was rather unusual, and from what we have been able to determine, she was in grave peril of sinking. The *Tacoma* sailed close enough to hail the Russians with loudspeakers. Apparently, the Russian boat had lost all of her radios and navigational aids. She asked that the *Tacoma* confirm its longitude and latitude coordinates, and when advised of their exact position in the Mediterranean Sea a few minutes later, their captain seemed genuinely shocked at the news. He then asked *Tacoma* to inform the nearest Russian surface craft of her position. Within an hour a trawler pulled alongside. The Russians requested that our destroyers not move any closer than one hundred meters, and we complied. Also, they said that for some unknown reason most of her crew members needed medical attention but declined our help."

Blizzard paused for a couple of seconds, then continued. "So, let me wrap up by saying that two guided-missile cruisers from their Mediterranean Fleet are steaming towards the submarine at the present time, so I think the Russians will be out of our hair for a while. Again, I want to extend my appreciation for the professional manner in which you all conducted yourselves. We will secure from general quarters and resume flight operations as scheduled."

Another pause, and the XO came on the speakers. "The chaplains wish to advise that church services will be held this evening, and times for the various denominational services will be broadcast later this afternoon. That will be all."

Blizzard had sounded relaxed, but that was far from the case.

* * * * *

"What is it, Al?" he had asked two hours earlier, racing onto the bridge.

The XO replied while keeping his eyes glued to a pair of binoculars. "Looks like a bogey submarine surfacing at two five zero degrees true, Boss. I immediately checked with the Combat Direction Center and they had no warning of a boat even being in the area! They became aware of her presence just moments ago," he added, still adjusting his binoculars.

"Dammit, Al, that's flat out impossible," Blizzard replied. "Somebody hand me some glasses!"

A yeoman jumped forward with a pair of binoculars. Blizzard trained on the target and sighted it in. The black shape took on an identifiable form.

"Looks like a Laika-class boat, Boss," said Paige, taking the words out of Blizzard's mouth. "Probably the *Yakutsk*."

The *LBJ* was already well on its way to coming into the wind, Paige having given the order immediately after calling for general quarters. The men gathered on the command bridge could see the pilots strapping into their cockpits while the various color-coded deck crews prepared the ship for launch operations.

"Tell CDC to get their shit together and come up with a damn good explanation as to why we weren't warned of that submarine in the first place. Also, I want to know why everybody on the escorts were also asleep. Why the hell didn't they squawk bogies in the area?' As Blizzard spoke, the red phone by his elbow rang. It was the admiral wanting to know what was going on.

It took Blizzard less than thirty seconds to apprise him of the situation. "Why wasn't I told of the Russian sub? I'm the strike group commander in case you've forgotten, Captain. While my flag's aboard, you're my eyes and ears, Blizzard." He was furious. "Stand by for further orders."

"Aye, Admiral," replied Blizzard, rankled that Taylor was blowing off steam at him, yet deep down fully appreciating the admiral's dilemma.

Blizzard studied the faces of the two officers who had appeared in the sail. Something was very wrong. He alerted his Executive Officer. "Al, zoom in on the captain; I want you to look carefully at his face. The guy hasn't shaved in days, his whole appearance is haggard, and you'll see he's shivering uncontrollably. That's the face of a man who's really ill."

"The same can also be said about his friend, Boss," the XO replied. "Did you see how they're dressed? Why would anyone be wearing a winter sweater in the middle of summer? It just doesn't add up. I'm thinking they've got some major problems. "

Later, Blizzard and his department heads met to try to piece together what had happened. Their answers were puzzling, and in many respects not answers at all. For some still-unknown reason, none of the sonar operators in the strike group had recorded the Russian submarine's presence until moments before she broke to the surface. There was no explanation for this egregious, impossible lapse, yet all monitoring equipment was found to be functioning normally.

A chief from the Combat Direction Center spoke for them all when he said in an exasperated voice, "Captain, it's like one moment the water was clear of all hostiles for a hundred miles, then in the next instant, *pow!* God created this one and popped it to the surface!"

Blizzard stared the man down with an icy look while silently admitting that his was as good an explanation as any. But all shared the same genuine concern. How could they not have known of the Russian sub's presence? What sort of new technology did the Russians possess that their submarines were now impervious to detection? It was enough to make the hairs on one's neck stand on end just thinking of the ramifications of such a game-changing possibility.

* * * * *

"Commander Hirshberger, you'd better come down here immediately, Sir." It was the duty weather officer.

"Is there a storm brewing out there?" he asked into the phone beside his bunk.

"Negative Sir, but it's real important.

"This Ensign Hoyle?"

"Yes, Sir."

"I'll be there in five." Three minutes later, Hirshberger hotfooted it into the weather station. He had noted the ship was riding with a barely perceptible roll, so he realized the problem couldn't be weather-related.

"Sir, I need you to take a look at the readings we're getting." He led the way to a bank of screens which were displaying in real time a readout of barometric pressure, wind velocity with direction and speed, temperature, dew point, and a satellite display of weather patterns for the entire Mediterranean and adjacent land masses. Hirshberger studied the displays, his eyes darting from screen to screen before speaking.

"How long has this been happening?"

"About ten minutes, Sir. Suddenly, everything began acting haywire. I immediately sent a technician topside to check and see if our instruments had been damaged, but the package is normal. I then asked the weather guys on the escorts if they were having the same problems, but for some reason our radio transmissions keep breaking up, and we're having a tough time confirming anything, so I decided to call you because of your standing order."

"That was the right move." Hirshberger knitted his brow, lost in thought. Glancing once more at the displays for confirmation that what he was seeing was indeed fact, he reached for a phone on the bulkhead and dialed up the communications center.

"This is Lieutenant Commander Hirshberger, let me speak to the duty officer."

A few seconds later, "Joel, Ed Sewell. What gives?"

61

"I might ask you the same Ed, or is it normal for you to be there at twenty-three hundred hours?"

"No, it's not." Sewell sounded serious. 'Frankly, we're having major problems with our comm."

"Across the entire spectrum?" Hirshberger asked.

"That's affirmative. HF, VHF, UHF, single sideband, infrared, and our all discreet frequencies. Radar and Sonar, same story. Also, the Internet is down. Fact is, I was about to call you to see if it was weather-related."

"My instruments are screwed up too, Ed, and I can't explain it. Do you know if the skipper has been alerted?"

"He has," Sewell replied. "Captain Blizzard, the XO, and the admiral are on the command bridge right now. We'll be recovering aircraft in about twenty minutes, and the brass is worried whether we can bring them down or not."

"How many are up?" Hirshberger wanted to know.

"Carrier Air Traffic Control Center tells me we have two, four-ship formations. Communications is kaput between us and them, so they're going into a standard holding pattern waiting for advice from the ship. The Tactical Air Navigation System (TACAN) and the Instrument Landing System (ILS) are also down."

"Knock wood we're back on the air by then," replied Hirshberger. "Got to run, Ed, stay in touch." He hung up the phone and told Hoyle to make another check of their outside instruments up on the island superstructure. His thoughts harkened back to what Ed Sewell had told him. The eight planes, some single seaters, most two-seaters, were now flying blind somewhere up in the darkness. But even if they were able to get back to the ship in the unlikely event that only a directional beacon was still operational, it would be impossible to land those big, supersonic jets without an ILS. It was moments like these that Hirshberger was glad not to be a pilot.

"Holy shit, Commander, come look at this!" shouted a sailor monitoring the panels.

Hirshberger jumped to the console. The instruments were all rapidly seeking new positions. The barometer went into a freefall, stabilized, then rapidly reversed itself as the temperature gauge began climbing. Within a minute the instruments had all settled onto new readings, doing in seconds what should have taken twenty-four to thirty-six hours.

He felt the hairs on his neck rise. He grabbed the phone.

"Ed, do you have your communications back up?"

"I do. Moments ago, everything came alive. We're back in touch with the aircraft aloft and have let them know our inertial navigation system and ILS are operational. We should be recovering shortly. There's no way I can explain this, and I know the boss and the admiral are going to want answers."

It was as if he were clairvoyant. No sooner had he spoken than he was paged to report to the command bridge. A similar call went to Hirshberger. Both men met a couple of minutes later and walked onto the bridge together.

"Standby to recover aircraft." The command echoed throughout the ship and the carrier completed her swing into the wind. Red lights were switched on all over the flight deck and the island, bathing the vessel in their glow. To anyone observing from afar, the *LBJ* appeared as a surreal ghost ship floating on a painted sea. The red light theme was not used for the purpose of creating strange, nighttime effects, but to save lives. And those were the lives of the returning pilots and the deck crews. White lights blind, and a blind man on a carrier deck working amidst moving jet fighters and whipsawing metal cables would soon be a dead man. For an unfortunate few, this has been a swift and final fate.

For the next forty-five minutes, they huddled in conference with the admiral, the senior ship's officers, the air wing staff, and the flag command staff.

The planes were recovered without incident, yet by the end of the meeting no one had answers. Manny Eisenhour believed they should cease flight operations until the problem was identified and solved, but the admiral nixed that idea. He argued that the flight crews should be thoroughly briefed on the continuing possibility of weather-induced communications problems, but the most important warning would be to stay alert while airborne.

"Gentlemen, we can't let this incident keep us from our mission, so let's get our planes back in the air." Admiral Taylor's tone of voice told everyone the meeting was over.

CHAPTER 9

Monday mid-morning – June 21ˢᵗ

Fleming and Lafayette were flying one hundred miles northwest of the carrier, and the Island of Sardinia stretched out below them to the southwest, while Italy's shoreline remained an unseen 220 miles to their east. They had been in the air for thirty minutes, one of eighteen planes the *LBJ* had launched.

"Repeat, I didn't get that," Fleming now said into his headphones.

"I asked if you get the heebie jeebies flying with us Navy types? Worries that you didn't have flying with the Air Force. Maybe it's a difficult question to answer," Lafayette added lamely. "Also, maybe it's a really dumb question."

"No it's not dumb, Chuck," Fleming replied. "However, there is one thing that *does* give me the heebie jeebies, and that's the thought of a "cold cat." But from listening to the other guys, I guess it's something most of them think about at one time or another. You ever seen one?"

"Not in person," said Lafayette. "Just the standard footage of the one on the *Oriskany* shot during the Vietnam War. It was a pretty grim thing to watch."

Both flyers knew that the "cold cat" they were discussing was a condition that might occur during one in ten thousand airplane launches from a carrier deck. And it's never a pretty sight. It happens when a catapult releases without a full head of steam, but still attempts to hurl a jet into the air. Because there is no power, or insufficient power at best, the aircraft flounders helplessly along the deck trying the impossible task of gaining enough speed to fly. Inevitably, it crashes into the ocean, and before anyone can react, the carrier traveling at well over thirty knots will churn the plane under its bow to be lost forever. This all takes place within a matter of seconds, and there is never any hope of recovering the crew. Little wonder carrier pilots don't like to dwell on that prospect, though oftentimes they will do that just before a launch while the plane is straining against its harness. The possibility this will be that one time flashes through many an unwilling mind. *It's a very uncommon occurrence,* Fleming now reminded himself, *and anyway, it's impossible with these new maglev catapults.*

Fleming and Lafayette had flown all their missions together and were now a team. Each implicitly trusted in the other's ability to perform his function smoothly and professionally. They weren't close friends, although they often chatted in the ready room. Each had his own circle of acquaintances, but in the air, they complemented one another perfectly.

"So, what do you make of the recent communications blackouts, Dave?" Lafayette now asked.

"Nobody seems to have an explanation," he continued, his mind primarily focused on monitoring his screens. "I spoke with a couple of the guys who were up there last night, and they admitted things got real hairy, real fast. Not just that they couldn't speak to the CDC, but for a few minutes, they couldn't even talk to each other. Some said that all their glass cockpit displays went completely black. And this was all happening while the weather was clear, and visibility was unlimited. Doesn't make a whole lot of sense, huh?"

Fleming frowned, remembering his conversation with Joel Hirshberger yesterday evening down in the meteorological department.

Hirshberger had told him of the meeting with the skipper and the admiral, and how both had expressed their frustration over the incidents and were deeply troubled by the lack of answers. "It's tied into the weather, Dave, I'm sure of it now," Hirshberger had said. "I've been in this business for more than two decades, and I've never seen anything like this. Something bad is going to happen, and when it does, it will be an unmitigated disaster."

"I'm starting to agree with you," Fleming had said. "CAG told us there had been thoughts of cancelling all further flying until we got some answers, but the admiral nixed that idea and said we would stay at flight quarters until contrary orders came from him personally. The mission briefers have warned us to be alert for possible communications blackouts and instrument malfunctions. Most of the pilots I know are acting like it isn't getting to them, but there's a palpable undercurrent of nervousness in the wardrooms. And then having that Russian sub surfacing right under our noses sure has added to the jitters."

Now, cruising at twenty-eight thousand feet and moving at five hundred seventy knots, his mind was on full alert. His eyes swept his instruments for the umpteenth time. Everything was normal, and communications between the other planes and the CDC were loud and clear.

The mission profile had called for a simple patrol. The eighteen aircraft would fly in pairs on equidistant headings from the carrier, each two-ship maintaining forty degrees of separation from the next pair, thus covering the entire three hundred sixty degrees of the compass. The flight plans called for them to fly outbound for forty minutes, execute an echelon turn to port, intercept their new headings twenty degrees less than the outbound one, and return to the carrier. Recovery would be in order of launch unless any aircraft declared an inflight emergency or squawked a critical fuel condition. Fleming was flying lead with Hamilton his wingman. There was no indication this would be anything other than a routine flight.

Within seconds that all changed.

"Major, I'm losing my radar return," said Lafayette, subconsciously signaling his concern by addressing Fleming by rank.

"Does it look like an equipment malfunction?" Fleming asked, instantly alerted to the potential seriousness of the problem.

"Negative, Sir, everything's normal, it's just that we're not painting anything. On the long range sweep I've even lost contact with the strike group."

"Stand by, let me check with Hamilton." He changed from intercom to transmit. *"Liberty two, this is lead."* He waited a couple of seconds No response. He called again. Nothing. The third time, he raised the Combat Direction Center. Their signal was weak and broken.

"Bigfoot, this is Liberty one," he said, identifying himself to the carrier. *"We're having comm difficulties raising Liberty two. We're inbound and experiencing radar malfunctions."* His eyes darted to the instrument panel. What he saw made him do a doubletake. The computer-generated instruments on his glass cockpit display screens were now all malfunctioning, even his primary flight instruments which were controlled by static and atmospheric pressure were giving patently false readings. And this had taken place within a matter of seconds.

Glancing outside, everything appeared normal. *Where was Liberty two?* There was no sign of his wingman. His eyes swept the sky on both sides of the Hornet and he checked both mirrors. Nothing! Hamilton had vanished! Visibility was unlimited with no sign of bad weather. A check with his magnetic compass assured him he was on course, and although his attitude indicator was showing he was in a fifteen-degree climbing turn to the right, all outside visual references said he was flying straight and level.

"Bigfoot, this is Liberty one. I've lost Liberty two. All my instruments are now totally unreliable, not just my radio-nav screens, but even my mechanical instruments. I'm resetting circuit breakers, but the problem is being caused from outside of the aircraft. Do you read, Bigfoot? Acknowledge."

There was no reply. He broadcast again. Only static. He switched back to intercom.

"We've got problems, Chuck. I'm heading directly to the last known position of the carrier. We should be back in the pattern within twenty minutes. Right now, fuel is not a worry, so if we have to divert to a land base in Italy, then that's what we'll do. How are you doing back there?"

"I'm not sure, Major." Lafayette said, sounding worried. "I'm getting a radar return showing like we're inside a barrel, and it's shrinking around us real fast. Major, my advice is to slow down to maneuvering speed. It's probably an equipment malfunction, but I sure don't like it."

Fleming immediately complied by easing back on the throttles and opening his speed brake. The whine of the engines became deeper as their airspeed bled off, and the deployed speed brake created a rumble uniquely its own. The fighter rapidly lost speed, and when the airspeed indicator showed one hundred and fifty knots. he came back with the power and retracted the speed brake. He had made the decision not to power all the way down to maneuvering speed simply because he no longer trusted any of his instruments. He wanted that built-in margin of safety in case he had to spool the engines up quickly, light the afterburners, and hightail it out of harm's way.

Before he had time to relay his intentions to Lafayette, there was a blinding flash of emerald-colored light followed by an external explosion. The Hornet was instantly flung violently onto its back and pushed into an inverted flat spin. For a couple of moments Fleming's world turned dark as he fought to control the plane. He realized he was blacking out from the sudden, acceleration-induced force-loading effects on his body, but before he could gather his thoughts, daylight returned, the plane was flying upright, and the air was smooth. He willed away the sensation of impending vertigo by fixing his eyes on the magnetic compass, a trick used by pilots to confirm their spatial orientation with their surroundings. The unsettling experience lasted less than five seconds. He nudged the Hornet back onto its original heading.

"You OK back there, Chuck?"

"Holy shit, Dave, what the hell happened? I must have blacked out for a couple of seconds. I was about to warn you to brace yourself, but before I could say a word, we were being tossed around like a kid's rag doll. And that green flash of light! I've never seen anything like it." He paused for a long moment, then added in a puzzled voice, "Check this out. My screens are functioning normally again, but I can't seem to paint the strike group, or any other airborne objects out to a range of forty miles. But I am getting a clear return from the small island grouping below, so I know the down looking radar is working again. I can also see a few blips on the surface which I'm guessing are fishing vessels. Man, this is way beyond weird."

Fleming scanned his own instruments, baffled by what he was seeing. Those which relied on atmospheric pressure to function, appeared to be operating normally, but all his radio-navigation instruments were dead. It was beyond weird.

"At least the plane seems to be in good shape," Fleming said, rocking the wings as he spoke. He tested the rudder and elevators, then brought the engines up to max military power while closely monitoring their performance. Everything checked out normal. His fuel flow meter showed he had enough gas on board for about thirty more minutes flying time, maybe more, if he conserved. He wasn't too concerned, knowing he would be back aboard the *LBJ* in half that time.

He tried raising the carrier again to no avail, and after a frustrating few minutes, decided to call Approach Control at Rome's Fiumicino Airport. He dialed in 125.5 and listened. Nothing. He shrugged, then dialed Naples International Airport Approach on frequency 125.35. Nothing. *Even the static doesn't sound right,* he thought, then began dialing in random channels. Nothing anywhere. As a last resort, he slowly worked through the AM band hoping to pick up any civilian broadcasts. The results were equally disappointing.

"Chuck, we seem to have lost our radios," he said in a matter-of-fact voice so as not to alarm his backseater. "Seems we're on our own, at least for the moment." He felt a cold sweat forming under his mask and flightsuit.

Wait until Joel Hirshberger hears about this little escapade, he thought, as he scanned the water below, looking for the carrier and the rest of the strike group. All he saw was an empty sea from horizon to horizon.

"See anything on your radar yet, Chuck?" Fleming asked, his voice hopeful. "We should be coming up on the strike group."

"Nothing, and I don't understand it because my radar is painting normally. There's no sign of the *LBJ* anywhere."

Fleming continued to visually scan outside the plane. This was now more than just spooky! Another check with the standby magnetic compass confirmed that he was still heading in the right direction, yet somehow an entire strike group of United States Navy ships had vanished. He realized fuel was definitely going to be a problem now, and he didn't have enough left to start hunting for the carrier. He made a decision and turned the plane eastward.

"Something's very wrong, Chuck," Fleming finally conceded, "so instead of trying to find the answers out here over the water, I think our best bet is to press on to Rome. We're still good on fuel, but I want you to prepare to eject in case the worst should happen, and we find ourselves having to depart company with this bird rather fast."

"Understood, Dave," came the reply from the rear cockpit. "Do you want me to broadcast an SOS as we head for the coast?"

"Negative. We know we aren't receiving, so in all probability we're not being picked up by anyone. I need you to concentrate on getting squared away. Doublecheck your survival gear."

"Dave, I have a thought," said Lafayette. "Maybe our transmitter *is* working, and possibly our receivers are also. Let me activate my emergency locator beacon while you monitor the guard channel, and let's see if my signal is getting picked up on our own radios."

Fleming thought the idea was brilliant. Lafayette would activate his survival radio which would automatically begin broadcasting a simultaneous distress signal on 121.5 MHz and 406 MHz. At the same time, he would tune his aircraft radio to the same frequency to see if a signal were coming through. These international distress frequencies,

71

known as guard channels to all pilots, were dedicated to civilian and military flyers, and continuously monitored by airports around the world.

"Good thinking, let's give it a try." Fleming dialed in the right frequency and waited. Seconds later he picked up the signal being broadcast from the rear cockpit. That left no doubt in his mind now. The Hornet's radios were functioning normally.

"Your signal's loud and clear, Chuck." This only added to Fleming's sense of unease. If the plane's radios were working, then why weren't they able to pick up any communications from the strike group, or any of the dozens of civilian stations throughout the region? He shook his head. The answer eluded him.

"Chuck, as soon as you have yourself squared away, and if I give you the word, start broadcasting a mayday and keep broadcasting a continual update of our position. Maybe someone out there will pick it up."

"Roger that."

Fleming concentrated on flying, and ten uneventful minutes later, the Italian coastline of central Italy slipped by beneath their wings. They now had fifteen minutes of fuel on board. He checked his own survival gear, which included his handheld radio, his 9MM Glock, and his iPhone and charger, which he always carried while flying. Most pilots he knew did the same just in case they had to divert to a land base from the ship. All agreed on one thing: nothing would be worse than being stranded in a strange city without a phone.

As they flew inland, Fleming began noticing that the land mass below didn't look quite right. And then it hit him. There were no primary or secondary roads, but the one most glaringly obvious fact was that there were no cars to be seen anywhere!

"Chuck, my compass must have precessed. We're slipping off course, so I'm going down on the deck for a better look-see, and to get my bearings."

"Roger."

With throttles back to idle and the speed brake extended, the fighter dropped easily towards the ground. Leveling off at a thousand feet, Fleming took up a new northbound heading, now hugging the coastline. A few minutes later he spotted a harbor below and made a low-level pass over the small bay dotted with boats, while taking in the clusters of houses and other types of buildings strung out along its waterfront.

Lafayette spoke first. "Where in the hell are we? I don't recognize a damn thing down there. It looks like a cheap, frigging movie set." The worry in his voice was now very real.

Fleming said nothing but banked sharply, made a shallow 360 degree turn while dropping further down to three hundred feet, then powered back to maneuvering speed. Both now saw a sea of upturned faces following their progress. Soon, some in the crowd began acting scared and confused, pointing fingers up at them. Then, as if on command, they all began running for cover.

Fleming's low fuel warning light winked once, winked again, and "Bitchin' Betty's" digitalized voice began ordering him to 'return to base' by repeating '*Bingo, Bingo,*' in his ear in her distinctive, Tennessee twang. The moment of truth had arrived. With nowhere to land, and less than 2000 pounds of gas left in the tanks, Fleming pushed the throttles forward and began climbing to gain as much altitude as possible.

"Chuck, we're going to have to punch out. I'll set the trim and engage the autopilot to take the Hornet out over water once we part company. It will crash harmlessly into the sea. Any objections or comments?"

"No, Sir. Something is very wrong down there. Is it even possible we're not over Italy?"

No, that's Italy all right," Fleming said, as they climbed through fourteen thousand feet with an indicated airspeed of two hundred and seventy knots. The terrain below was rolling hillsides, and the weather was clear.

"You all set back there?"

"I'm ready to go on your command," Lafayette said as he mentally went through his ejection checklist for the umpteenth time. '*Canopy. Visor. Mask. Seat Kit. Life Preserver Unit.*' Ready.

Three seconds later Lafayette heard the one word command, "*Go.*"

Instantly, the canopy blew away as he triggered the rocket-propelled Martin-Baker ejection seat. He was violently thrust up into the slipstream at a speed of sixty-five feet per second while instantly enduring a crushing force on his body equal to twenty times that of the earth's gravity.

One third of a second later, Fleming followed him, the tremendous roar of his own rocket seat blotting out all other sounds. Gravitational forces scrunched him low into his seat, but before he had a chance to react, the separating mechanism kicked him free, and one second after that he was snapped into an upright position as his parachute opened automatically. He remained conscious throughout the ordeal and, as he swayed below his billowing chute, he took stock of the situation. His eyes searched for the Hornet which was now over the water and out of fuel. It had started a downward death spiral toward the sea. He turned to look back over his left shoulder, and spotted Lafayette behind and below him, drifting peacefully toward the ground. He replayed in his mind the scene of the harbor they had overflown only minutes before. *I can't believe any of this shit, but dammit, Chuck saw it too, so I know I'm not hallucinating.* A chill ran through him. *One way or another, we'll have an answer soon enough.* The ground was getting closer as it rushed up to meet him.

CHAPTER 10

Monday morning – Monday night – June 21ˢᵗ

The Combat Air Wing Commander activated the ship's 1 Main Circuit (1MC) PA system. "Now hear this," Gowdy said over the intercom, his voice being piped throughout the ship, "this is CAG requesting Captain Blizzard to come to the Combat Direction Center. That is all." This was a call from one commander to another commander of equal rank and equal authority. Their interdependent commands were an anomaly found only aboard aircraft carriers.

In simpler terms, all shipboard operations fall under the sole authority of the ship's captain, and all vessels can only have one captain. And even though several of the senior officers aboard can hold the navy rank of captain, every one of the ship's crewmembers knows there's but one person called 'The Captain,' and he's also known as 'God' while commanding the ship!

So too, a Combat Air Wing (CAW) can only have one commander, and the CAG has sole authority over all of his sailors, and the 76 or more, aircraft in the CAW. He does not answer to the ship's captain, and vice versa. In the air wing, he too is God!

The phone by the watch officer's elbow buzzed. It was Blizzard. He turned it over to CAG.

"Miles, we're having a problem with one of our planes. It could be a repeat of Saturday. Please come to the CDC."

"I'm on my way."

75

A couple of minutes later Blizzard joined Gowdy in front on a huge plexiglass situation board. Every airborne plane's position was being monitored in real time, and all pertinent information was being posted by sailors writing in black markers behind the transparent board. Their scripting and numbering was written backwards, so that those standing in front of the panel could read it. Theirs was a unique skill that took months to master.

"What's the problem, Sean?" asked Blizzard.

"*Liberty one,*" replied Gowdy using a metal pointer to show Fleming's position relative to the *LBJ.* "A couple of minutes ago we received a signal from him stating that his instruments were malfunctioning, and that his radio-nav package had become unreliable. His transmission was patchy, and we missed some of it, but what we did hear we have on tape. We heard him trying to raise his wingman, so we broke in when we heard him call *Liberty two* a couple of times with no response. We're not sure whether he heard us or not."

"Where is he now?" Blizzard, asked, eyeing the entire board to grasp the big picture.

"Apparently he's gone down, Skipper," said Gowdy. Meanwhile, all around the two officers, men were working quietly and efficiently with the aid of the ship's computers, guiding the seventeen remaining planes back to the carrier. "One minute he was painting a good return on our radar, and the next minute he disappeared, just like that," CAG said, snapping his fingers.

"What about *Liberty two?* Did he experience any similar difficulty, and did he see *Liberty one* go into the water?"

"Yes, he had difficulties and, no, he did not see *Liberty one* go in. *Liberty two* also had radio and nav problems. He told us he experienced momentary, severe spatial disorientation at the same time he lost *Liberty one* on his surveillance radar. And apparently this all happened within a couple of seconds. Weather is unrestricted, and that's why I'm saying it looks like a replay of yesterday."

"Who's the pilot?"

"Major Fleming, our Air Force guest. He's flying a Super Hornet, and his backseater is a Lieutenant Lafayette."

"Have the angels launched?"

"Yes, Captain. As soon as we lost him, we sent two helicopters up." CAG studied his watch. "They should be over the area of last contact in about twenty minutes."

Blizzard rubbed his jaw, thinking through a host of possibilities and rejecting all in rapid succession. Without looking at anyone, he asked quietly, "Has the admiral been told?"

"Negative, Skipper."

Blizzard called Taylor on a direct line. "Admiral, we have a downed aircraft about one hundred miles north of our position. It appears to be a repeat of Saturday's problem. Spotty communications, total instrument malfunction, then the loss of any radar contact in a split second's time. We have angels airborne, and they're on their way to its last known position."

Blizzard heard a sudden intake of air, but when Taylor spoke, he was calm. "Two questions, Captain. What's the *Truman's* position? And how are her decks?"

"Stand-by, Admiral." A few seconds later Blizzard had the answer for the admiral. "The *Truman* is on station approximately fifty nautical miles to our west, and her decks are spotted for launch. Did you want her to recover our planes, Sir?" Blizzard was trying to second-guess the admiral.

"It was a thought, Miles, but no. Continue to recover. As soon as the last bird is down I want you to move the *LBJ* to the aircraft's last known position. Radio the angels our intentions. Also, Miles, I am ordering our screen of destroyers and escorts to rendezvous with the *Truman Strike Group*. We're going in alone."

"Am I sure I heard you correctly, Admiral? You want us to go forward unescorted?"

"Yes, you heard correctly, Captain." There was a momentary pause, then Taylor continued, "Miles, the US taxpayers have ponied up sixteen billion dollars to build this ship. There's nothing like her

77

on earth, not even the other carriers in her class. She's that unique. Now, if we can't operate for a few hours alone, then the public has effectively wasted our country's treasure. Also, I can't say I'm thrilled at the way our screen failed to find that Russian sub yesterday before she suddenly surfaced right on our doorstep." After a longer pause he said, "Miles, request permission to join you on the command bridge in five minutes."

"Of course, Admiral," said Blizzard. It was the expected reply, one steeped in naval tradition. Decorum called for the admiral to request permission to come onto the captain's bridge. There is only one captain on any vessel, and Blizzard was the only skipper of the *LBJ*. But to deny the admiral access to his bridge would have been unthinkable.

* * * * *

An hour had passed, and the *LBJ* command bridge was electric with anticipation. The executive officer was effectively in command of the carrier even though the skipper was on the bridge but engaged in next-step planning discussions with the admiral and his staff.

All the aircraft aloft had been recovered, most now securely tied down on the flight deck, others moved down to hangar deck for maintenance. The escort vessels in the *LBJ* carrier strike group would rendezvous with the *Truman* and fall under the direct command of the Strike Group Commander, Rear Admiral Barry Morgan, until further notice.

Hamilton had been debriefed personally by Admiral Taylor. He could not shed any light on the mysterious disappearance of his flight leader and spoke of his own confusion and problems in the air. The admiral insisted he go to sick bay along with his backseater for a complete medical check-up. Hamilton began to object, saying he felt fine, but Taylor cut him short stating that it was a direct order.. He was also told not to talk about the strange turn of events to anyone other than Captain Gowdy, or Captain Potter. Hamilton saluted and left.

When the helicopters were less than ten minutes away from the point of last contact with Fleming's plane, they reported back to the CDC that their instruments were malfunctioning and could no longer be considered reliable. Their radio transmissions were becoming noticeably garbled and broken, and this update was immediately telephoned to the bridge.

"Tell them to abort the mission and return to the carrier," Admiral Taylor commanded.

A few seconds later the CDC duty officer informed the bridge that both pilots requested to continue the search.

The admiral exploded. "I gave an order for those men to return to the carrier now, and that means now! Confirm immediately that they know where the order is coming from and have them report to me on the bridge as soon as they land."

"They're heading back here now, Admiral," came a reply moments later from the duty officer several decks below. "They should be on board within a half hour."

Taylor wasted no time in giving other orders. "Manny, contact Admiral Morgan and tell him I have ordered all flight operations on the *LBJ* cancelled immediately and recommend he do the same for the *Truman*. I will contact him shortly to personally brief him. Barry will understand that something big must be happening." He looked at Blizzard. "No aircraft are to be launched without my direct approval, understood?"

"Aye, aye, Admiral."

Commander Birdwell stood waiting a few paces from the group of senior officers, a collection of nautical charts under his arm. He placed the appropriate chart of the area on the metal table, marked the point of last contact with Fleming's plane and the present position of the carrier. "We should be there in just under two hours, Admiral."

Taylor nodded and studied the chart, all the while whistling tunelessly. Everyone waited.

"How's the weather there right now? he asked, surprising everyone with his abruptness.

Joel Hirshberger spoke up. "More of the same, Admiral. Visibility is unlimited with no isolated storms or cells within three hundred miles of our position. Seas are running two-to-three feet, and I expect everything to stay status-quo for the next twenty-four to thirty-six hours."

"Well, at least that's something in our favor," Taylor said.

He turned to recognize the two helicopter pilots who had just reported to the bridge.

They stood at attention, saluted in unison, and waited for the admiral to speak.

Taylor looked at the senior pilot. "Tell us what you encountered, Lieutenant. Keep it simple."

"For some unknown reason, our instruments began acting up as we approached the area of last contact with *Liberty one*. Our radio transmissions became unreliable, but the weather was VFR, with unlimited visibility." The pilot shook his head. "I have no explanation for the phenomena we encountered, Admiral. We exited the area on your orders and came right here after landing."

"I want you to report to Doctor Potter in sick-bay along with the rest of your crews for complete medicals. Tell your flight surgeons those are my orders. Also, say nothing about your experiences except to CAG and the hospital commander."

They saluted and left.

* * * * *

The sun was setting as the carrier approached the area where Fleming had disappeared, and the worry was that both men might be in the water. The senior staff officers were at a loss to understand why Taylor had ordered the *LBJ* to proceed without the escorts, reasoning they would have been invaluable in helping search the many square miles of ocean. Only once had the admiral given an indication of his thoughts, and that was when he had turned to Hirshberger and asked about the currents off the coast.

"There are no currents to speak of anywhere in the Med, Admiral." Hirshberger said. "The prevailing winds aloft flow in a northwesterly direction. However, at this time of year they're pretty soft, which means if those guys are in the water they won't drift far or fast. By morning they should still be within twenty to thirty miles of where they went down. It wouldn't be hard to spot them."

Alan Paige had sent down to the galley for sandwiches and coffee, and the assembled group now ate and drank in silence, watching a bright sun sink below a pink-streaked horizon.

At twenty-thirty hours the meteorological officer on duty below decks called up to the bridge to tell Commander Hirshberger that their instruments were starting to give intermittent false readings. His message was heard by all on the loudspeaker.

A few minutes earlier, the admiral had suggested to Blizzard that they bring the carrier around into the wind, what little there was, and hold close to that spot until daylight. They were now in the vicinity of Fleming's last known position, approximately thirty miles east, and slightly south, of the port town of Livorno. There were two hundred and forty-five fathoms of water beneath the keel. Search radar and sonar were indicating there were no obstructions on or below the surface within ten miles of the *LBJ*.

As they were digesting this update from the meteorology department, a message from the navigation duty officer was piped through for Lieutenant Commander Birdwell.

"Commander, all our nav-aids have gone on the fritz. It started moments ago, and your instructions were to report anything out of the ordinary immediately. Also, the ship is losing all communications with the rest of our strike group and with the Truman Strike Group. It's probably just an atmospheric anomaly," he added.

All the assembled officers crowded around the bridge's three radarscopes. Snowlike images danced across the screens while their operators worked diligently to clear the pictures.

Without warning, the sweep hands on the three screens began painting a clear return, showing a mammoth obstruction which appeared to have completely surrounded the *LBJ* for a full three hundred sixty degrees. It was ten miles from the carrier and closing in rapidly.

None spoke, all eyes glued to the monitors. Each man involuntarily held his breath and watched helplessly as the unknown raced towards the ship. Twelve seconds later it hit.

All the lights on the *LBJ* flickered, once, twice, then went out. The *LBJ* shuddered violently as if wracked by an explosion from deep within her hull. Everyone on the bridge staggered, and some fell to the deck, a few landing hard, but all feeling an unbearable pressure squeezing the life out of them. At the moment of explosion, the entire interior of the *LBJ* was bathed in a brilliant flash of emerald green light.

It was all over in less than three seconds, and the ship's lights came back on moments later.

Blizzard was the first to react. He staggered to his feet and grabbed the PA phone. "This is the Captain," he said, his voice piped to all areas of the ship. "Damage report from all departments; nuclear engineering, report immediately."

He made his way in hesitant steps over to a computer display terminal that showed the operational workings of all of the *LBJ*s systems in real time, updating themselves by the nanosecond. The information Blizzard was seeing told him the ship's functions were normal.

"Captain, this is nuclear engineering," came a concerned voice over the intercom. "Lieutenant Rodriguez reporting for Commander Castle. The reactors are operating normally, but the darndest thing happened. Both reactors actually shut themselves down for a few seconds. I know that's impossible, Sir, but the mainframe computer captured a permanent record of the exact moment it happened. Lucky for us the computer operates with a continuous parallel power source independent of the ship's electrical grid. It's part of the failsafe design.

Anyway, the reactors are running as if nothing happened. Also, for the record, we lost the continuous time signals from the GPS satellites' atomic clocks at that exact same moment, but so far, we've not been able to reacquire. I've never seen anything like it."

"But you're absolutely sure there's no leak or threat of any kind to either of the reactors?"

"Everything is normal, Sir. Not the slightest hint of any radiation leak, but of course, we're going over the entire system with the tech-reps right now. I'll call back with a full report."

"Very good, carry on, Mr. Rodriguez."

Over a span of the next fifteen minutes, departments began reporting to the bridge, each summarization was a duplicate of the one preceding: No scorch marks were found anywhere, and no damage was reported, except for some broken dishes in each of the galleys. No one had the slightest idea what had caused the phantom explosion, or if it had even been an explosion at all.

* * * * *

Captain Blizzard soon realized their troubles were far from over. Meteorology had reported all systems normal, but the same was not the case with Navigation or with Communications. The reports from both were disconcerting. Commander Birdwell had told him it was impossible to raise any station on earth. All of the navigation instruments were not only tied into the ship's mainframe computer but were likewise dependent upon earth orbiting satellites for precise positioning information. They were obviously malfunctioning, simply because any and all signals from the *LBJ* up to the satellites were not being returned. Yet the maintenance crews insisted there was nothing wrong with the ship's equipment. Birdwell had summarized the situation with the somewhat lame observation, "It's as if all of the satellites, in thousands of orbits, have been snatched out of the sky. And the same holds true for our more conventional navigation aids, Sir, such as our Global Navigation Satellite System (GNSS), and the Global Positioning System (GPS). These signals which blanket the globe are just not being received at all. And, lastly, Captain, the emergency hotline to the International Space Station (ISS) is not responsive either."

Blizzard gave a command to the helm. "All engines emergency stop."

The four huge screws slowed, then stopped. and the *LBJ* began its glide to a halt.

The admiral had remained silent while Blizzard was assessing his situation and that of his command. "What do you suggest we do next, Captain?" he finally asked.

"I suggest following your earlier recommendation, Admiral. Let's hold our position and wait for daylight. We're facing something that's beyond our combined experiences, and I don't relish the idea of thrashing blindly around the Med in a state of utter confusion." He paused and looked at the assembled group. "As stupid as this might sound, let me throw out an idea for all of you to weigh in on. Is there any possibility that the Russians have come up with the ultimate weapon that can black out our entire communications suite? I mean like some newfangled type of jamming, but it's being done on a scale never before thought possible?"

They all mulled the possibility. Taylor was the first to reply. 'I don't think so, Miles," he said with a shake his head. "I say that because we know for a fact that one of their nuclear boats was damn near blown out of the water right next to us only a few hours ago. No, I'm pretty sure we can bet the Russians aren't behind any of this."

The others slowly nodded their agreement.

Taylor turned back to Blizzard. "Captain, I would like your permission to address the crew. Rumors will start flying, especially since all communications to the outside world are down, even if it's only temporary. Right now, just a handful of us know how serious the situation is, but I don't think wild speculation on the part of the crew will serve any useful purpose. I would like to tell them that we have undertaken a special assignment ordered by the joint chiefs-of-staff, and that if things don't appear normal for a short while, then they must understand that this is precisely what we are wanting to achieve. I will further explain that this challenge calls for *LBJ* to operate without escorts."

"Good idea, Admiral, but I think as their captain, I should make the announcement."

Taylor's face reddened, and his jaw hardened. Finally, "Very well, Captain."

"Thank you, Admiral." As Blizzard reached for the microphone, a call came from the CDC.

"Captain speaking. What is it?"

"Sir, we've got something really strange to report. As you know, all our radios are dead, at least as far as receiving is concerned, yet we're now picking up a confirmed distress signal on guard channel. At first we thought it might be a false return, but it checks out. The signal's coming from quite a way off on the Italian mainland."

"Are you sure?" asked a visibly incredulous Blizzard.

"Positive, Sir. If we had a chopper up we could triangulate and pinpoint the location exactly, but it's coming from the mainland all right."

Listening to the conversation, the same thought was on everyone's mind standing on the bridge. Could it be Major Fleming? If, yes, then why was his distress call the only radio signal being received by the LBJ?

Admiral Taylor spoke up. "Negative on the chopper launch, at least until dawn. Get as close a fix as possible and keep monitoring it throughout the night."

"They might be badly hurt, Admiral," said Manny Eisenhauer, speaking for the first time. "Maybe they won't make it 'til morning."

"Nothing doing, Manny. This is my decision. There are over five thousand sailors on this ship, and another two thousand plus in the strike group. I'm responsible for all of them. I know how you feel, but my order stands. No aircraft are to be launched until further orders from me." He continued, but his tone softened. "The very fact that their signal, if indeed it is their signal, is coming from Italy, tells me that they somehow made it to the coast, and were able to have ejected over land. So, at least they're not in the water, and that's the main thing. Now, once we have daylight and know where we stand, then I'll allow a chopper up to triangulate a fix and recover the two flyers." He turned to Blizzard. "Captain, I'm going back to the flag bridge. Inform me of any change, no matter the hour."

The assembled officers stood as the admiral departed.

The uppermost thought on all minds was: What new phenomena would the morning bring?

CHAPTER 11

Tuesday morning -Early – June 22nd

It was as if nature was a mind reader. Shortly after midnight the skies turned leaden, and it began to pour. Since the moment of the explosion earlier, the temperature had dropped steadily, and by dawn the thermometer had gone from 81 degrees Fahrenheit down to forty-nine.

Lieutenant Commander Joel Hirshberger was embarrassed. He had assured the admiral the weather would stay clear with unrestricted visibility for at least twenty-four, and possibly as much as thirty-six hours. He had no good explanation for what had happened, so he just reported conditions as he found them.

The *LBJ* was cut off from the rest of the world; the only radio signal received was the distress call on guard channel which had continued uninterrupted throughout the night. All the ship's radar scopes were working in that they continuously painted a return of the Italian coastline, and showed a smattering of small fishing boats in the distance. No aircraft were seen, nor any of the larger surface vessels one would expect to see in the Mediterranean. Whatever the special test the admiral was conducting at the behest of the joint chiefs, it had crewmembers scratching their heads trying to figure out exactly how it was being done.

The navigation department, under Birdwell's personal supervision, plotted the carrier's exact position manually, and although they had tried to get star fixes throughout the night using sextants, the weather

87

had turned against them, so they waited, hoping to shoot the sun later in the day.

The hard-driving rain of darkness had turned to a light drizzle by morning, but coupled with the fifty degree temperature, life had turned miserable for sailors outside standing the boatswain's mates deck watch or those working on the carrier's flight deck.

At seven-thirty A.M., the same group of officers had reassembled on the flag bridge and were now huddled around a walnut conference table. They had been served coffee and croissants by stewards who had since withdrawn. The sole newcomer was Doctor Potter, who quickly briefed the others that the helicopter flight crews seemed to be in perfect health and would be released from sick bay later in the morning.

The conversation then turned to the distress signal still being received. Commander Sewell could not discount the possibility the signal was coming from the Emergency Locator Transmitter (ELT) in the wreckage of the Hornet, meaning its crewmembers were dead.

"Well, I intend to find out," the Admiral said. "I'm giving the go-ahead to send up one chopper to triangulate, and I'm doing so based on what Doctor Potter has just told us about the well-being of the two helicopter flight crews. However, it must be clearly understood it will return to the *LBJ* once they have a good fix." He looked at Blizzard. "Is CAG ready to launch?"

"Aye, Sir. A crew's been briefed and is standing by for your order."

Taylor nodded. "Tell Gowdy to send them up. We'll monitor their transmissions back to the CDC from here while we continue this meeting. Also, Miles, please direct the CAG to take command in the Combat Direction Center for the time being with your approval of course." He quickly explained, "I know the CDC is a ship's function and not a responsibility of the combat air wing commander, but CAG's aware of what's going on, the CDC personnel are not."

"Very good, Admiral."

They covered other topics for about a half hour, monitoring the conversation between the helicopter pilots and Gowdy with one ear.

When the crew reported its position to be some fifty miles east of the LBJ, and operating in heavy rain with almost zero visibility, the group became more attentive when it was announced that the helicopter and the carrier now had a good fix on the signal. It was definitely coming from the coast.

"Admiral, we put it one hundred ninety-four miles north of Rome," said Gowdy. No sooner had he spoken than the helicopter pilot came on the air. He was extremely excited. *"Ajax, this is Hound Dog. I'm picking up a voice signal, it's weak, but it's a definite contact. Request permission to fly closer to the coastline."*

All eyes went to Taylor. "Roger that. Permission granted to get in closer for a readable transmission."

The OK was relayed to the pilot via CAG.

Ten minutes later the jubilant voice of the chopper pilot came back over the airwaves. *"Ajax, this is Hound Dog,"* he fairly yelled into his mike. "It's affirmative! The contact is Major Fleming. Both he and Lieutenant Lafayette are high and dry, and report they are in good condition. I've told him exactly where he's located, where we are, and where the *LBJ* is. He sure sounds happy to hear from us." There was silence for a few seconds, then the pilot continued, sounding somewhat subdued, *"Standby, Ajax, we're getting instructions from Fleming."*

The officers in the conference room broke out in cheer at the good news from the helicopter pilot, then waited in silence for more news.

The anticipation lasted three long minutes.

"Ajax, this is Hound Dog. Major Fleming has just made a strange request. He asked if communications were normal between the *LBJ* and the rest of the world? I told him we were experiencing some intermittent difficulty but said it would be fixed momentarily. When he heard this, he requested that no attempt for a pickup be made until nightfall. He was quite adamant. He further states that it's vital he speak directly to the admiral and to the captain. I don't know what to make of it, *Ajax.* I await your instructions. Over."

"Stand-by, Hound Dog," came Gowdy's voice over the intercom.

Admiral Taylor spoke into the speakerphone. "'Gowdy, can the chopper pilot relay Fleming's signal to the *LBJ*?"

Moments later he had his reply. "Negative, Admiral, it's too weak."

Taylor spoke again. "CAG, what sort of officer is this Major Fleming? A straight shooter?"

"Aye, aye, I mean, yes, Admiral. If Major Fleming says stay away, then something is very wrong. He's got two tours of combat flying in the Middle East under his belt, and I trust his judgment implicitly." Gowdy let that sink in for a few moments then asked, "Admiral, how about us moving into voice range ourselves? That way you can talk direct to the major and find out what's on his mind."

"Good idea, CAG." Taylor gave the command to Blizzard to rendezvous with the helicopter's position. He told Gowdy that since the *LBJ* would be at their new position in an hour and a half, permission was granted for the helicopter to remain aloft and stay in radio contact with the two downed airmen.

* * * * *

The air was filled with static, and the radio link was faint, but Fleming's voice was audible.

"*Bigfoot*, this is *Liberty one*, do you copy?" came Fleming's voice.

"That's affirmative," replied the CDC. "We read you five by five. Stand by for the admiral."

Taylor sat next to Blizzard in a massive captain's chair. "Fleming, this is Admiral Taylor, we hear you fine. Tell me, what's this request about waiting until nightfall for a pick-up?"

"The request still stands, Admiral,'" came Fleming's reply. "Sir, before we ejected, I flew the coastline looking for an airfield, and found none. In fact, Admiral, if I didn't know better I'd say it wasn't even Italy! There is nothing here that's recognizable." He paused to gather his thoughts then asked, "Admiral, just before you lost all communications capabilities on the *LBJ*, did you hit something, or did something hit you which caused instant darkness for a second or so?

Was there a violent heaving aboard, an explosion, and then a blinding flash of green light?"

"Affirmative, Major. Why?"

The faint voice continued. "We experienced the same thing, and moments later found ourselves totally alone. I couldn't find the *LBJ*, so I headed for Rome as my alternate landing field, but when I got to the coast I became lost due to instrument malfunction. But before running out of gas, I overflew a sizable harbor some ten kilometers north of my present position and made two passes. Admiral, I was low and slow and what I'm about to say is going to shock you. The land below was not the Italy we know. We have somehow gone back in time. My best guess is this is the Fourteenth or Fifteenth Century. The reason all of us can't pick up any radio signals for either navigation or communication is that they simply don't exist in the here and now! Admiral, I know this must sound like the rantings of a fool, but that's the way things are. We all have one hell of a problem on our hands."

The group collectively felt their flesh crawl as they listened to Fleming.

It took the admiral some moments to digest what he had just heard, then he spoke. "Major Fleming, you have taken us by surprise, and, no, I don't for a second think you are deranged. There's a logical explanation for what you think you saw. Coming on the heels of a severe in-flight emergency, I'm sure things don't seem quite right, especially since we on the *LBJ* admit that we too are having difficulties with some of our electronics and comm gear, but putting that aside, our primary mission at the moment is to recover you and your radar intercept officer."

Fleming replied immediately. "Admiral, I respectfully request you delay our pick-up until nightfall for obvious reasons."

"And those obvious reasons are what, Major?"

"Admiral, if what I am saying is true, that somehow we have all gone back in time to some past century, then how would you expect those folks to react to the sight and sounds of a helicopter? Believe me, I saw their reaction when I overflew the port yesterday. Those

91

people on the ground were frightened out of their wits and started running for their lives." Fleming rushed on before Taylor had a chance to cut in. "Sir, Lafayette and I are safe. We're out in the boondocks, miles away from all habitation. The area is rolling countryside and well-suited for a night pick-up. I'll secure a landing zone and guide the chopper in by radio and flares from our survival packs. It's a no sweat operation, Admiral."

Taylor squirmed slightly in his chair, chewing on his lower lip as he gave Fleming's proposal some thought. He looked at Blizzard, then to Paige. Shrugging his shoulders, he spoke to the group. "Why not humor him? Apparently, they are both unhurt and won't come to any harm for the next ten hours, so I'll do as he requests. Meanwhile, I want a reconnaissance plane standing by for launch. As soon as the weather lifts, I want to make a run along the coast to collect imagery from Rome up to the Florence area." He quickly added, "This doesn't mean I'm buying what Major Fleming is selling, but I will go so far as to admit that something strange is happening, and I want to know what that something might be."

"You think this should be a low-level run?" Paige asked.

"Only if the weather forces us down low," Taylor replied. "And if that's the case, I suggest a fast run up north following the coastline, then head inland for a short ways, then back to the *LBJ* out over the water so no one down there gets his medieval codpiece in a twist. We'll be getting real-time imagery transmitted directly to the CDC, so we'll see what the pilot is seeing, and we'll have plenty of opportunity to get all the backup film processed and interpreted by the intel folks before we pick-up Fleming. But I'm sure we'll be back in communication with everyone else on planet earth by then, so, to repeat myself, I'll humor the major."

The admiral keyed his mike. "Fleming, this is Taylor. We'll go along with your request, but stay in contact with us, and if your situation changes and you need to be pulled out of there in a hurry, just holler, and we'll come running. I'll see you when you come back aboard. Out."

"Thank you, Admiral, I sure hope this all turns out to be a big nothingburger, but I have my doubts. Over and out."

For a couple of seconds, the ensuing silence was absolute, but quickly interrupted by the downed pilot's emergency locator transmitting its incessant, high-pitched plea for help.

CHAPTER 12

Tuesday morning -Later -June 22nd

CAG had convinced the Admiral that he should fly the reconnaissance mission. "Until we have a better understanding of what's going on, it makes sense to keep our misgivings to as small a group as possible," he had argued, "and also, because I know what we're looking for, I'm the best judge as to when to turn on the cameras and sensors."

The admiral agreed. Tom Dowling, the air wing Deputy CAG, was brought into the picture so that if anything untoward happened to Gowdy, he would be in the loop. His almost colorless eyes betrayed no reaction to the startling information he was now hearing from Admiral Taylor, and his only comment was to recommend that Gowdy fly with a Lieutenant Liam Prescott, the systems officer he considered the best in the air wing.

Taylor spoke directly to Gowdy by radio as he sat in the catapult a mere minute before launch. "Good luck, Sean. If anything happens to your radios and other nav aids, then your magnetic compass and your watch become your failsafe means to guide you to your Point Option. You and I know this crude method of navigating back to a carrier hasn't been used since the Pacific battles in WWII, and the kids flying our jets today have probably never heard of it. But if Major Fleming is right in his assessment of the situation, and you miss us for any reason, you will be lost forever. *Knowing how to get to your Point Option is absolutely critical to your survival! You read me, CAG?*"

94

"Aye, Admiral," Gowdy replied, "but I'll be back, never fear, I have all the information I'll need to make a good intercept of the *LBJ* written down right here on my kneepad, and my backseater has it too."

At twenty minutes past eight A.M., CAG roared off the carrier, circled once, climbing all the while, and headed south. Navigation had plotted his course to fly directly to Rome, turn north, then fly inland over Siena and Florence, and from there, he would head out to the coast to over-fly Pisa, then back to the *LBJ* over the water. Mission time was seventy minutes.

The weather around the carrier had cleared to the point there was now a fifty percent cloud cover, and the temperature had climbed to fifty-four degrees. Lieutenant Commander Birdwell had personally made a sun shot using a sextant to plot their position. He soon realized he must have made a mistake, because minutes later he was back on deck shooting the sun again. The results were the same. The information was then fed into the computer for a cross-check. It confirmed his computations. He took his findings to Blizzard. The skipper was with the XO, and both men listened to the navigation officer's report with disbelief.

"There's no mistake, then?" Blizzard asked.

"None, Captain. The sun is simply not where it should be for this date in June. My figures have been verified by the computer using an existing internal program, not one requiring downloading information from the Cloud. For some unexplainable reason we are smack-dab in the middle of March, only I just can't tell you which year."

"This is insane," mumbled Paige, looking from one to the other.

"I tend to agree," replied Birdwell, "but I'm relying on mathematics for my answers, and the numbers don't lie. This is March; last night was June." After a momentary pause, he added in a whisper, "Major Fleming could be right after all."

"OK, let's wait and see what CAG's recon flight produces. I'll pass your findings along to the admiral at that time." The worried look on Blizzard's face spoke volumes.

The carrier proceeded on a northerly course at twenty-two knots, churning its way through a leaden sea. A couple of wooden vessels were sighted far off in the distance, but the *LBJ* sailed on with no intention to intercept or to even maneuver closer for a better look.

* * * * *

CAG kept his transmissions to the CDC brief, giving no indication of what he was seeing as he flew up the coast from his starting point over Rome.

It was on his return flight that things began to unravel. CAG keyed his mike to report to the CDC that he was returning to the carrier.

"*Bigfoot*, this is *Ajax*, do you copy?"

Silence.

His backseater, Lieutenant Liam Prescott, came over the intercom. "CAG, I seem to have lost the *LBJ*'s TACAN signal; are you still tuned in up front?"

This was critical information, and CAG immediately checked his receiver. Without a TACAN signal beacon from the carrier he was in essence lost, and flying blind. The TACAN station gave him his bearing and distance from the carrier out to a range of almost four hundred nautical miles. Gowdy's immediate thought was that he inadvertently tuned into the wrong channel, but no, he could see the frequency selector was correct. Prescott came back on the intercom.

"CAG, I can't raise *Bigfoot* on any frequency. The Air Boss and the Mini Boss are both silent, yet we know the CDC has been tracking us since we launched." A few seconds later he was sounding more worried. "I've just lost all of my instruments. I mean, I'm looking at nothing but empty screens back here, especially my radar. I can't paint the carrier. How about you, CAG?"

"You're right, it's the same up here. My entire panel is also dark which means we need to get on the horn and declare an emergency. It's possible the carrier can still hear us even if we can't receive. I'm going to fly to our Point Option for recovery on the *LBJ*." Gowdy sounded calm, but inwardly was feeling anything but. His first thought was that something dire had happened to the carrier, something like what Major Fleming had encountered, which meant they were now alone in a very hostile world; a world Liam Prescott still had no idea even existed.

"CAG, I've broadcast an in-flight emergency and informed the *LBJ* of our intentions, but I can't be sure it's been picked up by the CDC. We can only hope, but I'll continue to update them as we head back to the boat. Also, I've plotted our new course. We know the *LBJ* is on a heading of 280 degrees and moving at twenty-two knots, which means we need to come right fifty degrees to intercept that track. We'll take up the 280 degree heading in twelve minutes at our present airspeed of three six five hundred knots. I'm also showing we have 7000 pounds of fuel from our initial load of 14000, so that's good news."

CAG stole a glance at the notes strapped to his thigh and agreed that Prescott's calculations looked right. He turned towards the new heading while maintaining his current flight level at three zero zero. His mind was racing at a million miles an hour, and it was all he could do to keep the darkest thoughts at bay. He physically shook his head as if to rid it of demons, knowing his prime mission was to keep his wits about him.

"CAG, my magnetic compass is starting to show a significant precession, and it's not just a turning error. I mean, it's now totally unreliable."

Gowdy's eyes immediately went to his own compass. The same thing was happening. His skin turned ice-cold. Without instruments, or at the very least a reliable standby compass to guide us back to the LBJ, we have no hope of ever seeing the carrier again!

The minutes slipped by until Prescott broke the silence. "Boss, my compass semes to have righted itself, so I suggest you begin your turn left to intercept the 280 degrees heading in thirty seconds. Drop down to two thousand feet, and maintain three six five hundred knots. I'll call out the seconds and the "go" command to begin your turn. That new altitude will put us below any cloud cover. We should come up on the *LBJ* in eight minutes, but we'll have a visual in five."

"Roger that. I see my compass has also stabilized," CAG replied.

One minute later the silence was shattered.

"CAG, CAG, check six, check six!"

Gowdy heard the raw fear in Prescott's voice as he looked into his left rearview mirror in time to see a swirling black mass closing in on them at an incredible rate. He only had enough time to brace before the plane was swallowed into a seething cauldron of something out of hell itself. The Hornet was flung violently onto its back, and a second later it began tumbling inverted towards the sea.

The huge mass blew passed them at supersonic speed, then, as if on command, abruptly changed direction and spiraled upward. It then self-destructed into an infinite number of glistening fragments, and disappeared in the blink of an eye. The Hornet righted itself, and once again began flying straight and level.

"Are you OK back there?" Gowdy gasped, his voice sounding like that of a runner who had just finished a marathon in record time.

"I … I think so," came the tentative reply. "What in the hell just happened?"

"I have no freaking idea, but I sure don't want a repeat of whatever it was. Right now I need to see if this bird is still airworthy."

Less than a minute later, Gowdy triggered his intercom mic. "Liam, did you happen to see a flash of green light, or hear an explosion right after that black cloud thing hit us?"

Prescott's answer was immediate. "Negative, CAG. Should I have?"

Gowdy breathed a silent sigh of relief. *Thank God!* He could safely assume they had not been thrown further back in time to where a rescue, or any hope of a return, would have been rendered impossible. "No, no, everything's good," he said. "Now all we need to concentrate on getting ourselves back to the carrier."

Four minutes later they were down to flight level two zero and flying just below the cloud cover on their designated heading when Prescott asked, "What are you showing for fuel, CAG?"

Gowdy looked at his fuel flow meter gauge. *"What the ...!"* he inadvertently blurted out.

"Boss, we must have sprung a leak when we hit whatever that thing was. I'm showing us down to thirty-five hundred pounds and dropping, but I suggest it could be way less."

Yeah, that's what I'm also showing," Gowdy replied, wondering how that particular gauge could still be working. His eyes shifted outside for any sign of the carrier, or its telltale wake. Nothing. The gray sea was empty from horizon to horizon. They should have spotted the *LBJ* by now. He willed himself to breathe normally. Things were starting to look grim. He knew there could be no talk of flying to Italy and bailing out; there was simply not enough fuel left to find dry land. And if they didn't come across the carrier in the next few minutes, they would be forced to eject to a certain watery death, or ride the plane down and suffer the same fate.

"BOSS! Do an immediate one eighty right-hand turn; I saw a flash in my mirror, there's something on the surface. It was at our four o'clock!"

Gowdy banked into a steep turn and peered down, all the while wondering how could they have overflown their Point Option? It was next to impossible, but apparently it had happened. He shuddered. *What if Prescott hadn't caught that flash out of the corner of his eye ...*

Bingo, Bingo, "Bitchin Betty's" twangy voice filled both of their earphones, warning they were coming up on minimum fuel, and to find somewhere to land immediately.

"CAG, it's the *LBJ*, she's at our two o'clock. Yes, sir, it's definitely the *LBJ*, Boss!' he repeated, his voice exploding with excitement, then immediately turned serious. "I'm now showing we're well below 2000 pounds of gas which means we'll have to fly a straight in approach and land. No time to do a no-radio fly-by to give the Air Boss a heads-up," Prescott said, reminding Gowdy of the obvious, which was their engines could flame-out any moment.

"Roger. I'm descending to 800 feet and setting up our approach. There's no time for them to deploy the emergency barrier, so we'll only get one crack at this. We definitely won't be a bolter, so prepare for a rough landing."

* * * * *

His plane was placed on the forward elevator and dropped to the hangar deck with both crewmembers still in their cockpits. While the Hornet was being tied down, photo technicians unloaded the camera bays and hurried off to the processing section, and to review by the intelligence officers.

"How did it go, Sean?" Blizzard asked as he walked along the hangar deck with Gowdy and Prescott, both loosening their partial G-suits as they went. They looked done in. "We heard all of your transmissions, so we had a good idea of what you were going through up there, but let's wait for a full debrief until we're with the admiral."

Gowdy nodded his agreement. "Miles, Major Fleming's one hundred percent right; we're in the middle of a frigging nightmare. Nothing over there is recognizable," he continued, jabbing his thumb toward the coast. "The only structure I recognized for sure was the Colosseum in Rome, and all I can say is that it's in one hell of a lot better condition than it was when I last saw it ten days ago. Anyway, you'll soon see for yourself once the pictures are downloaded into the computer. I flew low over Rome, Siena, and Florence, but climbed higher as I approached Pisa because the weather had improved. I got some pretty good imagery."

The admiral joined Blizzard, Paige, and Gowdy in the photo interpretation area, and while the digital film footage was being scanned onto a computer screen, Gowdy pointed out to the technicians which frames he wanted enlarged and printed.

Five minutes later, the digitally printed photos were passed among the group, each man silently comparing a print to a similar image being displayed on the large computer screen. Their silence was deafening. What they were looking at was Italy of long ago. Like CAG, none recognized the city of Rome except for the Colosseum. The same held true of the photos taken over Siena, and Florence. Absolutely nothing was recognizable. Each photo had a frame-counter in its top right hand corner, a digital clock readout of the time-date the picture was taken.

The color photo printouts of those frames shot over Pisa clearly showed the effects of the better weather. There was more activity on the streets and in the harbor. Gowdy pointed a finger to the lower left hand corner of the last print. Plainly visible was the tower which had made Pisa such a famous landmark for centuries. It was eerie seeing this historical building in a setting so stark and strange, but most shocking of all was seeing that the angle of the tower showed it to be leaning only slightly off vertical, and not its "ready to fall over" condition so well known to untold generations.

Admiral Taylor was first to comment. "*Tell me I'm not seeing ...!*" he whispered, his face the color of putty.

Blizzard looked to Gowdy. "Sean, was there anything you saw during your flight that would indicate what century we're now in?" Gowdy pursed his lips, then shook his head. "Sorry, Miles, I don't know enough history other than those important dates and places I had to learn for school exams, so your guess is as good as mine."

Paige offered up a suggestion. "Well, let's get rid of some centuries by a process of elimination. All we have to do is a Google search for the history of that tower in Pisa."

"We can't do a Google search, remember?" Blizzard said. "There is no Internet, which means we can't access most of our files because they're stored in the Cloud. The only ones we keep internally are those necessary for running the ship's day-to-day operations. No, Al, we're on our own in this brave new world."

"Tell you what," interjected the admiral, unwilling to dwell on that uncomfortable reality. "We'll call down to the ship's library and ask Father Caffarone to look up the Leaning Tower of Pisa in the hardcopy *Britannica Encyclopedia* we have onboard. Have him find out the date the tower was built, and then in what year it started to lean. That should tell which century we're now in."

101

"Can't hurt," replied Blizzard, "even though that presents us with another problem, Admiral, but I think you've just given me the answer. Those folks over there probably don't speak a language we know, so how are we going to powwow with them if it becomes necessary?"

Taylor answered while still studying the last photo. "We have five thousand sailors on board. There must be a bunch of second-generation Italians who speak the lingo. They should have no trouble making themselves understood."

Blizzard shook his head. "I don't agree with you, Admiral. Back in the day, most Europeans spoke localized dialects. Oftentimes they couldn't understand someone from only a couple of hundred miles away. And forget about the Italians understanding Frenchmen, or Germans, or Englishmen. No, the only language common to most of Europe back then was Latin. What we need is someone fluent in Latin."

Admiral Taylor threw up his hands. "That counts me out. I know less Latin than CAG knows about history." He looked questioningly at Blizzard. "But you say you have the answer?"

"I think so." Blizzard got on the ship's intercom. "This is the Captain speaking. Father Caffarone, please report to the bridge immediately."

The priest arrived five minutes later, his face reflecting a twinge of apprehension at being summoned so abruptly, and he thought, *for a meeting with the captain and the admiral no less.*

"Father, we need your help and expertise with something important ..."

"Yes, Captain," the priest said, cutting Blizzard short, "you requested information about the Leaning Tower at Pisa." He turned to Admiral Taylor. "Admiral, for your information, *Britannica* no longer publishes an encyclopedia. They went out of business years ago. There's only one company left that makes a print edition, and that's *World Book Encyclopedia* in Chicago. Along with universities and schools, the Defense Department is one of their best customers." Caffarone then glanced down at a sheet of paper and began reading.

"Construction of the tower at Pisa began in the year 1172 and continued until its completion 199 years later. The structure began to sink shortly after the second floor was added in 1174, and all activity was halted for almost a century to allow time for the unstable ground to settle. The bell floor was finally added in 1372, completing the tower."

"Good work, Father," said the admiral, "and fast too. Now, can you tell us how many degrees the tower is leaning, and what was the date when it stopped tilting?"

"I have that information right here also, Admiral. The angle of slant is 3.97 degrees, which places it exactly 12 feet 10 inches off of vertical. The sinking process actually stopped in 2001 when engineers finally stabilized the ground around the tower and managed to reduce the angle from 5.5 degrees to its current 3.97. They say there is no fear of it toppling over now."

"So, what you're suggesting is that we really can't tell what the tilt might have been in say, the year 1400, just to use that as a random date?"

"I'm no engineer, Admiral, but my guess is it would still have been pretty close to standing upright around then."

"I tend to agree with you, Father. Now, I have one other question. Do you speak Latin?"

"I do."

"And read and write it as well?"

"Yes." Caffarone now wore a worried look. *Where is this conversation going?*

The admiral read Caffarone's face correctly. "Relax, Father. You see, we have a big problem to solve, and your knowledge of certain matters will go a long way in helping us."

Caffarone let out a long exhalation, the worried look fast disappearing. He waited for Taylor to continue.

"Father, please sit. I'm going to let you in on a subject that's top secret, which means you cannot discuss it with anyone aboard other than these officers." For the next five minutes Admiral Taylor told the chaplain about the misfortune that had befallen the carrier and ended by showing him Gowdy's photos. Taylor waited for Caffarone's response.

Finally, "Well, well. All I can say is there'll certainly be some interesting times ahead."

"Yeah, maybe for the rest of our lives, Padre," said Blizzard. "I've got a wife and three kids I'd like to see again. However, that is only one of a *beaucoup* number of problems we're facing at the moment, but the biggest is this: How do we find the way back to our own time if we really are stuck in the middle of some earlier century?"

"Those photos seem to prove we've gone somewhere, Skipper," replied the priest.

"OK, we'll grant you that," said Taylor, "But because of the slight tilt of that tower in Pisa which we've all just seen, we can be fairly sure this is the Fifteenth century." He got up to pace, then began rattling off orders. "Miles, I want you to put together a team of tech-reps from IBM, Westinghouse, Bechtel, Boeing, and your department heads. They are to go over everything that's happened to the ship and crew since we weighed anchor. Look to things like our course, speed, weather, longitude, latitude, time, and date; in other words, everything of significance leading up to that moment the *LBJ* went over to whatever time we're in now. I have a gut feeling that if we don't manage to get back home soon, we'll be trapped in the Middle Ages forever. And lastly, they must know their work is top secret."

Each man listening to the admiral had no trouble creating a mental picture of the consequences. Their reverie was broken by a ringing phone. Blizzard took the instrument from a sailor, listened for thirty seconds, then ordered the individual to report to the bridge.

"It seems that something else has shown up on the digitalized copy of the film," he said. "It's on the way up now."

Three minutes later a lieutenant j.g., from the air wing intelligence office entered, saluted, and handed three prints to the admiral. He immediately went to work explaining the significance of each.

"That top one, Sir, it's the harbor at Livorno, just thirty miles south of Pisa, and as you can see, it's a pretty busy place. The second one is a closeup of the north end of the harbor."

By now the others were queued up behind Taylor, looking over his shoulders.

The lieutenant continued. "And the last picture is a blow-up of the area in question. I direct your attention, Admiral, to the vessel tied up at the wooden jetty away from all the other boats."

Everyone stared in disbelief. It was a modern pleasure cruiser!

"She's about sixty-five feet in length, and fully equipped with the latest satellite nav-aids and radar," the photo-intel officer said. "At least that's our conclusion from the looks and size of her antennae farm. In all likelihood she's a twin-screw, capable of doing about twenty-five knots."

Blizzard exhaled loudly and was the first to speak. "Now, how in the hell did this frigging boat end up in Livorno?"

"Better yet, how long has she been there?" said the admiral.

"Well, at least we're not alone," declared Paige, picking up the last photo and studying it closely. "Can you identify the make?"

"We're working on that now, Sir. We suspect she was built in this part of the world because of her low profile and sleek lines, but we'll have a positive ident shortly. You'll note her tender is still aboard, which suggests the crew and passengers are close by."

"Admiral, we need to get some better shots of this boat right away," said Blizzard, taking the photo from Paige. "If we can have a plane come in from the east, we stand a good chance of picking her name off of the bow; or we can make a pass from out over the water and get it off her transom. There's no flag flying, so we do need those pictures to figure out where she came from."

Taylor glanced at his watch. "There's plenty enough daylight to make a run today." He turned to Gowdy. "You up for another flight?"

"Absolutely. I didn't see this when I flicked on the cameras for my approach to Pisa. Livorno was just south of that when I made my turn and headed back to the carrier. I can be airborne in fifteen minutes, Admiral."

Not a word was mentioned of his earlier near-disastrous flight.

CHAPTER 13

Tuesday afternoon to evening – June 22nd

The rain stopped shortly before noon. Fleming had decided it would be safe to start a fire, heat coffee, and prepare some food from their survival packs. He was elated they had finally made contact with the carrier and that his request for a night pick-up had been approved by the admiral.

The only injury suffered by either was a cut on the bridge of Lafayette's nose. It had happened when he pulled off his helmet without first raising the plastic visor. The wound had barely bled, but he now sported a band-aid over his self-inflicted battle injury.

After they had eaten and were on their second cup of coffee, they built-up the fire to warm themselves and to dry out their clothes.

"All we'd need now would be for our flightsuits to catch on fire and have the chopper pick-up a couple of near-naked jaybirds," said Fleming. Both were huddled close to the heat and remarking on their good fortune.

"You know, what's happening to us is like some kind of a macabre hoax," said Lafayette, gazing into the flames, face somber, tone serious. "Ever since I was a kid, I've thought that time-travel made for great science fiction stories and even better movies, and now here we are with everything indicating that we've somehow crossed that impossible barrier. What's to become of us, Dave?" he asked in a mournful tone.

"Chuck, let's take it one step at a time, OK?" Fleming stood and examined their clothes. "They're dry. How about we get dressed and take a stroll around our new home. We'll douse the fire and leave everything here except for our weapons, compasses, binoculars, and radios. We'll make sure to keep this large oak in our sight at all times as a landmark for our campsite." Ten minutes later they set out, heading east. The land was rolling hillside with few trees and fewer bushes and shrubs. Small rocks and shale shards were strewn everywhere, and Fleming could not help but comment on the sizable rabbit population.

Something had been nagging at his mind, and as he studied a small clump of wildflowers, the answer hit him. He bent low to examine what he thought to be wildflowers. Many had still-unopened buds, while others were beginning to bloom. "Here's a new twist for us to think about," he said, snapping a bud from its stem. He rose and faced Lafayette. "Take a look around you, Chuck. Go on, take a good look, then tell me what you see."

Lafayette slowly turned in a complete circle, looked all around as directed, then shrugged his shoulders. "Grass, flowers, and tons of rabbit stew." He concentrated his gaze on the bud Fleming was twirling in his fingers. "So what do you see?"

"I see springtime. It adds up. The cold weather with lots of drizzle; flowers just beginning to bloom, the fresh greening of the landscape, even the new growth on the trees and bushes. Last night it was summertime, but today sure isn't summer. I'd say it's more like late March, maybe April, but definitely not June."

Lafayette took another, longer look around. "I think you're right. I would have thought that if we've gone back in time we'd have stayed in the same month." He let loose a small, mirthless laugh. "At least that's how it happens in all the sci-fi flicks."

They continued walking, making a large circle, all the while keeping their campsite's oak tree in view. Turning in a westerly direction, then climbing a small hill, they spotted a stone hut with a thatched roof a couple of hundred yards away. They studied it in silence with their binoculars for a few minutes, and seeing no sign of life, Fleming decided they take a closer look.

The hovel was rough and old. Fleming guessed it at twelve feet by fifteen feet, and six feet in height. He pronounced the roof to be beyond repair. There were no windows, and one entrance on the southside. Peering inside, he spotted a pallet of leaves and twigs on the dirt floor. There was no furniture, and the place emitted a really foul odor. In one corner he saw a small cluster of mushrooms struggling to grow. "Must be a shepherd's hut," he murmured, turning his face towards some welcomed fresh air.

"Glad that isn't my permanent address," added Lafayette as they backed away.

The rest of the journey held no additional surprises, other than observing several plumes of black smoke dotting the horizon, evidence of human habitation somewhere off in the distance. A half-hour later they were back in camp with the sun getting low. Fleming looked at his watch. Almost six. He called the carrier, and his signal was picked up immediately.

"Fleming, this is CAG, are you reading me OK?"

The air was filled with static, but Gowdy's voice was clear.

"Roger, CAG, five by five."

"Here's the plan. We'll make the pick-up at nineteen hundred, one hour from now, and you'll be back on board in two. Anything new to report?"

"Negative, CAG. No signs of habitation within five miles of our position. Should be fine for the extraction. As soon as we hear the chopper coming we'll light a flare. The wind is zero at the moment, but if it changes dramatically, we'll provide smoke. Over."

"Roger. Continue to call every fifteen minutes. Will you need a flight surgeon on board?"

"Negative, CAG. We're good. Just need a shower."

"Keep the faith. CAG out."

At three minutes past seven Fleming heard the first thump, thump, thump of the helicopter's blades as it beat its way through the air. A minute later Lafayette fired a flare. The pilot acknowledged by flicking his landing light on and off a couple of times.

Fleming and Lafayette tossed their gear into the helicopter, huge grins lighting up their faces beneath helmets. Both gave a thumbs up signal to the pararescue sailor, then climbed aboard.

A fastidious Fleming had made sure their campsite was scrubbed of all signs of their ever having been there. The fire had been extinguished and its ashes scattered; empty food packages had been secured inside zippered flightsuit pockets.

Fifty minutes later they were greeted with hoots and hollers and slaps on their backs by scores of jubilant Tiger Sharks squadron members.

CHAPTER 14

Tuesday Evening, later – June 22ⁿᵈ

Fleming's mind began to wander, blocking out the sound of droning voices. He was sitting in conference with Admiral Taylor, Captain Blizzard, CAG, and Lafayette. Both flyers had been given a perfunctory physical once-over by Dr. Potter, and now, ninety minutes later, his tiredness was beginning to tell. The three senior officers were discussing a plan of action and had asked Fleming for any input he considered important. He now mentally detached himself from the group and willed his thoughts to turn to his wife. Would he ever see Susan again? The realist inside said probably not. To escape such dark thoughts, he harkened back to their early days.

* * * * *

Their first date had been an outing on the water with two other couples. He remembered how she had cancelled an earlier one for dinner in the middle of the week by telling him she had a sore throat. It was only much later she confessed that although her throat had indeed been sore, her reticence was more of a case of cold feet. But when he called and asked her to go boating with two other couples for the following Sunday, she enthusiastically agreed. Safety in numbers was how she phrased it when reminiscing about their early dating, as starstruck lovers often do.

Throughout the month of May he saw her as many times as he could, and then the school term was over. She had not signed a contract for the following year although the school principal had let her know she would be most welcome to return. He had gone out of his way to persuade her to come back, telling her he would wait until the middle of August before signing a contract with her replacement. Her roommate also begged her to reconsider, telling her that she too would keep the apartment open for her. And, of course, Fleming added his two cents' worth. Susan Renninger made no promises to any of them.

"Dave, I'm going to Indianapolis at the end of the week," she announced in the first week of June, "and then to Chicago to see my mother." They were lying on the living room floor in her apartment after she had cooked a fantastic Mexican dinner. The roommate had gone to Las Vegas for a long weekend with her boyfriend.

"How long will you be gone?" he asked, dreading the answer.

She raised herself onto one elbow, rested her chin in the palm of her hand and stared into his eyes. "I don't know," she replied softly, "I haven't seen mother in a while, and I know she would really enjoy the visit."

Susan had not volunteered him much information about her family. He knew her father was dead, that she was an only child, and her mother worked long hours. He had suspected her childhood had been financially precarious, and that her single mother had often struggled to make ends meet.

"Would it be possible to visit you in Chicago? I have a ton of leave time built up and need to burn off some days."

"We'll see. But of course, we can talk and text whenever we want, so that'll be nice." She smiled, squeezed his hand, and offered her lips for a kiss.

She drove away the following weekend in her five-year-old Toyota. David Fleming's social life slipped into slow gear, then into neutral. He soon found he was miserable without her and took little joy in joining his squadron buddies in an off-base bar-and-grill after a day's flying.

They spoke a couple of times each day and texted often, sometimes well into the night.

In the middle of the third week, he received a letter from her. Yes, she was in Chicago, yes, her mother was delighted to have her home, and she ended with the admission she missed him. She had also jotted down her mother's home phone number and suggested that she would like to see him very much. He never stopped to think that he could have just called her cellphone to say yes, but instead, he called Susan on her mother's home phone to tell her *yes, yes, yes!*

Ten days later she met him at Chicago's O'Hare International Airport, along with a woman who appeared to be in her early fifties. One glance, and Fleming understood where Susan had gotten her fabulous looks.

Susan ran to him as soon as she spotted him and throwing her arms around his neck breathed deeply into his ear, "Oh, how I've missed you. It's seemed like forever."

He held her tight for several long seconds then kissed her. Passengers smiled as they walked past the happy couple.

Susan introduced her mother. "Dave, this is the best mother in the whole world, Theresa Renninger. Mom, this is Dave Fleming."

"Welcome to the Windy City, Dave," Theresa Renninger said, smiling warmly as she shook his outstretched hand. "It's a pleasure to finally meet you. All I've heard for the past few weeks is Dave this, Dave that, or Dave says." She ended with a full-throated laugh.

"*Mother!*" said the shocked daughter, turning crimson with embarrassment, but within moments was laughing alongside her mother and Fleming.

With a beautiful woman gracing each arm, Fleming floated through baggage claims and out to the terminal curbside parking zone. It was here that he received his first surprise. Waiting for them was a chauffeured Bentley Flying Spur. Forty-five minutes later came the second surprise as the limousine glided up a long paved driveway to a stately mansion gracing the shore of Lake Michigan.

A butler greeted them at the front door. Fleming was now thoroughly stunned and knew that it showed. He turned to face Susan and managed a disbelieving shake of his head.

"I never told you," she said quietly, coming to stand close to his side. "I had to be sure." She squeezed his arm and led him inside.

It was during this week that he learned of Susan's family and upbringing, and it was also when they made love for the first time.

He discovered that this working mother was the Chairman of the Board and sole stockholder of Rentran Industries. Had it been a publicly traded company, Rentran would have appeared on the Fortune 500 List with its annual revenues of twenty billion dollars. The company made the transmissions and industrial gearboxes used in large electrical trucks and buses for automotive manufacturers in a dozen countries. Paul Renninger had started the company at twenty-two years of age with a stake of one hundred eighteen thousand dollars borrowed from his father. It was at a time when only a handful of visionaries foresaw a future that included large numbers of Electrical Vehicles (EVs). Twelve years later, Rentran was becoming a major force to be reckoned with in the specialized world of EV transmission manufacturers, but two days shy of his thirty-fifth birthday, Paul Renninger collapsed from a cerebral hemorrhage. He was dead before his body hit the floor.

Theresa Renninger refused all buyout offers, and soon after the funeral, announced that she would run the company. The competition bet among themselves that Rentran Industries would flounder and go under in no time, but she fooled the skeptics. The woman worked sixteen hours a day, sometimes seven days a week, year after year. Five years later the competition grudgingly agreed on one thing: Theresa Renninger had indeed fooled them all.

Susan spoke of a lonely childhood. She had attended private schools in Chicago and described herself in those early years as being an all-legs, skinny kid adorned with a mouthful of braces. Yes, she had friends, but spent most of her time in lonely pursuits. It troubled her mother to see her child pass the days in such solitude, but, to her credit, she tried everything to make the daughter's life as normal as possible. School friends were invited for weekends to the huge home, yet nothing could pry Susan from the shell she had ensconced herself. Finally, in desperation, Theresa had Susan visit a psychiatrist to determine if there was some deep-rooted flaw in the girl's character, but after a few consultations he assured the mother there was nothing wrong with her child. He recommended she attend a university away from home when the time came, and upon graduation from high school, Susan was accepted to the University of Arizona.

Four years later she graduated *cum laude* with a bachelor's degree in Primary Education, then spent the following year at UCLA where she received her master's degree, again graduating *cum laude*. She was now twenty-two-years of age and had blossomed into a beautiful young woman. The braces she had so hated were long-gone, and although she was still very much a private person, she had at last come out of her shell. There was no special man in her life, and with nothing to tie her to Los Angeles, she accepted a teaching post in Indianapolis. She stayed there three years, fell in love, and became engaged to an up-and-coming attorney with the city's most prestigious law firm. Then, inexplicably, just one week before the wedding she called the whole thing off. Her mother was justifiably upset and acutely embarrassed by the sudden turn of events, yet no amount of questioning would pry from her daughter the reason for her decision. The local society mavens now dubbed her the "runaway bride" behind her back. Susan Renninger returned the engagement ring to the now heartbroken attorney and quietly left town.

She found a job for the coming school year in the small Southern California town of Lancaster, close to Edwards Air Force Base, where she dated little, sometimes young officers from the airbase, but towards the end of the school term had met a man she knew she could easily fall in love with. The feeling truly scared her, and though she fought it at first, somewhere deep within her soul she knew that such an opportunity and such a man might never come her way again. His name was David Fleming.

* * * * *

At a few minutes past one, Gowdy roared off the carrier and headed for the harbor at Livorno. Liam Prescott insisted he should go, too, and Gowdy didn't object. Ninety minutes later, CAG, Blizzard and Paige were studying prints of the vessel. CAG had made a low pass from out over the water and had captured the name on the ship's transom. FÉLICITÉ-CANNES was written in bold, black letters.

"I'll bet there's more than one very confused Frenchman down there at the moment," Blizzard said as he studied the photographs. "Their world has really been turned upside down, and they haven't a clue what's happened." He glanced at Gowdy. "Were there any signs of life aboard? I really can't tell from these photos."

"I made our first pass from north to south, and one hundred feet off the deck. We were clocking three-twenty knots and scared the crap out of everyone in the harbor. It had a handful of folks on board, but from the way they reacted, I'd have to say they were not the owners or crew. Lieutenant Prescott saw two jump into the water, and the rest scrambled onto the pier and disappeared into some buildings nearby while I was executing a climbing three-sixty overhead with full afterburners. I think it's safe to say that any modern-day sailor would have stood in the open and waved to us. These guys acted like it was the end of the world. Bottom line? There were no Frenchmen on board."

"Yeah, that makes sense," Blizzard said, then turned to Paige. "Before I forget, Al, Doctor Potter says he wants our entire crew checked for current plague shots, and those whose records indicate none, they're to be vaccinated at once. Same goes for the air wing, CAG. He also wants us to let him know of any plans we have to send people ashore so that he can update their shots or vaccines for other diseases. If this really is the Fifteenth century, then there's a lot of bad stuff out there, and the last thing we'd need is an old-fashioned epidemic breaking out onboard, or even something like that Corona 19 virus thing from a couple of years ago."

* * * * *

Later that evening, a plan was submitted to Admiral Taylor for his approval. All day the temperature had remained in the mid-fifties, confirming that it was indeed early spring. At fifteen hundred hours, Commander Hirshberger reported to the bridge that the meteorological department was again experiencing unexplainable readings on its instruments, and the electronics folks noted that the ship's radar had become unreliable, then totally inoperable for a few tense minutes before turning operational again without warning.

Captain Blizzard had ordered the carrier north, the admiral wanting the *LBJ* to be positioned off the coastline by midnight, but near the port of Livorno. With the admiral's approval, Blizzard had briefed his staff on the unexplainable turn of events. And, for the first time, select senior tech-reps from Westinghouse, IBM, Hughes Aircraft, Bechtel, and Boeing, were brought into the small group.

Throughout Blizzard's briefing, Lieutenant Commander Birdwell had been working alongside two IBM reps armed with old-fashioned slide rules, and after double-checking their work, he feverishly transferred their findings to paper.

When Blizzard was finished, Birdwell stood up. "Captain Blizzard, Gentlemen," he began, "I've been working on this problem along with Joel Hirshberger, and we think the warning signs and red flags were all there from the moment we started this deployment. However, because none of us had ever confronted such happenings before, we failed to notice the obvious."

All those around the conference table leaned forward in anticipation of what was to come.

"It's clear now that the weather abnormalities and the communication failures we've experienced since Thursday were but a prelude to Saturday's main event." Birdwell paused, his intention being to maximize the effect of what he was about to say. "Gentlemen, we are living proof that the fourth dimension really does exist!" He held up a hand to stave off the ridicule and objections he fully expected but showed genuine surprise when none were forthcoming.

He rushed ahead before any skeptics could weigh in. "The only possible conclusion we can draw is that *time and light are somehow similar*, even though theoretical physicists up until now have insisted *they're not interchangeable*. However, Einstein proved with his famous $E = mc^2$ theorem that *light and mass are interchangeable*, the key which unlocked the door to usher in the Atomic Age. And gentlemen, our being here at this very moment *proves that time and light are energy fields which are interchangeable, and that both last forever!* Just as a star explodes into oblivion, the light emanating from that dead celestial body will race unimpeded through the universe for all time, so that when we gaze through our telescopes into the night sky we will see that very same light coming at us from billions of light-years in the far distant past."

Birdwell stole a quick glance down to his notes. "But let's now do a one-eighty and turn our attention to the plane's crewmembers who both died last Saturday. They encountered what we later ran into, but were not nearly so fortunate as we were. Instead of passing cleanly into the fourth dimension, they hovered on its fringe, and that indecision of nature killed them. Their on-and-off, garbled, then finally broken radio transmissions prove that. They were teetering on a cusp, caught somewhere between the present and the past. How far into the past had they traveled, I can't be sure. But what I do know it was the past because they aged terribly, and hours later when they actually died, they were truly old men. And their plane aged at a similar rate. So, I would venture to guess they went back in time less than two hundred years, because if they had traveled as far back as the Fifteenth century and then managed to return under those same on-again, off-again conditions, they would have returned as mummified corpses. In summary, their misfortune was that they did not pass cleanly through that fourth dimension, and it killed them."

While his listeners were digesting his remarks, Birdwell grabbed a quick drink of water, then continued. "But Major Fleming and Lieutenant Lafayette were a whole lot luckier. They made a clean pass through that time portal, and so did the *LBJ* a day later. Major Fleming spoke of seeing a fog, and his backseater told him his radar was painting a barrel-shaped object closing in on their position at an alarming rate. The *LBJ* passed through that same portal at night, so even though none of us actually saw a fog, it most assuredly was out there. Also, both Fleming and the *LBJ* experienced an explosion and saw a brilliant flash of green light upon entering the fourth dimension. Saturday's Hornet crew never experienced an explosion, nor did they witness an emerald green flash, which tells us the absence of both phenomena cost them their lives. All the pilot could remember was a strange fog he found himself flying in and out of.

"But we have the resources to help ourselves. Because of our nuclear capability, we can function self-sufficiently for a helluva long time and, with our computers and scientists, we have a fighting chance of making it back. God only knows how many people throughout history have had the misfortune to do what we've just done. They were all doomed to a terrible fate because they did not have the wherewithal to initiate a return. Which means we must seize the moment when it comes, because in all likelihood we will only get that singular chance."

"That was quite the speech, Commander," said Blizzard, breaking the long silence that followed. "I have no evidence to dispute what you suggest, so until something better comes along, I'm buying what you're selling. And I agree that time will be of the essence, no pun intended, and that we must be prepared to act on a moment's notice. You tell us that the weather instruments are still acting up," he continued, "along with most of our telecom, which could suggest that our 21st century is still battling the 15ᵗʰ century for dominance." Blizzard smiled. "Believe me, gentlemen, that all sounds just as farfetched to my ears as I'm sure it does to yours, but I'm afraid I can't express myself more clearly at the moment. I've never been a good extemporaneous speaker, especially when it comes to talking of things I know nothing about!"

The assemblage laughed, then Blizzard continued. "Nevertheless, we have things we must do, and do in an extremely limited amount of time. Our first order of business is to recover that French pleasure cruiser from Livorno. Naturally, that means recovering the owner and crew as well. We will not leave them behind to fend for themselves in Medieval Europe."

Heads nodded. Empathy with the unfortunate Frenchmen was easy to come by; each man present could only imagine his own terror upon finding himself alone in a world as foreign as those folks from the *Félicité* surely must now be finding themselves.

Taylor approve the rescue plan when Blizzard presented it, but with a caveat. "OK, Miles, get that boat and bring her back to the *LBJ*. My only change to your plan is this: If the crew isn't on board, I don't want the boarding party going ashore to find them. Recover the boat and come back to the carrier immediately."

When Taylor pressed Manny Eisenhauer for his opinion he replied, "Admiral, I don't know what to think."

Some help you are," said Taylor, but not in a nasty way. He turned to Blizzard who obviously had something he wanted to add.

"Admiral, we have a moral obligation to rescue those folks."

"Overruled, Captain. You're the captain of the *LBJ*. That's your command. Anything outside the operation of your ship is my responsibility." Taylor sighed deeply. "Miles, I have no intention of leaving those men behind," he continued in a quiet voice, "but we can't go off half-cocked in the middle of the night to rescue folks who might already be dead. And if not dead, they could be anywhere. No, do it my way. Get the boat first, then we'll tackle finding its crew."

Blizzard was momentarily tempted to press for his point of view but admitted to himself that Taylor was right.

"Aye, aye, Admiral."

"Good. Now, who do you plan to send ashore?"

"I'll lead, Admiral. There'll be five of us: Four SEALs and me, all sailors with backgrounds working as crewmembers on private yachts before joining up. Lucky for us we have SEAL Team 3 aboard for an exercise scheduled to begin later in the week. We'll take a rubber Zodiac by oar up to the harbor's entrance, slip into the water, and board the *Félicité*. I intend to crank her up and drive her right out to the *LBJ*." He then made a back and forth cleaning motion using both hands. "It'll be done, just like that!"

"*Done? Just like that?* What of your command?" asked an incredulous Taylor. "Sometimes I don't understand you at all, Miles."

"Supposing I did get killed?" Blizzard countered. "So what? Al Paige is more than capable of commanding the carrier. For that matter, *you're* also a fully qualified carrier commander, Admiral."

"OK, I'm not going to argue with you anymore, Miles," said a visibly exasperated Taylor. "Go get the boat; be a hero, and report back to me. But remember, Captain, only the boat."

One half-hour later, Admiral Taylor sat alone in his stateroom staring into space, the weight of the world pressing down on his shoulders.

CHAPTER 15

Tuesday night – Wednesday morning, June 22nd – June 23rd

Fleming was in his stateroom, enjoying the profound sense of relief that he was again among friends and in familiar surroundings. He had taken note of the multi-colored bruises on his torso when showering, trophies acquired when he had been violently blown away from the ejection seat. And aching muscles in his back foretold of more such souvenirs yet to be discovered.

Like many military officers, Fleming kept a daily diary, a habit picked up while a cadet at the Air Force Academy. Some entries were longer and more detailed, others no more than a single sentence. But in the fifteen years of faithful recordings, he could only remember missing a handful of days, and most were recounted later. These diaries were actual hardcopy books and not merely electronic logs in computer files. Fourteen were now stored in his parents' home in Sedona, Arizona, the fifteenth, and current one, was with him now on the *LBJ*. He harbored secret visions of one day turning them into a best seller, or a blockbuster movie, or even … ?

It took him an hour to transcribe the events of the last two days. Because the admiral had placed a TOP SECRET blanket over the incident, he had been extra careful with his choice of words. Satisfied, he closed the diary and snapped shut the locking mechanism.

Fleming picked up a magazine which had been on his desk since his arrival. The banner headline read: *"PROPERTY OF USS LYNDON BAINES JOHNSON PLANKOWNERS."* He flopped down on his bunk and snapped on the reading lamp. Speedreading through the introductory *Welcome Aboard* message from the Captain, he settled in to learn some of the more interesting facts about the world's most potent warship.

'The *LBJ* has much more room for storage than her older generations of sister carriers simply because she is not required to carry thousands of tons of ship's fuel just to keep the screws turning. This has freed up much more space for additional aviation fuel and weaponing, enabling her to roam the seas for extended periods and strike an enemy repeatedly.'

Fleming put the magazine aside, snapped off the light, closed his eyes, smiled into the darkness, and thought, none of this impresses the average eighteen or nineteen-year-old plankowner. Nope, those kids live only to go from one shore leave to the next, and dream of scoring while guzzling gallons of local beer.

* * * * *

It was now shortly after midnight, and the carrier lay three miles from the mouth of the harbor at Livorno. Captain Blizzard was talking quietly with his XO, who had just remarked that the fathom depth readings and channel markings on their paper charts weren't worth a damn.

"Miles, I've been thinking about that Russian sub. Birdwell's on the right track about time warps, fourth dimension transitions, and what have you. The submarine incident supports his theory. One second she wasn't there, and the next moment all hell was breaking loose. And from what little we learned from our loudspeaker contact with the captain, it was evident his crew was in a really bad way. My bet says they met a fate similar to that of our two dead pilots."

"I agree." Before Blizzard could say more, his portable radio came to life.

"We're ready for you, Captain." It was the senior SEAL in the boarding party.

"I'm off, Al," Blizzard said with a quick handshake. "We should be back in a couple of hours, but I'll keep you posted. We can talk freely on the radio because there won't be any eavesdroppers." Blizzard zipped up his wetsuit and checked his gear. "I've decided we'll paddle the Zodiac all the way to the dock. There's a rising moon, but lots of cloud cover, so I can't see the need for us getting into the water and sneaking on board. We've got our night vision glasses, so we'll be fine, and I'll drive the *Félicité* back here like the admiral said."

"Sounds good, Boss. See you in a couple."

Blizzard told the team of his decision to use the paddles all the way in. Each team member had been assigned a number. Blizzard was one, the others, two through five. They untied the line fastening the Zodiac to the ladder and began a rhythmic paddling toward the shore. The sea was running slightly with them. Blizzard had requested that a light be flashed twice every minute from high up on the LBJ's island to help them keep their bearings.

For twenty minutes they paddled in silence, each lost in his own thoughts. The team had been briefed that violence was to be avoided at all costs, but if they had to engage an armed enemy they would respond only to the degree necessary to protect themselves.

Number Four was the first to break the silence. "Man, this harbor smells like an outhouse."

"Makes me glad I decided not to abandon the Zodiac and swim the last couple of hundred yards to the boat," Blizzard whispered back. He checked his watch and wrist compass. "OK, keep a sharp look-out, Number Five. I'm figuring a couple more minutes. Remember, when we get to the transom, the grappling hooks go over the rails, then it's me, with Two and Three going onto the *Félicité*. Four and Five, you're going onto the dock to cast off her lines when the time comes, and to keep anyone from boarding. As soon as I fire up the engines, you two climb aboard and secure the Zodiac to any rail, even if it bounces around behind us until we can hoist her on to the deck. Now, let's take thirty seconds to do an equipment buddy-check."

Five paddles came out of the water simultaneously. The men checked themselves and each other. Less than a half-minute later the paddles went noiselessly back into the filthy sea, silently propelling the Zodiac toward the quay.

Every minute, two short flashes from the *LBJ* kept Blizzard on course, and just when instinct was telling him they were nearing their objective, they heard a noise and froze. From out in the blackness came a deep, phlegmy cough, followed by the sound of water being poured into the harbor. Blizzard stifled a laugh. Someone was taking a leak!

Number Five motioned with his arm, signally for a turn to a more westerly direction.

The man emptying his bladder finished and, after another coughing jag, quiet returned, save for the barking of a solitary dog off in the distance.

The Zodiac continued toward the *Félicité,* with Number Five sitting in the bow giving directions with his hands. Number Three had readied the two lines to fasten the Zodiac to the boat, and now waited for the signal from Blizzard to throw them over the railings.

The Zodiac bumped to a gentle stop. No lights were seen from behind any of the portholes, and as the team worked its way back towards the transom, no voice rose to challenge them.

With a silent nod from Blizzard, both lines were tossed and landed with a muffled thud. Number Three yanked them taut, their rubber-coated grappling hooks finding secure holds around deck stanchions.

Blizzard began working his way hand-over-hand up the side with Two and Three following him, while Four and Five paddled the Zodiac toward the pier. And still their presence had not been detected. Once aboard, the three instantly searched about for any signs of guards. None. Blizzard shrugged, then pointed downward. The other two nodded behind their night vision goggles that they understood, then double-checked their holsters and knives. Blizzard gave a thumbs-up signal, and the trio padded their way toward the hatch.

125

He opened the hatch and descended into a spacious, but darkened drawing room, the two SEALs close behind. He wrinkled his nose. The air was thick with the stench of sweat, garlic, and cheap wine. Blizzard wanted to retch.

A loud coughing fit from somewhere in the darkness caused the three to instinctively spread out, ready to engage any threat. Number Two stumbled over a figure curled up on the floor beside a settee, but before the man could react, a gloved hand was clamped over his mouth and an Ontario MKIII Navy Knife pressed to his throat. His eyes opened and he froze, releasing a clutched wine jug which began gurgling its contents onto very expensive carpeting.

Blizzard and Number Three crept on toward the coughing sound. A voice called out, and a shadowy figure appeared in the companionway only to be instantly overpowered and tossed onto the deck. Like his companion, he immediately understood the knife held to his throat. He lay quietly for a moment, then began an uncontrollable shaking. Blizzard pressed forward alone. A minute later he returned. "Looks like they're the only two aboard, so let's get him into the salon to join his pal."

Blizzard held a finger to his lips, the universally understood command for silence, and beckoned the quaking man to get up. He rose on unsteady legs, but immediately doubled over, and began coughing.

"I'm going topside to get the grappling lines and to radio back to the *LBJ*. We'll bind these two and leave them on the pier, but with their legs hobbled. They'll be able to walk slowly to look for help, but we'll gag them as well so they can't start yelling before we're gone."

"Roger that, Captain," Number Three replied, nudging his prisoner to join his mate.

Blizzard went up on the deck. "Four, Five, how goes it?" he called softly into the night.

"All secure, One," came a low voice from the pier. "No opposition. What's next?"

"There are two prisoners below," Blizzard said. "We'll take them off the boat, then you guys stand by to cast off the lines. We should be ready within three minutes. Secure the Zodiac to the *Félicité* and wait for my order to board." Blizzard then keyed his radio. "Paige, do you copy?"

"Roger, Boss, what's the word?"

"Everything's good here. We'll cast off in a couple of minutes. Al, I want you to move the *LBJ* over the horizon so that she's out of sight from land before daylight. The folks here are going to freak-out when I fire-up these marine noisemakers. Keep the ship blacked out except for the signal light up on the bridge. We'll come up on your starboard side, and once we have daylight we'll get this boat up to the hangar deck for safekeeping."

"Right, Boss, I'll inform the admiral."

Blizzard ordered the two prisoners bound, then went to the bridge to check batteries, electrical circuit breakers, navaids, gauges, and the amount of fuel aboard. He returned to the salon to see the two Italians were now bound, seated on the deck, and still very much in fear for their lives. Blizzard told the other two to remove their night vision glasses, then switched on a sizeable table lamp. The soft glow lit up the room, startling the prisoners. The wide-eyed look on their faces spoke volumes as they stared at the bulb. *What magic can make light without fire?*

"Everything's good topside," Blizzard reported. "Batteries are still fully charged, and the fuel gauges show we have about one thousand gallons in two tanks. She's fitted with twin six-hundred-horsepower GM Diesels, which means we'll make one helluva racket leaving this place. I've already cranked up the bilge blowers."

He turned to study the captives. Their appearance shocked him. Both were probably in their twenties and incredibly filthy. They were short, thin, maybe five feet tall, both with faces scared and pitted from the ravages of smallpox. The cougher had mucous oozing from his nose, and every few moments his tongue would dart out to lick at the slime. Blizzard wanted to choke.

"Captain, have you ever seen anything like this in all your life?" said Number Two. "I haven't ever smelled an animal as ripe as these guys. You just gotta know they're covered with fleas and lice, and all sorts of other creepy-crawly things." He shuddered at the thought.

"I don't want to even think about that," said Blizzard, busy opening windows. "This whole boat is going to have to be fumigated after these two. Anyway, without us touching them more than we have to, we'll leave them on the pier, then get the hell out of here."

Once on the quay, the prisoners stood motionless and allowed themselves to be gagged.

Returning aboard, Blizzard took the helm, started both engines, and gave the command to cast off. *Félicité* responded smartly, backing away from its berth as if alive, seemingly glad to be underway once more. Navigation lights were switched on, and once clear of the dock, Blizzard lit the two powerful spotlights on the forward deck. He immediately spotted huge amounts of garbage and flotsam of all description bobbing in the filthy water, but nothing of sufficient size to damage the vessel. He turned the *Félicité* westward and headed toward the open sea, its twin diesels sounding like rolling thunder as the craft gained speed. He set a course for the carrier.

Torches were now seen flickering near the dock. Livorno had come to life.

The stiffening breeze soon drove away the awful smells, and for the first time in days fresh air began circulating belowdecks. Between gales of laughter and the cracking of corny jokes, the boarding party drew in welcoming gulps of clean air, and released their pent-up stores of adrenaline-stoked energy. They became a momentary band of giddy kids.

Blizzard maneuvered the *Félicité* into a position one hundred yards off the carrier's starboard side, and a half-hour later Paige radioed that the carrier would be powering back. Blizzard acknowledged, and worked his way over to the steel mountain as it came to rest on the open sea. He peered at his watch. It was now three o'clock, Wednesday morning.

"At first light we'll get her up and out of the water just as soon as we can place a cradle around her. Meanwhile, I'll make sure you have plenty of hot coffee and sandwiches. Post your watches as you see fit and continue to monitor the radio." He paused and looked at each man in turn. "Thanks for a job well done. You guys are the best. Now, remember, when you get relieved in the morning, you say nothing about any of this to other members of the crew. They'll be told when the time is right. Of course, they'll all see the *Félicité* come daylight, but still, say nothing." He returned their salutes and headed up the ladder to report to the admiral.

CHAPTER 16

"Hey, I'm talking to you!"
"Whatdya want?"
"I asked what day it is?"
"How should I know! Do I look like a calendar?"

A third voice piped up, ringing with all the authority of a chief with twenty years of service under his belt. "Knock it off, both of you, and get back to work."

"I only wanted to know what day it is, Chief," came a whiny reply.

"It's Wednesday, Murdock," said the Chief Petty Officer now sounding angry.

There followed a long moment of silence, then, "It can't be Wednesday, Chief."

"And why not?"

"Because we had fish last night, and we always have fish on Friday!"

"I'm warning you ..." the chief threatened.

Blizzard heard it all as he stepped into the ship's printing plant. He appreciated the confusion of life below decks with its jumble of days and nights. For some crew members the only knowledge as to what shift and which side of the clock they were working at any given moment was that the lights were always dimmed throughout the ship during the night.

The chief spotted Blizzard, but before he could call the area to attention, Blizzard spoke up. "As you were, Chief. Good morning."

"Good morning, Captain, anything I can do for you, Sir?"

"No, just sort of an informal inspection tour to see how things are going. What's cooking?" he asked with a nod of his head towards a huge copier which had begun spitting out copies of something into a wire basket.

"Oh, that's the newsletter, Sir, except there's really not much news." He picked up a copy and handed it to the captain. "Just some junk filler. Ever since the radio blackout started, we haven't received any sports scores or the international news updates from Armed Forces Radio, and we haven't seen a mail plane either. Of course, you know all that, Sir."

"Well, hopefully that will change soon." Blizzard turned to the two sailors. "Chief's right. Today *is* Wednesday, and for the life of me, I don't know why they served fish last night either!"

The duo stood at attention and grinned.

Blizzard spent the next hour dropping in on various departments and was often surprised at the questions he was asked, not by the older men, but the younger sailors.

"How come we've ceased air operations, Captain?"

"Saw a boat being hoisted aboard, Captain. Did the admiral get a new gig, Sir?"

"Is it true the ship's been quarantined?"

"Some of the guys working topside said the weather has turned real cool all of a sudden. That a fact, Captain?"

"Can you tell us where we are, Sir?"

He answered them all, and at the same time listened to their gripes. The sailors all knew he was the son-in-law of the chief of naval operations, and no doubt a few thought he would phone the CNO later that day and report directly to the top sailor what was on their minds. The gripes which he saw to be valid, Blizzard jotted down in a small leatherbound pocket notebook and promised to rectify immediately. Others would take longer, especially items concerning the *LBJ*. He reminded them that the carrier was still considered a brand new vessel, and that

131

this voyage was really an extension of the shake-down cruise. It could be months before all the kinks were worked out, but he reminded them that for the most part she was trouble-free and that they were privileged to be plankowners of the greatest warship ever built.

His last stop was to the squadrons' ready rooms just as eight bells rang; then it was on to Gowdy's office. CAG ran a tight wing, and kept his officers busy studying tactics and carrying out the many additional duties each must perform to keep the air arm humming smoothly.

Blizzard brought Gowdy up to date as to what had taken place during the night, and just as he was finishing, Major Fleming walked by the open door carrying a sheaf of papers.

"Fleming," he called out, and the Air Force major entered. He stood at attention and saluted both senior officers.

"Good morning, Captain, CAG."

"At ease. You get a good night's sleep?" Blizzard asked.

"Yes, Sir, I'm fine. So's Lafayette. He might be developing a bit of a head cold, but we're both in good shape."

"Close the door a minute," said Blizzard. "CAG, Major, both of you know the score. In fact, both of you have seen first-hand what it is we're facing." He then spent a couple of minutes repeating to Fleming what he had told Gowdy moments ago about last night's recovery of the French vessel, but not its passengers. "So, we're going to have to land a group either in Livorno or Pisa to rescue them. Our party must be kept to less than a dozen, and I think it'll be wise to bring as few new faces into the picture as feasible. I'd like both of you to be ready on short notice to be a part of a rescue." He glanced at his watch. "I have a meeting at ten hundred with the admiral to go over other matters, but I'm thinking that would be a good time to come up with a plan to get those folks freed. I'd like you both to be there for input. Any conflicts?"

Both said that there were none.

* * * * *

Blizzard made his way onto the bridge, returning the duty Marine guard's crisp salute. This was the nerve center of his multi-billion dollar command. A clock on the aft bulkhead told him it was not quite nine-thirty. He had been too keyed up to sleep because of last night's adventure, and after tossing and turning fitfully for a couple of hours, he rose with the first light.

At seven he watched as two scuba divers went over *Félicité's* side to check her hull for damage. Satisfied with what they saw, the duo worked two cradles under her, and secured the boat by steel cables to winches that had been swung seaward and lowered from the hangar deck.

The sixty-foot craft came slowly out of the water. Blizzard took note of the scores of curious sailors looking down. He had to admit, the *Félicité* was a beautiful boat. Her sleek, ultra-modern silhouette bespoke of an Italian pedigree, and as she inched her way up toward her temporary drydock berth, Blizzard saw that her hull was almost pristine, suggesting of a recent bottom job in Sicily or possibly Sardinia.

The bridge was quiet. The duty officer gave Blizzard the ship's eLogBook to bring himself up to date. The carrier was lying motionless in the water, the reactors sending just enough power to the turbines to keep the *LBJ* stationary and to generate electricity for the ship's functions.

As Blizzard was reading, his phone rang. His face turned hard as he listened to obviously bad news, but he continued to nod while the caller droned on, until finally, he'd heard enough. "And what do you recommend doing? Throwing him into the brig? Use your head. Get him down to the hospital and have them take care of him." He put the phone down, then immediately picked it up again and punched a button on the console, connecting him to the ship's PA system.

"This is the Captain. XO, call the bridge."

It took Paige mere seconds to respond. "What gives, Boss?"

"Drop whatever you're doing and get over to the hospital."

"What's happened, Miles?"

133

"Nothing serious, but even so, Taylor's going to have my head. Seems we have a stowaway. Apparently he was well-hidden on the *Félicité* and only discovered moments ago. And *I* was the one who didn't find him last night."

"Why the hospital? Did someone shoot him?"

"Not you too, Al," Blizzard said, trying hard not to sound exasperated. "Just where would you recommend putting a little boy?"

"Yeah, I see your point."

"Al, just go take a look-see, and report back to tell me what the hell's going on."

CHAPTER 17

Wednesday Morning – later -June 23rd

"You have a what!" Admiral Taylor exclaimed. He had been updating a journal of his daily activities, a task he hadn't missed in thirty years. "You have a what?" he repeated, the incredulity in his voice genuine.

"A stowaway, Admiral," Blizzard replied, slumping low in his chair. "Seems he was hiding on the Félicité and discovered only minutes ago. I ordered him taken to the hospital and sent Al Paige down there to get a full a report."

"Tell me you jest, Miles."

"Admiral, he's twelve years old, or thereabouts. I've weighed all the possibilities, and I've concluded he's not going to take over my ship."

Taylor shook his head, ignoring the veiled sarcasm, and busied himself by locking his journal and placing it in his desk. "All right. We'll wait to see what Al Paige has to say." He changed the subject. "What have you decided to do about the folks from the French boat?"

Blizzard shook his head, "We don't have much of a choice. We're going to have to go ashore and get them. They're entitled to the same fighting chance of finding a way home as we do, and I'm not that optimistic any more about our chances. Our scientists aboard are suggesting we stay close to the spot where we came across with the hope the same conditions will reoccur to somehow transport us back."

"And what's that got to do with the Frenchmen?"

135

Blizzard shrugged. "Well, while we wait, we may as well do something constructive, and I think that would include rescuing those people."

"How many do you think there are?"

"Four, maybe six." Blizzard poured a cup of coffee, took a tentative sip, and continued. "We have a meeting scheduled to start in a few minutes, Admiral, and I've asked CAG and Major Fleming to join us to help come up with a plan that will meet with your approval. I want to put a party ashore, do what needs to be done, and be back on board well before nightfall."

They spoke for a few more minutes on ship's business, and at ten were joined by Paige, Eisenhauer, Gowdy, and Fleming.

"Let's hear it, Al," said Blizzard.

"The little fellow's doing fine. Doc Potter personally checked him over, and other than being frightened and hungry, he's in good shape. They're getting him cleaned up and having his clothes sent to the laundry. You were right about one thing, Boss These people understand Latin, at least our boy does. Father Caffarone was able to chat and convince him he'll be OK. He's a sharp little tyke, and he gave us some good information."

"Like what?" said Taylor.

"Well, for starters, today is March 19th, and according to our guest, it's the feast of St. Joseph, or *Josephus* in Latin as the kid said. Apparently, it's an important feast day in the Catholic Church's liturgical calendar, and Father Caffarone says that's indeed correct."

"And the year?" Manny Eisenhauer asked.

"The year of Our Lord, Fourteen hundred sixty-three."

The news was met with a profound silence. Wide-eyed stares circled around the room. There was no avoiding the truth any longer. They had indeed gone back in time.

"Well, at least that's something," Gowdy said, the first to speak. "I don't know how the hell it helps us any, but at least we know the year."

"Anything else?" the admiral asked, sounding deflated at that last bit of news.

The XO smiled. "The little guy won't tell us his name. Father Caffarone says he ran away from home and doesn't want his uncle to find out. So, the kid suggested we call him *Josephus* in honor of the saint's birthday. He also admitted that he sneaked on board the *Félicité* out of curiosity, but that he got frightened when the guards came back early from lunch yesterday afternoon. He hid in a forward locker and stayed there until we found him. There was a small porthole, and he saw the scuba divers getting the boat ready for hoisting aboard. Said the ride in the air really scared him."

"Does he know anything about the Frenchmen?"

"No, he hadn't seen them, but they're the talk of the town. The people are saying they came from the devil, and the bishop, or cardinal, or prince, or some other muckety-muck, is deciding what to do with them. Public opinion is that they're going to be burned at the stake soon!"

"Jeeze!" The admiral's face turned pale. He turned to Blizzard, "Looks like you'll have to move fast after all, Miles."

"Agreed." Blizzard looked at Paige. "Have Father Caffarone report here right now. Whether he likes it or not, he's going to have to come with us because it's going to be his job convincing the bishop or whoever's in charge that their burning at the stake party ain't such a good idea."

When Caffarone arrived, he reported that *Josephus* had eaten a hearty meal and was now fast asleep.

"It's obvious he's being well-educated because he speaks Latin like a churchman, and only the nobility and the rich do so. He can also read, which is something of a rarity, even among the upper classes. He says the prisoners are still in Livorno, but thinks they'll be taken to Pisa at any moment for a formal sentencing. Then they'll be put to death."

After forty minutes of back-and-forth, all agreed that the best approach would be the most direct and to the point. The group going ashore would consist of Blizzard, Gowdy, Fleming, Caffarone, two SEALs, and Lieutenant Silver, a flight surgeon, just in case any of the Frenchmen required immediate medical attention.

They would all wear battle gear, except Father Caffarone, who thought it best he wear a cassock, the long black robe worn by most Catholic priests down through the centuries, so that the local powers would recognize him as a cleric.

The agreed-upon plan called for the group to fly to Livorno by helicopter and land as close to the center of town as possible. The idea was to catch the locals off guard by appearing to descend from Heaven, which would strike the fear of God into them. Blizzard, Fleming and Gowdy, would carry Glock 19s, as do all pilots, while the SEALS would be armed with M4A1 automatic carbines and sidearm Glocks. The two non-combatants would carry only strobe lights, plus the flight surgeon would bring along his emergency medical kit. The helicopter crew would wait in the town square for their return, staying in radio contact with both the search party and the CDC. It was agreed that two Hornets would be armed and ready on the flight deck in case their support would be needed in a hurry. Finally, two additional helicopters would stand-by if they would be needed for additional transport. Al Paige would assume command of the carrier and, for obvious reasons, Admiral Taylor would move down to the CDC for the duration.

"We'll meet on the flight deck in thirty minutes," said Blizzard, rising, while saluting the admiral, with the others following suit.

* * * * *

Fleming made his way to his cabin, eagerly anticipating the adventure ahead. Caldwell had questioned him last night as to what it had been like ashore, and Fleming told him little without divulging the fact that they were smack in the middle of a much older Italy. Like all the other officers in the air wing, Caldwell knew something unexpected was happening, made obvious by the fact that flight operations had been abruptly cancelled in the middle of an exercise. Rumors ran rampant, but no one had any hard facts to fall back on. It was all very strange.

"Hey old buddy, slow down, slow down," Hamilton called out, leaving his cabin. He joined Fleming. "What's happening? I hear you've been up in Admiral's Country with the captain, CAG, and all the other brass. Something's popping, that's obvious, even to this dumb old country boy."

Fleming unzipped his flightsuit and pulled a utility uniform out of his locker.

Hamilton wore a puzzled look. "Going somewhere?" His tone was suddenly serious.

"Yeah, going ashore for a spell, Bud. I'm sorry I can't tell you any more right now, but that's the way things are."

"At least tell me this: Has it got anything to do with your bailing out a few hours back?"

Fleming nodded. "Yes, but only indirectly. Bud, as I said, I am not at liberty to discuss it. I'm sure you'll find out soon enough from Gowdy or Dowling, but I can't say anything more."

"Well, can you tell me this? Does it have anything to do with that big-assed Chris Craft that was hoisted aboard this morning?"

Without looking up from strapping on his shoulder holster, Fleming nodded, checked himself in the mirror, and as he was about to leave, Susan's photograph caught his eye. He picked it up and studied the beautiful face for a long moment. "If anything should happen to me Bud, please let Susan know that I loved her more than life itself."

The tone in Fleming's voice sent a shiver up his spine. "That's a promise, Dave," he replied in a low, somber voice, now knowing that something was very, very wrong.

* * * * *

Fleming was the first one to arrive on the flight deck and went directly to the waiting helicopter, it's mission name, *Firefly one*. The others arrived a minute later, and on Blizzard's signal, the pilot lifted off and set a course for Livorno, forty miles away.

Taylor waited patiently in the Combat Direction Center for word from the shore party. He had asked that Volume R of the *World Book Encyclopedia* be brought from the library, and was now refreshing his knowledge of Renaissance Italy and Europe.

The continent was emerging from both the Dark Ages and the catastrophic upheaval brought about by the black death which had first decimated the population of Asia in the east before sweeping its way westward, unchecked to the shores of the Atlantic. The Church fathers held the view that this was God's punishment for a sinful mankind, and by the time the Renaissance was in full bloom, the power of the Church over Europe was absolute.

Italy was a hodgepodge of city-states, each with powerful ruling families fiercely competing with one another for ever-greater wealth and even greater power.

Architecture saw a rebirth, and the period spawned the building of many imposing edifices, all directed to the greater glory of God, and of course, His chosen few. But the one dark blot on this picture of perfection was the fall of Constantinople to the Turks in 1453. The reign of Pope Nicholas V came to an end in 1455, and the new pope was crowned Pius II. He was the most powerful man in Europe in this Year of Our Lord, 1463.

Taylor now turned his attention to a map of Italy. He saw a country divided into twenty-five city-states. The Kingdom of Naples dominated the south, while the Patrimony of St. Peter, and Florence, held center stage. Milan was the evident power to the northeast, with Venice holding a similar authority in the northwest. He read that the city of Pisa lay within the boundaries of the State of Florence and, by deduction, so too did the port town of Livorno ten miles to the south.

He closed the book with a resounding thump, startling those around him. He looked up apologetically, rose, and walked over to a plotting board where two sailors were busy adding aircraft identification numbers in crayon onto the Lucite surface.

"What's this?" he asked.

The duty officer answered. "Admiral, flight ops has just moved two Hornets onto the mag-levs. CAG's orders."

"What armaments are going on 'em?" Taylor asked.

The lieutenant referred to an Apple notebook before replying. As he read from the screen, his eyes opened wide. "Looks like they'll be loaded for bear, Admiral. Each has a mixed bag of air-to-ground missiles, two-hundred fifty-pound bombs, and napalm cannisters. Funny thing though, Sir, they don't appear to be carrying any air-to-air missiles. That must be a mistake," he murmured to himself, but loud enough for Taylor to hear.

"That's no mistake, Lieutenant. Carry on."

Several decks below, a small group of officers and in-the-know tech reps tasked with finding a solution to the problem were weighing the many variables. They constantly fed information into the computer, but the answers coming back were less than heartening. The biggest unknown was the *Félicité*. When, where, and how had she been transported back in time? Birdwell had scoured the boat looking in every conceivable place for the ship's log, but it was nowhere to be found. "The captain *must* keep a log on a boat this size," he had complained to Joel Hirshberger.

The group now had charts of the area spread out before them, marked with the exact dates and times of every weather and communications anomaly they had encountered since the morning in Naples when things were first noticed as being odd. They had drawn lines connecting all waypoints, hoping to find some commonality between them and the track the *LBJ* had followed while underway. Nothing. They had marked red circles around the two most important points: the exact position of Fleming's Hornet, then that of the *LBJ* at the precise moment each had been transported back in time. The computer revealed that both incidents had occurred within one hundred yards of the other, and that the *LBJ* and the Hornet had been on identical headings at the time. Which left the group with two very important unanswered questions regarding the *Félicité*. Had she been in that same spot and on that same heading when she too

141

had crossed the time barrier? And exactly at what time of day had that happened?

Commander Birdwell was convinced this would prove to be key to finding the answer.

CHAPTER 18

Wednesday Afternoon – June 23rd

The Sikorsky MH-60S helicopter hovered three feet off the ground before finally settling down onto *terra firma*. The ride from the *LBJ* had been uneventful other than flying over a two-masted vessel tacking on a course towards the carrier. The pilot radioed back to the CDC which acknowledged they had radar contact and were keeping an eye on it. Plot determined it was a good five hours sailing time away from the ship.

The pilot decided there was no safe landing zone (LZ) near the center of town, so after a sweep of its entire perimeter, he settled down on a cobblestone road connecting Livorno with the city of Pisa. Blizzard gave the crew instructions: "If anyone approaches, fire up the engines; that should scare the crap out of them. But if not, and it appears you could be overrun by hostiles, then get off the ground and back away. And if we should run into trouble and a safe pick-up looks impossible, then as a last resort come in prepared to shoot to kill. We'll stay in touch, and you can relay any messages back to the carrier if needed. Any questions?"

Both pilots gave Blizzard a thumbs up to signal that they understood.

Fleming looked at his watch. Fifteen minutes to one. There was no activity around them. He had thought it had seemed unreasonably quiet as they had circled the town. Less than a handful of people were about, and those that were, had scurried into buildings on spotting the helicopter.

"Smells like the inside of a toilet bowl," Gowdy said, wrinkling his nose in disgust.

"I bet this must be a fun place during the summer when it gets really good and hot," replied Fleming, looking all around. "I'm kinda surprised we haven't seen much in the way of a welcoming committee. Not that I had expected to be greeted by adoring hordes with open arms, but I did think there would be more signs of activity. There's no one on the road, and this has got to be a well-traveled route."

Father Caffarone spoke up. "I've been thinking along those same lines, and I believe I have the answer. Odds are one in seven that today is also Tuesday in this new time zone." He chuckled at a thought. "*Josephus* could have told me the answer, but it slipped my mind to ask. Well, no matter. My point is this. It's St. Joseph's feast day, but more importantly, this could well be Holy Week, which means everyone's in church. Not just here, but all over Italy."

"Makes sense," Blizzard replied, "so let's act on that assumption. We're going to church."

The group started off for the center of Livorno under a cloudy sky. The temperature was hovering in the low fifties, and a light wind was pushing out of the east. Fleming was surprised to see that the road was in such good repair, knowing it had probably been built by Roman slaves ten centuries earlier.

They approached the town's outskirts, and still no one was out and about. The first building they passed was a rundown wooden hovel, and like the shepherd's hut he had come across with Lafayette, this too had no windows, one narrow, doorless opening, and an appalling stench. They hurried past in silence, and as they released their collective breaths, a mangy cur appeared from around the side of the building. Startled, she stopped short, the hackles rising on her spine. She bared her teeth and growled menacingly but chose neither to advance nor retreat.

It was an impasse, until suddenly, and without warning, Fleming sprang forward with both arms swinging wildly and screamed, *"Move!"*

The startled dog yelped once and fled back around the building.

"That's all we'd need," said an obviously relieved Gowdy, "to get bitten by a freaking, rabid dog from the freaking, Middle Ages. Sorry about that Father," he quickly added.

"My feelings exactly, CAG." Caffarone replied. He was dressed in his black clerical cassock and walking alongside the flight surgeon.

Dr. Silver turned to the priest. "Padre, how do you think these folks feel about Jews, especially if this is the week Christ died?" Before Caffarone had a chance to reply, Captain Blizzard, a couple of paces ahead, spoke without turning his head, "Relax Doc, we don't plan on trading you for the Frenchmen, that is unless it becomes absolutely necessary."

"Well, that sure is comforting news for my ears, Captain. I'm feeling better already."

The group laughed. Buildings were now closer together, most incredibly old, but noticeably cleaner than the first one they had passed. These too were mostly made of wood, but some had decorative stone fronts now blackened from years of neglect and soot from an untold number of chimneys. It was obvious Livorno was a poor community whose citizens relied entirely on eking out their livelihoods from the sea. The harbor lay in plain sight below a sloping, rocky hillside with dozens of fishing vessels at anchor, some tied alongside wooden jetties, others high and dry on the shore. The tide was rising, and the wind off the water carried with it the smell of fish.

The sound of running feet drew the group up short. They caught a glimpse of three hooded figures scurrying toward the church, and heard voices rising in chant from within. The trio dashed up the side entrance steps and disappeared inside.

"Well, we can assume our presence is now known," said Blizzard, who relayed the information to the helicopter crew. They came to a stop ten yards from the front entrance.

This is no cathedral, Fleming thought, *but it's by far the finest building in Livorno.* Where the others were grimy, in various stages of disrepair and with garbage strewn about, the church sparkled like a jewel. *This is God's home,* he realized, and the faithful took an obvious pride in keeping it immaculate. The hewn-stone structure rose more than forty feet, it boasted several stained glass windows, and was topped with a spired belltower. It was the obvious epicenter of life in Livorno.

Two heavy, metal-banded wooden doors opened slowly; a head appeared for just an instant, then was immediately withdrawn. The chanting stopped.

"Get ready to do your thing, Padre," Blizzard said. "Let them know we come in peace and only want the Frenchmen. Tell them we will leave as soon as we have them."

Caffarone nodded, waiting to see what the congregation would do next.

The same figure reappeared at the door and peered out. His head turned sideways as he spoke to unseen others in the shadows, all the while keeping a wary eye on the strangers.

Caffarone stepped forward and lifted his right hand in greeting. He spoke in Latin. "Peace be with you. We come as brothers in Christ, with charity in our hearts and malice toward none. We ask to speak to your priest on a matter of the utmost importance." He quickly translated his message to the others.

Blizzard nodded, but cautioned the group. "Stay on your toes. I don't know what they're planning but be prepared for anything. It's possible they might try to divert our attention, then surround us."

The doors opened wider, and three men slowly ventured out. The one in the center was obviously a priest. Several others now appeared behind the trio, most of them jostling for a better view of the strangers. The side door opened, and a half-dozen more men descended the steps and stood in sullen silence, staring at the foreigners.

"Who are you and where do you come from?" the priest shouted in Latin, his deep voice ringing with authority.

"We come from far away," Caffarone began, speaking slowly to make sure there would be no misunderstanding of his words. "I am Father Eugenio, and like you, I am a servant of his Holy Father in Rome. "These men are my friends," he added with a sweep of his hands. "We have come searching for people who came to this town a short while ago. We only want to take them with us and return peaceably to our homes."

"Those people are infidels," the priest screamed back at Caffarone. "They speak in the tongue of the followers of the infidel Muhammed," he continued, wagging a finger, his face empurpled with a righteous wrath. "They are spies for the Ottomans, and you are the same!"

Caffarone translated quickly for the others.

Fleming was the first to speak. Looking straight ahead but addressing Blizzard, he spoke softly. "Captain, it's my guess the *Félicité* might be registered in Cannes, but it's probably owned by an Arab sheik. I can only imagine the reception they got when they landed looking for help."

"I think you're spot on, Fleming."

The group loitering by the side entrance of the church had grown considerably, and seeing the outrage on their priest's face, were showing a newfound courage. They began moving toward the Americans. Several openly held knives, while others stooped to pick up rocks. The crowd was waiting for a signal to attack.

"Caffarone, warn them to stay back," said Blizzard, keying his radio. He spoke rapidly, ordering the helicopter crew to over-fly the church. "The chopper should scare them, at least momentarily," he added for all their benefits.

"Do not come any closer," warned Caffarone in Latin.

The remainder of the congregation was now pouring out of the church, women and children forming in loose ranks behind the men. They paid no heed to Caffarone's warning, and he immediately realized it was because they couldn't understand him.

"Get that helicopter here, and fast," commanded Blizzard into the radio. They could hear the spooling whine of the engines as the pilot revved up to liftoff power. The harsh noise stopped the crowd in its tracks, and all heads turned toward the sound.

The Sikorsky flew into view, thumping its way just above the roof tops, heading directly for the church. Fingers pointed skyward, and a frightened murmuring rose from the crowd. Mouths opened in awe, and children began shrieking in fear. All signs of hostility had vanished, and, on some unspoken command, the rabble turned tail and ran back inside.

The helicopter went into a hover twenty feet above the church, the frightening noise from its engines and huge rotors terrifying those hearing such sounds for the first time.

The priest stood his ground on the steps of the church, his mouth moving, his arms gesticulating wildly, but his words were lost to the din.

"This is Blizzard," said the captain, holding the radio close to his mouth and looking up.

"Back off, but stay in view. We can't hear, and their leader is trying to tell us something."

The craft climbed higher, all the while moving southward. With the noise fast-fading, the prelate yelled again, only now he had taken a crucifix from around his neck and held it high.

"You are sons of Lucifer, monsters from the depths of hell. In the name of Jesus Christ, the Savior of all men, I command you to return to the fires from whence you came." As he spoke, he made a sweeping sign of the cross with the crucifix, apparently expecting them to immediately disappear. When they continued to stand before the crowd, the cleric's face began to show genuine traces of fear for the first time.

"OK, Padre, I'm getting tired of this circus," said Blizzard, after Caffarone had translated. "No offense intended to your religious beliefs, but we have a job to do, and we're getting nowhere. Tell that fellow I'm giving him one minute to let us know where the crew from the *Félicité* is being held, and if he doesn't come up with some answers, he's really going to see what the fires of hell look like, right here in living color."

As Caffarone spoke, the priest dropped to his knees, the crucifix still held aloft.

"Heavenly Father, what is the reason for this test?" he beseeched of the Almighty. "First the unbelievers reach our shores in a vessel created of Satan's hand having neither oar nor sail, and now these fallen angels come forth to add to our anguish. Our holy cardinal from Pisa has been struck down by their sorcery. O heavenly Father," he continued to lament, "what do you want of us? Give me a sign that I might understand."

Father Caffarone translated.

Blizzard had reached the end of his patience. "He wants a sign. Well, son-of-a-bitch, he's going to get one." He called the helicopter. "Tell *LBJ* to launch the two Hornets immediately. I want them in afterburners, I want them to buzz the town from north to south, I want them down on the deck, and I want to hear some sonic booms. Then I want them to make a pass over the harbor and dump napalm onto the group of fishing vessels moored furthest from shore. Did you copy all that?"

The helicopter crew acknowledged.

"Caffarone, tell that clown to get his congregation back outside right now," Blizzard said. "I don't want them missing the show."

"Captain, don't you think..."

"*Dammit*, I gave you an order, Commander," Blizzard shouted, using Caffarone's military rank for the first time. "Now repeat what I just said."

Caffarone relayed the order. The Italian priest rose slowly from his knees, visibly shaken in the realization God was not going to answer his prayer.

"Tell him to empty his church, *now!*" Blizzard roared.

The priest must have guessed at the nature of Blizzard's command, because before Caffarone could speak, he turned and entered the church. Moments later he reappeared, followed by a trembling congregation.

"Now tell them to stay put, no matter the noises they hear, and whatever they see." Blizzard paused before adding in a quieter voice, "Tell him the women and children can stay inside if they wish, but all the men must come out. And, lastly, tell him we promise that no one will get hurt if they do as they're told."

It wasn't long before two dots appeared low on the horizon, growing, and moving amazingly fast. The priest blessed himself, and as if on cue, the gathered men did likewise.

The two jets raced toward the crowd, then came ear-splitting, double sonic booms as both craft streaked over the church.

"Tell them to keep their eyes open," said Blizzard. "I don't want them missing the next act."

The planes had slowed while making a wide turn over the harbor in preparation for their bombing runs on the boats. Water vapor contrails spiraled off their wingtips.

Flying in trail, the lead aircraft released a napalm cannister from a height of three hundred feet. It turned end over end as it fell, and scored a perfect hit, spewing its jellied fire over a dozen vessels. Within an instant, the boats disappeared inside a man-made inferno.

The second plane dropped its load a little short, but the pyrotechnical display was just as impressive.

Both Hornets made a second approach over the city, flying so low Fleming could clearly see the helmeted heads of the crew. The planes banked sharply right, emitting a long, whining sound.

Gowdy spoke into his radio as they began another large circle over the water. "CAG to fighter cover lead. Do you read?"

"Roger, CAG, this is lead. What next?"

"Lead, return to the *LBJ*. Your firepower demonstration was just what the doctor ordered. Relay to CDC that everything is fine here but tell them to continue to hold two aircraft fully armed and ready to relaunch on a moment's notice."

The pilot acknowledged, then relayed a message from Taylor. "The admiral wants to know if he should prepare a landing party to back you up in case of serious trouble?"

Blizzard thought for a moment. "Yes, good idea," he replied, thinking of the one hundred marines on board his carrier. It couldn't hurt to have them ready to move in a hurry should things really turn sour.

The pilot again acknowledged, wagged his wings in salute, and headed out to sea with his wingman in trail.

Blizzard saw this as the moment of truth. "Gentlemen let's take advantage of the situation. Follow me."

The others fell in step beside him, forming a line seven abreast. They walked until they were within touching distance of the priest who now looked like death itself.

Father Caffarone stepped toward his fellow cleric and reached out his right hand in blessing.

"*In Nomine Patris, et Felii, et Spiritus Sancti,*" he intoned in a quiet voice, making the sign of the cross over the other man's head as he spoke in Latin. "In the name of the Father, the Son, and the Holy Spirit."

Women and children were slowly coming out of the church, curious to see what was happening. The fishing boats furthermost out in the harbor had already sunk, but a still-rising column of black smoke gave mute testament to the destruction that had recently taken place.

"We mean you no harm, Father," said Caffarone hoping to calm the man with his words. "We are not from the devil, but are God-fearing men like yourselves. It is true we possess powers you cannot imagine, but we do not use them to conquer. We could destroy the entire town in minutes if that were our intention, but it is not. We only want the men who came on the strange boat. We wish to take them home."

"And wh…where is th…that?"

"It's a land far away across the sea."

"Ch...Chi...China? Th...They do not look like y...you."

"Not China, but a land even beyond China," said Caffarone, hoping this answer would satisfy the cleric.

The Italian priest nodded, although his wide eyes betrayed the fact that he could not conceive of anything beyond China, a land which he knew lay at the very edge of the world.

The citizens of Livorno listened in silence to the exchange between priests, taking advantage of the opportunity to study the foreigners at close range.

Fleming stared back, trying to imagine the thoughts going through their collective minds. *These strangers are so tall! Their faces are smooth; there's no sign of pox.* Fleming remembered reading that very few adults in Medieval Europe had escaped the ravaging punishment of smallpox, and those lucky enough to be alive after the disease had passed, were left with disfigured faces. But this was life, and the survivors' countenances were mute testament to a destructive disease that knew no cure.

Fleming in turn examined them. *The tallest guy can't be much over five feet.* He could see and smell their poverty. Most were dressed in clothes that were old, threadbare, and dirty. He turned his attention to Caffarone and listened, though he had no idea what they were saying.

"And where are you holding those men?" Caffarone pressed, smiling as he spoke.

The priest paled again. "Y ... you are a priest?"

"I am a priest."

"Then you will understand." He paused to gather his thoughts, then began slowly. "The Cardinal from the great city of Pisa happened to be in our town when the infidels came. He had come to honor us with his presence for Holy Week. Never had the cardinal come to our humble town for such an important occasion. It was his plan to celebrate the feast of the resurrection of Christ with us, but the evil ones changed all that! Within one hour of their arrival, they cast a spell from Lucifer, and His Eminence became ill. He is growing weaker by the hour. It was he who told us that the sons of Lucifer have placed a curse upon him, and that they must be put to death at the stake. He said they are soldiers in the army of the Prince of Darkness, and enemies of the Holy Father in Rome. His word is final, and only he now holds the power to rescind that order. But he is dying and cannot speak. His orders must be carried out under pain of mortal sin. He speaks with the authority of the Holy Father in all such matters. I must obey."

Caffarone turned to the others and repeated what had been said.

"This is going from bad to worse," said Gowdy.

"Ain't that the truth," added Blizzard, his mind racing, trying to figure out their next step.

The Italian priest spoke up, his voice shaking. "We have been bound to silence by His Eminence, and even if you should put us to the sword, we cannot tell you where the infidels are being held. We must obey our cardinal."

Caffarone translated.

"Tell him we have no intention of killing anyone, God damnit!"

"Captain, I must protest your profanity on the very doorstep of the House of God," Caffarone said, his voice filled with righteous anger.

Blizzard reddened with embarrassment. "You're right, Padre. I'm sorry."

Fleming spoke up. "Captain, we have a doctor here. See if this fellow will allow Doctor Silver to take a look at his cardinal. Maybe there's something we can do."

"Padre, explain to him that maybe we can help his cardinal. It's worth a try."

Just then both Blizzard's and Gowdy's radios came to life. "Ground party, this is *Firefly one*. Everything OK down there?" It was the hovering helicopter's pilot.

The people murmured in wide-eyed amazement. Voices were coming out of the little black boxes held by the strangers. It was incredible. They could speak, just like the men holding them.

Gowdy replied. "Everything's fine, *Firefly one*. Return to the LZ but stay in touch. Out."

The helicopter swung away and headed north.

Caffarone turned back to the priest. "It is possible we can help the cardinal. This man," he added, pointing to Lieutenant Silver, "is a physician, just like St. Luke, and he has great powers of healing. Please trust him to look at His Eminence."

The prelate wrung his hands helplessly as Caffarone correctly read his dilemma. *What should I do? If only I had someone in higher authority to consult. I'm but a simple parish priest and know nothing about such important things.* Finally, he nodded his assent, while dropping his shoulders in a show of utter despair.

"Father Caffarone, tell him to have his parishioners return to their homes," said Blizzard in a quiet voice. "Assure him no harm will come to anyone."

The parish priest relayed the message to his congregation, speaking now in dialect rather than Latin. They obeyed without protest and slowly walked away.

The overwhelmed priest beckoned the Americans to follow him around to the back of the church to what was obviously the priest's home. It was two story, built of stone, and unlike any other house they had seen in Livorno, this one actually had glass windows.

Blizzard nodded to the SEALs. "I need you both to remain outside in case a mob forms."

Fleming and the others followed the Italian priest into a small foyer. The drab interior had been whitewashed to present a brighter appearance, and in a niche stood a marble statue of a woman holding an infant in her arms. To her side was a pedestalled marble basin of holy water.

A young girl who had been standing in the shadows took a step forward and bowed low to the visitors. The priest spoke to her in whispers and pointed to Lieutenant Silver. She beckoned the strangers to follow her upstairs.

The house was cold and damp. Fleming saw little evidence of any items for creature comfort. The meager furnishings were strictly utilitarian. He spotted a fireplace but noted that it hadn't held a fire in ages. "Not the best of comforts for a dying patient," he murmured to Lieutenant Silver as they entered a darkened bedroom. He could see an old woman holding a cloth to the head of a figure lying bundled beneath a mound of covers.

Silver went over to the one small window and opened its wooden shutters, allowing in the rays of waning sunlight along with much needed fresh air.

The physician reached out to the Italian priest and placed a hand lightly on his shoulder. "Tell him I'll be gentle with his cardinal," he said, and Caffarone relayed a translation.

The cardinal lay on his back, eyes closed, mouth agape. His face was ashen, and beads of perspiration dotted the thinning hair line. The patient appeared to be in his early fifties.

Silver picked up a limp wrist, looked at his watch and began a pulse count. When finished, he slipped a thermometer under the cardinal's tongue. Next, he opened the eyes one at a time, checking each with an ophthalmoscope. Silver read the thermometer, shook his head, then spoke. "His pulse is one hundred and fifty, and his temperature is one hundred and four. We have an extremely sick man here."

The parish priest spoke rapidly to Father Caffarone. The American nodded and turned to the physician.

"He says that the cardinal has been like this since last night. He could not hold down any food or water. Everything keeps coming back up."

Silver nodded, and gingerly pulled aside the covers. The patient groaned once, but otherwise remained motionless. He was covered with a long, coarse, grey gown. "Help me get this robe up as far as we can, Father." Silver lightly probed a large mass in the groin, studying the protrusion with his fingers. The skin was dry and hot to the touch. The man groaned again, this time longer and louder. Still, the eyes did not open.

Silver turned to Blizzard. "He has a hernia, Captain, and highly likely it's strangulated. This means the intestine has intruded into a body cavity, and in the process has become wrapped around itself. My best guess is that gangrene has already set in, and if we want to save him, we're going to have to operate within the next couple of hours. We wait any longer, he'll die."

"Right here?" said a surprised Blizzard.

Silver shook his head. "No, Sir. His only hope is for us to get him back to the carrier where we can do the job properly. It's his only chance, and a slim one at best."

"Damn!"

"How long would the operation take?" Fleming asked.

Silver pursed his lips and glanced down at the swollen figure on the bed. "At least an hour, but with unforeseen complications, maybe two, or more."

Blizzard walked over to the window and looked out. He stood there for fifteen seconds then turned to the doctor.

"OK. Prepare him to be taken out to the carrier."

"Captain, I'll need you to radio the ship so I can speak with Doctor Potter. I'll tell him the problem so that he'll be ready to move as soon as the patient is aboard."

Blizzard nodded. "CAG and I will go outside with you to see if the chopper can get down here between the house and the church for a pick-up. It'll be a tight fit but will save us a long bumpy stretcher ride to the edge of town."

After giving instructions to *Firefly one*, Blizzard handed the radio to Silver. CDC patched him through to Doctor Potter who immediately grasped the seriousness of the patient's condition. Silver ended by saying he would be injecting 10 milligrams of morphine and to let the operating room anesthetist know.

Blizzard signaled to Silver that he needed to talk to Potter. "This is Blizzard, Clarence. How long is post-operative recovery for something like this?"

"I'm reading your mind, Miles. Post operatively he should do fine, that is if you can get him here in time. There should be no need to keep him on the carrier. He can be flown back to shore and recuperate there. We'll perform the operation laparoscopically, which means there'll be no post op drains to contend with, and anyone can administer the antibiotic capsules we'll leave."

"That's good to hear because the *LBJ* must be prepared to move on a moment's notice. And, Clarence, please do your best, because your patient is the Cardinal of Pisa, and he holds the key to us saving the crew from the *Félicité.*"

"Understand, Captain. If that's all, then I'm signing off and going to scrub. Doctor Datzman will be the one doing the actual surgery using our newest da Vinci machine. I consider him the best surgeon in the Navy, so that cardinal of yours will be in good hands."

Another voice came over the net. "Miles, this is Taylor. I overheard what you said. Is this the only way?"

"It's the only way, Admiral. I'll explain when I see you, but we're going to have to move fast. I want us out of here as close to sundown as possible. I've got the helicopter coming in now for the pick-up. Out."

A minute later they heard the helicopter's engines, and while Blizzard and Silver returned to the house, Gowdy directed the pilot into an LZ. Five minutes later the cardinal was on board, sedated and secured.

Father Caffarone had told the Italian priest that it was going to be necessary to take the cardinal away to be treated. He further explained that Lieutenant Silver knew what was wrong, but that other doctors were going to be needed to make the man well. He promised that the prelate would be returned safely in a couple of hours.

Overwhelmed by events, the priest began to cry. These men possessed such powers that even if he objected, he knew there was nothing he could do to stop them. He nodded his head in mute agreement.

Blizzard spoke directly to Caffarone." I need you to stay here with CAG and Major Fleming. That way our new friend will know we intend to come back. I'm going out to the carrier with Silver and the patient, but I'll return with the cardinal. Is that OK with you?"

"Of course, Sir"

He turned to CAG. "Sean, I'll stay in touch, but if you need anything, just holler."

"I'm not anticipating any trouble, Miles. My only request is that you leave us some water. I don't relish the thought of drinking the local brand."

Blizzard grinned. Water bottles were handed over, and the helicopter lifted off, slowly inching its way upward to a safe maneuvering height, and once clear of the buildings, headed out to sea homing in on the *LBJ's* lone TACAN radio signal.

CHAPTER 19

Two corpsmen inched their way forward in a crouch to meet the helicopter as it settled onto the deck. Even before the rotors had stopped turning, they eased the patient onto a metal trolley and started down to the hospital situated amidships on the second deck. Silver was one step behind, while Blizzard headed off in the opposite direction towards the island. The medical crew descended by an elevator connecting the hospital to the flight deck, one used solely to transport injured pilots and deck crew.

A corpsman held open the swinging door leading into the Number One Surgery Operating Room. The cardinal was lifted onto the table, and through it all remained in a deep sleep.

Doctor Potter and Doctor Datzman, the surgeon, were waiting along with a nurse anesthetist, two surgical nurses, and two corpsmen.

"Let's see what we have here," said Potter studying the cardinal, "but first I need some scissors." He began cutting off the patient's clothing.

"I'm going to start with Propofol," the anesthetist said, and Potter simply nodded. Silver stood in the observation room, listening to the piped-in conversation. Potter glanced at Silver behind the glass barrier as he removed the last of the clothes and discarded them into a stainless-steel drum marked, *Surgical Waste - Burn Only.*

"You're right, Saul. This fellow's in a bad way. How long has he been like this?" Potter asked as he sterilized the exposed belly.

159

"Onset was forty-eight hours ago, but he really turned sour yesterday evening."

"Let's get started," Potter said, nodding to Datzman now seated at his surgeon's console and studying the monitor before him. He flexed his fingers for a moment, then began maneuvering the four robotic arms of the da Vinci Surgical System.

It was a well-organized team. Working steadily, the surgeon was soon inside the body cavity. The intestine had penetrated the peritoneum and had become badly tangled.

"It's gangrenous all right," said Potter, mainly for Lieutenant Silver's benefit, although the flight surgeon could see the problem for himself on the observation room TV monitor. "Doctor Datzman will have to do a resection. I don't think he would have lasted another hour."

They worked steadily, saying little. Twelve inches of infected intestine was excised, and the two exposed ends robotically reunited. The tear in the peritoneal wall was repaired, and after a thorough review of their worksite, Potter gave the OK to Datzman for withdrawing the 3-D cameras from inside the patient and start the closing procedure. "Looks good, Saul," he said for the flight surgeon's benefit.

* * * * *

Blizzard arrived on his bridge a half-dozen paces ahead of Al Paige. "The admiral is staying down in CDC for the time being," said the XO by way of greeting.

"Is he getting in everybody's hair?" asked Blizzard.

"No, he's staying pretty quiet, Miles. He has Manny and a couple of other senior staff with him. Frankly, I think he's really worried about our whole situation."

Blizzard sat down in his captain's chair. From this vantage point he had an excellent view of the flight deck far below. He noted the two Hornets were again secured and loaded, ready to be moved onto the mag-lev catapults for launching on a moment's notice. Further back, two helicopters were also waiting, their crews on full alert, ready to liftoff immediately should the word be given. A third helicopter had been sent back to shore to provide a communications link between Sean Gowdy and the *LBJ*.

Blizzard let loose a sigh. "Al, I'm worried too." He looked at his watch. "It's been just over three days now, and I'm getting a bad feeling that even though it's the right thing to help those folks on the *Félicité*, we just might have blown our chances of ever returning to our own time. Maybe if we had stayed in place, the same conditions would have re-occurred and we'd be out of this mess already." A moment later, he added quietly, "I just don't know."

"The same thought has crossed my mind too, Boss, but I rejected the argument. We simply had the misfortune of being in the *wrong* place at the *right* time. But so was that Russian sub, so were our Hornet crewmembers, ditto those folks on the French boat, and God only knows who else. What's more, who can say there aren't scores of other people, boats, and planes forever lost after being transported through a time portal into how many other centuries? Those folks have no hope of ever returning."

"That's a grim thought all right," agreed Blizzard, with an involuntary shiver.

"Indeed, it is, but back to my original point. Other than for the *LBJ*, Major Fleming, and the Russians, those other anomalies took place hundreds of square miles apart, which means this is no localized phenomenon. How it's happening, I don't know. Maybe it's a one-off and won't happen again for a thousand years, but there's one thing that's certain."

"And that is?" asked Blizzard, a quizzical look crossing his face.

"That it sure happened to us!" Paige laughed at his own gallows humor.

Blizzard eased himself out of his seat and began pacing. There was little to occupy the watch crew as the carrier was lying stationary in the water and had been since early morning.

161

"No reasonable person would ever believe us," he began. "This is the grist of the mill for cheap movies and comic books. It's a fantasyland; it's the dreams of madmen throughout the ages; the ultimate imaginative journey to free us all from the drudgery of the moment. But like you just said, it sure has happened to us!"

"Miles, do you remember hearing or reading about an incident that happened before our time; I mean like back in 1950s England?"

Blizzard stopped his pacing and stared at Paige.

"It was about 1953," Paige continued, "when the inhabitants of a town woke up one day to find that they were receiving television signals which had been broadcast from several thousand miles away, *and three years earlier!* This phenomenon didn't last just a couple of minutes or even hours. Oh, no, I seem to remember hearing it lasted a week, and the signal was coming from Station KLEE in Houston, Texas. For some reason those call letters have stuck in my mind all these years. Anyway, for those few days the people in that town in England were living in two time zones: the present, and the past. Well, the scientific community was rife with theories trying to explain away that one. Some suggested the TV signals had just yo-yoed for years in the atmosphere until finally returning to earth at that particular moment in time. Others claimed that the signal had beamed far out into space unimpeded for years, until it hit something, a planet or an asteroid, which then bounced it back to earth." He shook his head in wonderment at the recollection. "I don't remember hearing of anything like that happening before or since. It's considered a classic tale in the sci-fi community."

"So, you're saying that time is like a TV signal?" challenged Blizzard, with no scoffing tone in his voice. "Maybe that story was a complete hoax from the get-go, but over time it's morphed into an urban legend?"

Paige shrugged. "Who knows? Maybe there is a physical form of energy called time, and like all other forms of energy, it's perpetual." He paused, then added, "But here's a scarier possibility. Supposing someone or some nation has actually cracked the time-travel cosmic code and have developed the wherewithal to transport themselves backwards or forwards at will. I don't mean as passive time travelers like we are right now, but they've found the way to actually take an active role in their transport. Heck, they could destroy their enemies then make a getaway by zipping off into the future or skedaddling back into the past! How's that for some nitty-gritty, science-fiction to pack in your pipe and smoke?"

Blizzard laughed aloud. "It's a scary thought all right," he managed, then changed the subject by asking a serious question. "Al, does the crew suspect anything?"

"We have over five thousand nosy minds aboard, so, yes, rumors are flying, and some of them are hitting pretty close to the mark. The crew knows something's up, and I would counsel that if we don't find a solution within the next forty-eight hours, they're going to have to be told the truth. They have a right to know, Boss."

Blizzard nodded his agreement. "You're right. This morning I made some rounds and answered questions, and I could feel an uneasiness starting to manifest itself. If we're still in the same situation forty-eight hours from now, I'll break the news."

"What about the admiral? Where does he fit in?"

Blizzard let loose a mirthless laugh. "He's a strike group commander without a command at the moment. In fact, he's an admiral of a country that won't even exist for another three hundred years, while on the other hand, I sure do have a ship!"

They went to work on ship's business, going over the scores of items that daily make demands of their time until the phone rang. It was Doctor Potter informing Blizzard that the surgery had been successful. The time was 2:45 in the afternoon, and the weather was turning noticeably colder. It was time to move.

CHAPTER 20

Wednesday, afternoon to dusk – June 23rd

"CAG, the priest is asking if we want some food?"

Gowdy shook his head. "Better not, Padre. Chances are we would come down with something but thank him for the offer."

The group was killing time walking slowly through the heart of Livorno. They were being followed at a discreet distance by a smattering of townsfolk. The Americans were becoming used to the smell.

"When did you learn Latin, Father?" Fleming asked.

"Years ago. It was a requirement in my senior year at the Catholic high school and for two semesters in college. I was a terrible student back then, but somehow managed to get passing grades. In the seminary things were different. In order to be ordained I had to learn Latin fluently. Oh, how I struggled, but then I was fortunate to spend two years at the Vatican and that's when I fell in love with the language."

"But I thought Latin wasn't used in the Church anymore?" pressed Fleming.

"On a day-to-day basis, that's true," Caffarone agreed. "And sad to say, many of our younger priests can't speak it at all! I suppose you could say a streak of pride lies within me because I try to read the scriptures in the Vulgate as written by St. Jerome back in the fourth century. All my hard work seems to have paid dividends these last couple of days, wouldn't you say?"

164

"It sure has, Father, and in spades." replied Fleming.

Gowdy was the first to spot *Firefly two* and radioed landing instructions. Five minutes later the pilots reported that all was quiet on the road and stated there were no new messages to be relayed from the carrier. It was now fifteen minutes to three; the sun was beginning to cast long shadows, and the day was turning noticeably colder.

Their host told them of life in the small town. The people were simple, hard-working, God-fearing Christians who eked a meager living from the sea. Many had never ventured far from the outer edges of the town, and it was more the rule than the exception to say that the majority had never even been to Pisa. Politics meant nothing to them; they had no time to follow the goings-on of the princes and nobles in the surrounding city-states.

Only a handful could understand a little Latin, but he alone in town could read and write it, at least that he was aware of, but confessed that even those skills were barely adequate.

He went on to tell them that out of every ten babies born, two would live to five years of age, then only one would survive beyond that. It was God's plan, he explained, and all accepted the ways of God with a stoic humility. Most had contracted smallpox, and those who survived, bore the defacing scars of their hard-won battle. He remarked how rare it was to find the man or woman with a beautiful face and sparkling white teeth such as the strangers had.

Girls were married by twelve, fourteen at the latest, the men a few years older. So many women died in childbirth that it was not at all uncommon for a man to have three and four wives in his lifetime. And that life usually ended around thirty. By then, most of one's teeth were long gone, and the eyes were no longer capable of good sight. Life was harsh, but it was God's plan.

Food mostly consisted of fish, bread, and a few simple vegetables. Fruit was a treat enjoyed only in the fall. Rare was the day that anyone sat down to a meal of meat because just the rich could enjoy such a feast, and there were no rich people in Livorno. Life was hard, he repeated, but his people were content just knowing that God had prepared places for them in heaven.

In turn, however, the priest could not glean much information from Father Caffarone about his faraway country and its customs but was surprised to learn he was fifty-one years old.

"But you have all your teeth!" he exclaimed.

Caffarone then shocked the man by removing both uppers and lowers and grinning widely to show his naked gums before slipping his dentures back into place. Gowdy and Fleming had laughed heartily, and the Italian prelate joined them a few moments later.

He marveled at their clothes, but spent a long time examining their boots. "A man could walk in those until he fell off the edge of the world," he told Caffarone, "and still the boots would be as good as new." He believed a small person lived inside Gowdy's radio, and the Americans did nothing to disabuse that belief.

They strolled leisurely for the next twenty minutes, seeing the town from one end to the other. Only the main thoroughfare was cobblestoned; the others no more than dirt tracks leading down to the wharf and to the various pockets of homes. They saw an untold number of rats picking their way through piles of refuse while warily avoiding the group, but none scurried off to hide in the lengthening shadows.

When they were within a few feet of the priest's house, Gowdy's radio came to life.

"CAG, this is *Firefly two* with a message from *LBJ*. You prepared to copy?"

"Read you five-by-five. Go ahead."

"*LBJ* says the operation was a success. The patient will be transported back at sixteen hundred hours on *Firefly one*. Captain Blizzard and Doctor Silver will be accompanying. They'll put down behind the church."

CAG keyed his radio. "Acknowledge to *LBJ* that we understand the message. Out." He turned to Caffarone. "Tell our new friend his cardinal is doing fine and will be back shortly. Also, remind him the prisoners must be released to us so that we can leave."

The Italian prelate's face broke into a wide grin. These strangers had performed a miracle.

Fleming stood next to CAG as he guided *Firefly one* in for a smooth touchdown. It was a few minutes past four-thirty, and the chill in the air was becoming more evident.

Two SEALs removed the stretcher from the helicopter and followed the Italian priest into the residence. The cardinal was a changed man. Color had returned to his face, and his breathing was no longer labored.

The priest took one look and broke into tears. Clutching Caffarone's arm, he managed, "You have the grace of God within you. There can be no other explanation."

Father Caffarone simply nodded and followed upstairs. The cardinal's bed had been remade with clean linens, and the two women stood silently and watched as their patient was transferred from stretcher to bed. His eyes flickered open for a moment, then closed again.

Dr. Silver reached into his pocket and took out a clear plastic envelope. He signaled to Caffarone. "Tell our friend here that his cardinal will be well soon. He's still groggy and should sleep through the night. He can have food and water, but make sure he only has small meals to start with. Also, it will do him good to get up for brief periods just as soon as he can. And I'm leaving this antibiotic. He'll have no idea what it is, but he must be made to understand how important it is to give the cardinal one pill with water every morning, and one again at nightfall. There's a ten-day supply here and they will stop the cardinal from getting sick again."

Father Caffarone translated slowly, making sure the man understood the instructions clearly. He nodded vigorously that he did.

"Well, now for our payoff," said Blizzard. He turned to Caffarone. "Padre, please have the priest talk to the cardinal, and get his approval for the release of his prisoners."

Caffarone looked to Silver and the doctor nodded. "My patient's awake, or close to it. He can certainly understand what's being asked, so go ahead."

Caffarone spoke to the Italian priest. The man nodded, then approached the bed.

"Eminence, it's Father Angelo. Can you hear me?" he asked in a soft whisper.

The cardinal stirred, opened his eyes, and focused on the man kneeling beside him. His head moved slightly.

"Eminence, you must give me permission to free the infidels. They have friends here to take them away. These people are enormously powerful, but also exceedingly kind. You have been ill, but these people saved you. Now you must see it in your wisdom to repay that kindness, and let the infidels go."

The cardinal had closed his eyes while the priest pleaded his case, but now opened them again. He turned his head far enough to stare at the Americans. His face took on a frown as he peered at them in the dim candlelight.

"Who are these strangers?" he asked, hoarsely. "More followers of Muhammad?"

"No, Eminence. They are Christians like us. They have saved your life and ask in return that you free the infidels to them."

"Will they execute them?"

"No," replied the priest, and again explained to the cardinal how his life had been saved and that he should repay such kindness with a charity of his own.

"I'm very tired," the patient mumbled. He licked his lips, "And thirsty."

Dr. Silver understood, and without waiting for a translation he poured some water from a clay pitcher and handed a metal cup to the priest.

The cardinal drank sparingly, then fell back heavily against the pillow.

"If you believe it should be done, Father Angelo, then so be it," he muttered. "I will spare their lives, but only on the condition that they leave Italy, never to return."

"Yes, Eminence, I shall tell them. Now rest." The priest rose and spoke rapidly to Caffarone, who in turn relayed the good news to Blizzard.

"We've got to move fast. I can only hope they're not miles away."

The priest spoke rapidly to Caffarone who nodded, then turned to Blizzard.

"Captain, they're right next door in cells beneath the church. They've been under our noses this whole time!"

The group of officers rejoined the two SEALs and hurried over to the church. As they passed by the helicopter, Blizzard and Fleming took a moment to grab two powerful handheld lamps. Night was closing in fast.

They followed the priest up the steps and into the side entrance of the dimly lit church. Candles flickered on sconces dotting the walls, illuminating a drab interior devoid of seats. The priest genuflected as he hurried passed the altar, so too Father Caffarone. The others just nodded their heads in respect. The Italian led them along the nave toward the main entrance.

"We would have torn this town apart brick by brick," Blizzard said to no one in particular, "but would have left the church as the only building standing when we were finished."

Fleming laughed at the irony of it, and replied, "And who would have guessed that God's house is also the town's prison?"

The Italian priest opened an ancient wooden door held fast by three huge, iron bolts. They peered down to see a dozen steps hewn into solid stone, the surfaces visibly slickened from a constant dripping of water seeping in from seams in the rock formation overhead, and from the walls. The place was barely lighted, only one torch flickering at the top of the steps, a twin at the bottom, and a third marking the entranceway to a corridor veering off at a right angle.

The Medieval dungeon was dank and cold, yet there was definitely fresh air coming into the passage, and not just from the still-opened door up to the church's vestibule. The corridor led them for some twenty feet where it abruptly turned ninety degrees to the left. Here too a solitary torch flickered, this one in its final stages of life.

Blizzard and Fleming switched on their high-intensity LED lamps, flooding the place in a stark blue-white light. All shuddered at the terrifying thought of imprisonment in such a place. Several large rats scurried from the light by squeezing themselves under a sizeable metal grid and disappearing into the darkness beyond. The breeze coming from behind it spoke to the fact there was indeed fresh air circulating within.

The men now heard voices as they pressed forward along a corridor with four doors spaced a dozen feet apart on both sides. The Italian priest stopped at the first one, took a large key from a hook on the wall and inserted it in the lock. The rusty hinges groaned as the door swung inward to the sound of rattling chains.

Holding his light high, Fleming entered first. He was stunned by what he saw: Five men shackled to the wall, all shielding their eyes from his lamp's glare.

"Do any of you speak English?" Blizzard called out, looking from one to the other. The prisoners squinted in their direction. Finally, one took a single step forward, his chains clanking noisily against the stone. His feet were buried in straw, the only insulation from the cold floor.

"What now?" he asked in a Middle Eastern accent. "What new devilment have you arranged?"

"We've come to take you home," said Blizzard, holding his lamp low to shield the prisoners from its direct glare. "My name is Miles Blizzard, I'm a captain in the United States Navy, and commanding officer of the nuclear aircraft carrier *Lyndon Baines Johnson*. As I said, we've come to take you home."

"Praise Allah!" the man replied in a voice filled with a simultaneous disbelief, and a profound sense relief. He turned and spoke rapidly to his cellmates, their dazed stares proof of their difficulty in understanding what was happening. They began to chatter.

"Does anyone need immediate medical attention?" Blizzard asked, interrupting their babble.

"No, Captain, nothing that can't wait."

"Is this the lot of you?"

"No. There are two women in another cell somewhere."

"Sean, can you get these men unshackled? Fleming, come with me."

The priest handed a key to Caffarone who gave it to Gowdy.

"Father, tell him to take us to the women," said Blizzard. "In fact, I want you and the doctor to come along as well."

Fleming handed his lamp to Gowdy, then hastened after Blizzard and the others.

The Italian priest led them further down the passageway and stopped at the last door. Again, he took an oversized key off a peg, inserted it in the lock, and swung the door inward.

Two women were lying on straw pallets, and like the men, instinctively turned away from the unexpected light. Neither were chained. "Do you speak English?" Blizzard asked.

They rose slowly, holding onto one another for support. They were shivering, as much from fear of this new and yet unknown menace as from the cold.

Blizzard stepped forward and gently touched each on the shoulders. "It's all right," he said in a calming voice. "It's over. Everything's going to be fine." He turned to Fleming and Caffarone. "Take each of them by the hand, and let's get them out of this hellhole."

Halfway on their journey down the corridor, a spine-chilling scream brought them up short.

"What in the hell was that?" said Fleming, jumping at the sound.

The Italian priest spoke rapid-fire to Father Caffarone, who then explained to the others.

"It's a prisoner who's been here for two months. He killed his wife and three daughters with an axe and has been locked-up ever since. As soon as he repents for his sins he will be put to death, but has shown no inclination in wanting to do so. And he never will," Caffarone added in a subdued voice, "because the poor fellow is completely mad."

"Well, there's nothing we can do," said Blizzard, "so let's go before we all end up like him."

They hurried along, and as they turned the corner the doomed prisoner began his terrifying screeching and howling again.

It was a sound Fleming knew would stay in his mind to the end of his days.

As the two groups joined together in the clearing beside the helicopter, Blizzard turned to the just-freed prisoners.

"Which one of you is the Captain of the *Félicité?*"

"I am," replied the spokesman. "These two are my crew, and those two gentlemen are the owners," he added, nodding toward the two men who were now comforting the women. "The ladies are their guests, and all of us are citizens of the United Emirates Republic."

"I see," said Blizzard. "Captain, I have your vessel aboard my aircraft carrier. It's in good shape, so don't be concerned on that score, but I was not able to find your logbook. Where did you put it?"

The other man wrinkled his forehead. "Why do you ask, Captain?"

"I don't really have time for lengthy explanations," Blizzard said, trying not to sound short. "Just answer me this. Did you experience any strange events immediately before you found yourself in this mess?'

The man nodded. "What day is this, Captain?"

"Wednesday."

His face reflected genuine surprise. "Ah, it seems like we've been here for a week, but it's only been three days." He thought for a moment, then said, "We were sailing from Rome to Monte Carlo in smooth seas and warm weather. Just after dusk, our radios went dead, and so did our radar. There was no warning, they just went dead. My first mate knows about electronics, but he could not find a reason for the malfunction. Then there was a huge explosion, along with a flash of green light and then everything was quiet. The weather turned cold in an instant. I did not know what was happening, so I headed due east toward the Italian shoreline using my magnetic compass. I also wrote about this strange turn of events immediately in the logbook while it was still fresh in my mind. We motored for three hours until we came to the harbor. I thought it was Livorno, you know, just south of Pisa, but obviously it was not. There is much that is going to have to be explained to us, Captain, but I intend to complain most bitterly to the Italian authorities about our barbaric treatment."

"Your logbook, Captain. I need to know where you hid it so that I can figure out your exact position when you first experienced those problems. Or maybe you use an electronic logbook?"

"We do not use an electronic logbook. The owners insist on having a physical book, and I left it on the *Félicité's* bridge. I did not hide it, Captain, so if it's missing, then one of these thieving Italians must have stolen it."

"*Damn!*" Blizzard thought for a second, then asked, "You said that you were about three hours west of Livorno when your radios and nav aids went dark?"

"That is correct."

"At least that tells me something." said Blizzard. "OK, we'll talk later." He turned to Caffarone. "Please thank the priest for us, Father, we couldn't have done this without him."

CHAPTER 21

Twenty minutes later they were flying back to the *LBJ*. Night had fallen, and their helicopter was guided onto a flight deck bathed in the red glow of night operations lights.

Blizzard thanked the shore party and suggested they hit their respective galleys for a well-deserved meal. He turned to Fleming. "Major, would you join me on the bridge after you get a hot shower and some dinner? There are things I need to go over with you, but no rush. A couple of hours from now will work." He looked at Gowdy. "If that's OK with you, CAG?"

"Of course, Miles."

Fleming stood at attention. I'll be there, Sir."

The XO escorted the seven guests from the *Félicité* to their quarters.

Blizzard went to his in-port cabin on the 03 deck rather than his at-sea stateroom on the island, and following his own advice, luxuriated in a long, hot shower. He savored the time, clearing his mind as the water cascaded over him, and only reluctantly turned off the faucets when he felt he was becoming waterlogged.

Ten minutes later he was on the bridge and clicked up the ship's E-log on a mobile pad as he had done countless times before.

"Can I order you some dinner, Captain?" asked the Officer of the Deck.

"What's on the menu?"

"The steak and fries look really good, Sir. We still have several up here."

"Sounds great! Two helpings, I'm famished."

"Aye, Captain. Two steaks with all the trimmings, coming up."

It took a steward less than five minutes to heat up the meal. Blizzard ate seated in his captain's chair which was designed for having a meal tray snapped into its sides. *Things could sure be a hell of a lot worse*, he thought, making short work of his double order. As he swallowed his last mouthful of coffee, the phone rang.

"Captain speaking,"

"Birdwell here, Captain. I'm in the CDC. Take a look at the long-range radar."

"Hold on." Blizzard walked to a bank of large radar screens being monitored by sailors under the watchful eye of the helmsman.

They were scanning out to distance of forty nautical miles. Everything seemed normal. The coastline was well-defined, and there were only a few scattered showers within range.

"Run her out to max," Blizzard ordered.

The young rating toggled a switch, and the display became smaller in scale but larger in scope. The electronic beam swung the full three hundred sixty degrees of the compass, once, then twice.

Blizzard frowned. "What do you make of it, Commander?"

"Don't really know, Sir. At first, I thought it might be a malfunction, but both back-ups are painting the same return."

Any guesses, educated or otherwise?"

A moment's hesitation, then, "Yes, Sir. I think we're seeing the beginnings of a fusion between time zones. It's my guess that this is exactly what we ran into a couple of days ago."

"Is it static?" Blizzard asked, running several possibilities through his mind.

"No, Captain. It's a very strange forcefield, but it's definitely not just static."

"I meant static as in stationary, you know, not moving."

"Oh," came the reply. "No, we think it's moving north, but because we don't have any weather satellites to tell us exactly what we're seeing, that's our best guess. Also, the speed seems to be about twenty knots, but that's picking up."

"I want you to plot an intercept. My plan is to turn the *LBJ* to meet it. Your theory just might be correct and, if it is, this could well be our last chance to return home. Get on it right away. I'm on my way down." He pressed a button on the console to hook him into the ship's PA system.

"This is the Captain. Executive Officer please meet me in the CDC."

Paige greeted him as he entered. "An intercept course has been plotted, Boss."

"Good work, Al. Let's take another look at the main radar screen."

As both men studied the radar return, they were joined by Birdwell and Commander Sewell. The liquid crystal display monitor (LCD) clearly showed an arc thirty miles across, and behind that line was a void the radar beam was unable to penetrate. It was as if a portion of the screen's pixels had inexplicably burned out.

"At first, I thought we had a malfunction," said Birdwell, "but a couple of simple tests proved that not to be the case. We then tried to penetrate it with a laser-directed signal, but all we got was our own signal being returned, as if it had bounced off a solid object. But you can see that's nothing solid."

"How about a helluva storm?" asked Paige.

"No way, Sir. Joel Hirshberger also agrees, and he'll be right back. He's gathering up-to-date weather data from below. Because there's no satellites to tell us what's really happening, he flew a weather drone up to flight level one-five-zero fifteen minutes ago and got a good look out to three hundred forty statute miles. The drone was recovered a couple of minutes ago; that's the information we're analyzing now."

"Then we'll sail the intercept heading. What'll our course heading be?" asked Blizzard.

"One six three, true," replied Birdwell reading the information off a computer printout. "We're presently one-niner-four nautical miles from the unidentified target, and with the *LBJs* speed of twenty-five knots and our target closing on us at two-zero knots, we should intercept in a little over four hours. Seas are light, and winds are out of the northeast at ten."

Blizzard reached for a phone. "Bridge, this is the Captain. Prepare to get underway. Course is one-six-three true, speed, twenty-five knots, and have the ship piped to flight quarters."

"Feels good to be underway again," said Paige, still studying the screen. "Right or wrong, at least we're taking some kind of action to help ourselves, and that's all that counts."

"I'll drink to that," replied Blizzard. "Let's get our butts upstairs, Al. I'll speak with the admiral from the bridge and let him know what's happening."

* * * * *

Forty minutes later the aircraft carrier was cutting a path through the night seas, throwing up an impressive wake as she headed for her rendezvous point. The *LBJ* had come to life as thousands of sailors below decks acted in concert to bring the ship to flight quarters. The busy twenty-four-hour schedule had started again after a two-day standdown which had still not yet been explained, but to a man, the crew understood *theirs was not to reason why.* Hopefully, the admiral and the skipper both knew the score was the thought racing through most of their minds.

Blizzard stood engrossed with the strange arc formation on the radar scope, and still puzzled by the void being left in its wake. He had never seen anything like it in his twenty-plus years at sea. Sure, the radar return had been unusual just before the *LBJ* had passed across the time-barrier forty-eight hours earlier, but nothing compared to this. Previously, the radar screens had painted a picture of the carrier sailing headlong into a barrel, but events had happened so fast there hadn't been time to understand what was happening. This scenario was immeasurably different, but he realized now that only time would tell whether or not they were embarked on a fool's errand. Major Fleming stepped onto the bridge, and as he was about to render a salute, Blizzard was interrupted by a yeoman. "Captain, a call for you." He held a phone for Blizzard.

"Captain speaking."

"Captain, this is Senior Chief Petty Officer Clarke in engineering."

"Yes, Senior Chief, what's the problem?"

"We have a stowaway, Captain. At least I think he's a stowaway, Sir."

"What do you mean, a stowaway?" Blizzard asked absently, studying the picture on the radar scope.

"Captain, I'm holding onto a kid right now. He wandered in here dressed in a hospital gown about two sizes too big, and he's got some sort of a medical journal and a *Popular Mechanics* magazine tucked under his arm. And he refuses to say a word."

Blizzard's face turned white. *Josephus!*

In the confusion and rush of the afternoon's events, everyone had forgotten about the boy, and now they were plowing through the seas, sailing away not only from Livorno, but hopefully from the year 1463 as well.

"Oh Lord," thought Blizzard, a pit forming in his stomach. *What in the name of God am I going to do?* "Hold on, Chief, I'll be right back to you." Blizzard put the senior chief on hold and switched on the PA.

"Attention, attention, this is the Captain. CAG and Commander Caffarone, call the bridge immediately." He repeated the command then reconnected with Clarke.

"Senior Chief, take the kid to the hospital immediately and wait there with him. Don't let him out of your sight. Father Caffarone will meet you. I want you to turn him over to Father Caffarone, and only Father Caffarone. Understand?"

"Understood, Sir."

Blizzard held the receiver in a vicelike grip and spoke with Gowdy who was waiting on hold. He explained the problem, then said, "Sean, get a helicopter ready to launch, and I mean like yesterday, to take that kid back to Livorno. I suggest using the same pilots we had this afternoon because they're familiar with the town and will know where to land. Have the computer prepare their flight plan based on our present course and speed. And, Sean, make sure those guys know how to find their Point Option, because our radios and navigation aids could go down any moment. *Remember, if they miss Point Option, good chance they'll be lost forever!*"

"We'll be ready in ten minutes. I'll meet Caffarone and the kid on the flight deck."

Caffarone was next on hold. Again, Blizzard explained the problem and told the priest to meet *Josephus* in the ship's hospital. "Take him up to the flight deck, Padre, a helicopter will be waiting to take him ashore. I want you to go with him, so he won't be too scared." After a moment's pause, he added, "Padre, I'll meet up with you on the flight deck. Now hurry."

"You want me to get his clothes from the ship's laundry, Captain?"

"There's no time for that. He's going to have to travel in hospital PJs. Get him some warm socks and a heavy sweater to wear underneath a robe. *Move, move, move!*"

Blizzard hung up and turned to face Paige and Fleming. "*Can you believe it? Damn!*" He slammed his fist into his palm. "Of all the frigging bad luck, and at the worst possible moment."

He turned to the helm and ordered the speed reduced to fifteen knots. "As soon as the helicopter is clear, I want you to return to twenty-five knots, then maintain the same heading and speed. We're not coming around into the wind. The pilots are just going to have to manage with the existing conditions."

Blizzard watched the forward elevator bring the helicopter up to the flight deck. A couple of mechanics were still working underneath it when one gave the signal to start the turbines. The huge rotors began turning, slowly at first, then faster and faster as power built up. A minute later, under the glow of the red night lights, the pilot taxied slowly away from the elevator and back towards the center of the flight deck.

"You have the bridge, Al. I'll be back in five minutes." Blizzard hurried down from the island to join CAG, Caffarone, and the boy.

"Everything set?" he yelled in Gowdy's ear.

"Ready. The crew's been briefed and told to expect the worst. They know how to find Point Option and will stay in radio contact at all times."

Blizzard nodded and turned to Father Caffarone who was holding the boy's hand in a firm grip. If the lad was scared because of the noise, he didn't let it show.

"Ready, Padre?" Blizzard yelled at the priest.

"All set, Captain."

"Thanks, Padre. I'll see you when you get back." He then looked down at *Josephus*, smiled, and tousled his hair. "Good-bye, son, and good luck."

The boy smiled back, obviously understanding the meaning, if not the words. Caffarone helped him into the helicopter then climbed aboard. The pilot spooled the turbines up to full power and slowly lifted off the deck, hovering close, all the while turning the huge machine into the wind, then started forward, the nose down while picking up speed and altitude. When the helicopter reached one hundred feet, it turned, and set a course for Livorno.

Blizzard returned to the bridge to be told by his XO that the admiral had called about the helicopter. "He just wants to be kept apprised of what's happening."

"We'll keep him in the loop," replied Blizzard, turning his attention to the radar screen. The strange arc was still there but closer, and it was becoming more circular in shape. He rang down to the CDC and asked for Birdwell.

"Birdwell here, Captain."

"Reece, I'm studying the radar return and it's dawned on me that we never saw this kind of display on Sunday." After a momentary pause he added in a not-so-sure voice, "Or did we?"

'No, you're right, we didn't. I've been kicking that around with some Raytheon reps, and they kinda remember seeing something similar earlier in the week, but said it lasted for less than a few seconds. It was as if two time zones were about to fuse with each other, but that an unknown, repelling counterforce finally won out. The only reason we know this is because the mainframe computer sounded an alarm."

"And now?"

"And now, Captain, for some inexplicable reason our radar returns are suggesting a second time zone is coexisting in real time with the time we're in now, and as that arc moves across the screen and becomes more circular in shape, it's literally casting aside other centuries, other time zones if you will, and leaving them behind in its wake. And that explains the expanding void we're seeing on the radar screens." After a momentary pause, he added quietly, "That' s our theory, Sir, we just can't say for sure."

"Keep me posted, Commander."

Paige, who had been reading the ship's eLogBook, paused, pointed a finger at the electronic pad, and asked, "Miles, what do you plan to do about this if and when you return to the real world? Entries for those days spent in 1463 will look mighty odd."

"I don't know," Blizzard replied. "When Washington hears about this, the brass will demand that our eLogBooks be slapped with a top secret classification and impounded."

"Captain, could you come here, Sir?" said the helmsman's mate standing by the radar display. No sooner had he spoken than the intercom from CDC came alive.

"Get that, Al," Blizzard said, heading over to the radar scope. He looked, blinked, and looked again. *The arc was gone! Vanished!* The entire screen was lit up normally, the sweep of the electronic finger only showing a return of the coastline of Italy.

"Is that Birdwell on the phone?" he asked Paige, without turning his head.

"Aye, Boss" replied Paige.

"Put him on speaker." A second later, Blizzard asked, "What gives down there?"

"I don't know, Sir. We're now painting a normal return. One moment the expanding arc was there, then in the next, *poof*, just like that, it was gone!"

"Sounds like your bounce theory might be right," said Blizzard, stunned by this unexpected turn of events. His mind raced for answers but found none. For the first time since Sunday, he honestly believed they had just lost their last chance of ever returning home.

CHAPTER 22

The phone call from the flag bridge demanded immediate attention. "Al, tell the admiral we're aware of what's happened. His radar scope is showing the same as ours: one big fat zero. Ask him to standby; I'll get back to him as soon as I can." Blizzard turned to Birdwell. "We'll remain on this heading because I'm not about to start flailing around in circles. How long would it have been until we intercepted that arc if it were still out there?"

"One hour, forty minutes," Birdwell replied.

"Stay with it, at least until we recover the helicopter," Blizzard said, then added, "Do we still have a good radio link with the chopper?"

"We do, Captain. In fact, they're approaching the shore right now."

* * * * *

The cockpit radar screen in the helicopter showed they were eight miles from the center of Livorno. The pilot banked left and headed toward his planned landing zone on the open road leading to Pisa. When he was one hundred feet off the deck, he switched on his landing light and studied the terrain. Everything looked clear.

Father Caffarone sat close to *Josephus*, the boy obviously not scared in the least by the noise from the turbines and rotating blades. They had been chatting as best they could, and *Josephus* had said how he would have liked staying on the big iron ship a while longer.

183

He was enjoying the flight, nodding his head to signal he understood Caffarone's explanation as to how the strange metal machine could fly like a bird. Caffarone smiled to himself, knowing it was impossible for any child to understand the physics involved.

As they made their descent, he checked *Josephus* one last time to make sure that his clothes were tightly fastened. The night was chilly, and he was concerned his young friend could catch cold, or worse.

Caffarone placed his lips close to the boy's ear. *"Nunc, oportet pergens ad avunculus tuus domus."* "Now, you must go straight to your uncle's house."

"Etiam, Pater. Promitto. Non me diu." "Yes, Father, I promise. It will not take me long."

"Good boy." As he spoke, Caffarone spotted the corner of a magazine cover peeking out of the boy's hospital robe pocket. It was an illustrated quarterly from the Merck Pharmaceutical Company printed for the American College of Surgeons. How *Josephus* had gotten a hold of it Caffarone had no idea, but knew he couldn't let the boy keep it.

They were now in a hover, flying mere inches off the ground. *"Josephus, erit tibi dic mihi verum nomen tuum?"* "Josephus, will you tell me your real name?" Caffarone asked. "I'd like to know the name of my young friend in Livorno." He smiled as he spoke. "I promise I would never tell your uncle where you've been. That will be our secret."

The lad thought about this, his small face reflecting the struggle within. Finally, he nodded, and told Caffarone. The priest's eyes widened. He placed his mouth closer to the boys ear and asked him to repeat what he had just said. He looked closely at the youth in the dim light, then seeing the look of alarm flitting across his face, quickly patted him on the shoulder and smiled reassuringly. "You've been a good boy, and I'll always remember you, *Josephus*," Caffarone shouted above the din of the engines. The helicopter was now on the ground, and the co-pilot had come back to see the boy out safely.

"Tell him to run far away from the helicopter, Father. We don't want him tossed around by the wash from the turning blades."

Caffarone explained this to the boy. He nodded, reached over, and gave Caffarone a hug.

"Goodbye, Pater Eugenio."

"Goodbye, son, and may God go with you."

The co-pilot watched *Josephus* run off into the darkness and disappear. "All clear," he called to the aircraft commander, and settled into his position in the left seat. The huge blades began rotating faster as power was applied. The helicopter lifted off slowly and turned into the wind.

"Steve, set the course to our Point Option," said the pilot-in-command, "and you'll fly this return leg to the *LBJ.*"

"Roger that, I have the helicopter," Steve replied, placing his hand firmly on the stick between his knees. "We'll be on the deck in forty minutes."

CHAPTER 23

Wednesday late evening to night -June 23rd

"**C**_aptain, it's back,_" the seaman monitoring the radar screen shouted in an excited voice.

Blizzard was beside him in an instant. And there it was! The strange arc was back, only now much closer. He punched the intercom to the CDC. "Birdwell, what's the distance?"

"Forty nautical miles and closing, Captain."

"How about the chopper? What's her position?"

"About ninety-four nautical miles out, Sir. She's indicating one fifty-five knots, and we should have it recovered and secured before rendezvous." No sooner had he spoken than all the radar screens went blank.

"What the hell's happening?" asked a startled Blizzard as he began a fine-tuning of the dials on the radar screen.

The sailor beside him shook his head. "I don't know, Sir."

"Captain, this is Birdwell. We've just lost all radar and radios, which means we're no longer in touch with the helicopter."

"Keep this line open," said Blizzard while turning to Paige, and the duty officer. "Plot our location relative to the last known position of that arced wall and to the chopper. I want to know how soon we'll recover the helo before we hit that thing."

The three were working on the problem when a call came from the meteorological division.

"Captain, this is Hirshberger. The outside temperature has risen ten degrees in the past five minutes, and barometric pressure is rising. I have no explanation other than to say our instruments are not malfunctioning. And, Sir, if you look outside you'll notice there's a fog or mist closing in around us."

Blizzard peered into the night. Mere minutes earlier the visibility had been unlimited. Now he could barely see the bow.

His thoughts immediately turned to the helicopter. If they were flying into this fog without radar or radios, there was a very strong possibility they could miss the carrier completely, even if they flew to their Point Option with absolute precision. He made a quick decision.

"Duty officer, light up the ship," he commanded. "Not the night lights, but everything we've got, including our searchlights, but direct them forward and not upward so that we don't blind the pilots. I want the *LBJ* to be seen no matter how bad this fog gets."

Within moments, the fog-enshrouded ship was bathed in an eerie white light, while the beams from the huge forward-facing searchlights cut two brilliant paths into the night.

"Birdwell, talk to me. What's going on?" Blizzard wanted to know.

"We're now inside a very disruptive forcefield of some kind. I'm thinking it's because that arc is closing in on us, but without any radar images, there's no way of knowing for sure."

Blizzard got on the ship's loudspeaker to command the helicopter recovery team on the flight deck to stand by for a hard landing. He glanced at the bulkhead clock. Time was running out. The three officers on the bridge now turned their eyes outside, willing the helicopter to appear.

"Captain, this is Lieutenant Diebold on the flight deck," came a shouted metallic voice over the intercom. "We're seeing a landing light being switched on and off at our six o'clock, directly off the stern."

"You sure?" replied Blizzard.

"We're sure," came the reply. "We can barely hear the engine above the wind noise."

"Dowse all white lights and go to red. No, on second thought," he corrected himself, "keep one searchlight on, but tilt her up forty-five degrees. It'll act as a beacon but won't blind them."

Blizzard, the XO, and the duty officer stood shoulder to shoulder with noses pressed to the large shatterproof bridge windows and squinted into the fog to watch the helicopter land.

Admiral Taylor came onto the bridge with Manny Eisenhauer one step behind.

They all saw it at the same moment. The helicopter suddenly appeared like some otherworld apparition from inside the swirling fog, hovered momentarily, then scurried crablike across the pitching deck before slamming down hard abeam of the island.

Two yellow-shirted sailors raced toward it, leaning low into the wind, and disappeared underneath to secure the Sikorsky to the metal deck.

A blinding flash of emerald-green light turned night into day, followed a split-second later by a deafening explosion. The shockwave rippled through the carrier, causing many sailors on all decks to grab at handrails, while those less fortunate stumbled and fell like skittles. The lights on the *LBJ* went out. One second passed, two seconds, then three, and the lights flickered back on.

Blizzard had been thrown to the bridge's deck, landing hard on top of Manny Eisenhauer. He slowly picked himself up and staggered to the intercom. "This is the Captain," he shouted. "Damage report from all departments. Nuclear engineering, report immediately." It was a replay of Sunday.

Commander Castle answered moments later. "Castle in nuclear engineering. No damage here, but I think both reactors shut down for several seconds. We're still checking everything, but at first glance the entire system seems to be one hundred percent safe."

"Thanks, Walt. Give me a full report as soon as you can."

The other departments began calling in to confirm only minor damage.

Then a jubilant Birdwell came on the line. "Captain, look at the radar screens. We're back in our own time! The whole freaking strike group is out there!"

Blizzard limped to his screens and let loose a whoop. Birdwell was right. They were home!

Commander Sewell cut in. "Captain, this is the communications officer. All radio and nav aids are functioning normally. The *Truman* is calling, Captain. They say that we disappeared completely from their radar screens for almost two minutes, and they're saying they couldn't raise us on any channel. They want to know if anything's wrong over here?"

Two minutes? thought Blizzard, his mind racing for an explanation. *We've only lost two minutes?* Commander Sewell needed an answer. "Ed, inform the *Truman* that everything is fine over here, but don't volunteer anything more."

Sewell came back less than a minute later. "Captain, the *Truman* is asking for a position report from us. They say the satellite shows we're eighteen miles from where we were just two minutes ago. They're sure sounding puzzled. Also, Captain, we've reacquired the signals from the atomic clocks on the satellites and they all show we've been disconnected for two minutes."

I'll bet the folks over there on the Truman are puzzled, thought Blizzard. "Tell *Truman* we've been having some minor glitches with our nav equipment and radios, but everything's OK now. Stand by one, Ed. Don't hang up." He turned to the admiral. "Sir, I recommend we rendezvous with the *Truman* in the morning, and then rejoin our strike group after first light. We should have been in touch with the Chief of Naval Operations by then, and maybe have a sense as to what's coming next."

"Fine, Miles, that's great," replied a beaming Admiral Taylor, clapping his hands in a rare display of emotion. He then danced a little jig. "Gentlemen, we've made history by actually doing what folks have dreamed of since time immemorial. We've traveled into the fourth dimension and returned. I know, I know, that's physically impossible, all sane people would tell us that, to which I would reply: *"Then we've just done the impossible!"*

Everyone joined the admiral in a round of congratulatory handshakes. Blizzard disconnected from Sewell, then ordered the helmsman to reduce speed to fifteen knots. He turned to the officer of the deck and told him to set a course to rendezvous with the *Truman*.

All eyes turned as Father Caffarone came onto the bridge. He was cradling his left arm at the elbow, a bloodstain spreading on his shirt at the shoulder.

Blizzard strode towards the priest. "Padre, what in the heck happened? You should be down in sick bay."

"I'm going as soon as I leave here. I stupidly cut myself when we landed," Caffarone said.

"It'll require a few stitches, but nothing's broken ... at least I hope not."

Blizzard wasn't having any of that talk. "Father, nothing is so important that it couldn't have waited until you were patched up," he said with genuine concern in his voice.

"Not so, Captain," Caffarone replied. He turned to face the entire group. "Gentlemen, we traveled back in time and we returned, yet we managed to accomplish what every Grade B movie admonishes against: Do nothing to affect the course of history. We tried to follow that advice, but failed on a grand scale."

"How so?" Admiral Taylor asked, brow furrowed, tone skeptical.

"The boy, *Josephus*," Caffarone replied.

"Oh poppycock, Padre," replied a visibly relieved Admiral Taylor with a dismissive wave of his hand. "For a moment I thought you were going to tell us something truly earth-shattering." He laughed in obvious relief. "That youngster is just a child, Commander. My goodness, he'll remember the whole affair as nothing more than an exciting dream."

"Well, how's this for a big, fat nothing, Admiral," Caffarone replied, then waited a couple of beats to say in a hushed voice, *"Our young visitor was none other than Leonardo da Vinci!"*

"Josephus?" This one word response from a stunned Manny Eisenhauer.

"Yes, *Josephus.* I asked him his real name as he was about to get off the chopper and his exact words were '*I am Leonardo, from the town of Vinci.*' The same Leonardo we know as the world's most famous inventor, scientist, painter, dreamer, or whatever else you choose to add. And now we know why. That twelve year-old saw the twenty-first century from the vantage point of a nuclear carrier, and he remembered everything his young eyes beheld. And boy oh boy, did he ever get an eyeful! Helicopters, airplanes, scuba divers, cannons, machinery of all stripes, and even anatomy books," he added, fishing a medical journal from a pocket with his good hand and placing it on the chart table. "This was in his pocket. God knows what else he might have had hidden under his clothes, there simply was no time for me to search him."

A deflated Father Caffarone paused for several seconds to look at each man individually, then said, "Leonardo da Vinci got to peek behind the curtain, and we in turn got to uncover the truth behind his brilliance. *Leonardo da Vinci, the Renaissance Man, was an utter fraud!"*

None spoke, all too stunned by the revelation.

Caffarone shook his head and shuffled silently off the bridge without a backward glance.

A shocked Major David Fleming kept hearing Caffarone's damning indictment ringing in his ears: *Leonardo da Vinci, the Renaissance Man, was an utter fraud!*

CHAPTER 24

Thursday early morning – June 24th

Fleming stood by the railing on the hangar deck flanked by Hamilton and Caldwell. The three were watching the *Félicité* being lowered into the water.

The day was young, but already the temperature was seventy degrees, and not a cloud marred the sky. It was ten minutes past six. The *LBJ* lay still in the water, and the trio could clearly see the *Truman* standing-by some three miles in the distance.

Blizzard and his XO appeared, escorting the rescued group of five men and two women. Their clothes had been laundered during the night, and as they made their way toward the stairway, they showed no physical signs of their recent hellish nightmare.

Probably still don't know what to make of it all, Fleming thought as he studied them, knowing what their fate would have been had Blizzard not intervened.

The *Félicité*'s captain carried several nautical charts tucked under his left arm, but before descending, saluted Blizzard, then proffered his hand. Blizzard's words carried to the three pilots.

"We've provisioned your boat with food and water, Captain, and we've thoroughly checked your radios and navigation aids. You already had plenty of fuel on board, and my weather officer tells me you can expect clear sailing all the way to Monte Carlo." He paused to look down at the *Félicité* before continuing. "I suggest you, your crew, and your passengers forget your unpleasant experience of the past couple of days. Should you tell your story to the press and mention my ship in any way, I would deny everything. I would counter by telling how the *LBJ* had come to the aid of a stricken luxury yacht in the middle of the Med and discovered everyone aboard incapacitated from partying with alcohol and illegal drugs. You see, Captain, what happened cannot be revealed at this time, and possibly never."

The sailor stared a long moment at his rescuer. "Then so be it, Captain. I understand what you say, but I don't for the life of me know why. None of us have suffered lasting injuries, praise Allah, yet you are telling me that those days we spent in that filthy dungeon never existed. And you have shown me that today's calendar supports what you are telling me. It is beyond my grasp." He glanced back at his passengers standing a few feet away, then lowered his voice. "I do not think the two owners would want to explain to their wives back in Bahrain just who their female companions were when the incident took place. Nothing will be said of our experience."

Fleming watched the *Félicité* cast off and remained at the railing as it motored away, a frothy white rooster tail blossoming as it gained speed.

Caldwell suggested they go below for breakfast. "I've been in this man's Navy a long time, Dave, and I've never experienced a week like this. First, we stood down from flight quarters, just like that," he said with a snap of his fingers. "No explanation given. Next, we hoisted a civilian pleasure cruiser on board like it's an everyday occurrence, and a day later a bunch of Arabs from God knows where arrive in one of our helicopters accompanied by Captain Blizzard, CAG, you, and a couple of SEALs. Aircraft carriers on station don't do those things, yet we sure did." After a long pause, he asked, "Will us peons ever find out what really happened this week?"

Fleming exhaled loudly. "I honestly don't know," he replied. "I was ordered to keep my mouth shut, and until I'm told otherwise, I'm afraid I can't say anything more about it. But I can tell you with certainty it's over, and life should be back to normal before day's end."

At ten o'clock the captain announced that a return to flight quarters would resume at twelve hundred hours and continue for the next three days.

Fleming's Tiger Sharks launched first. The day's flying schedule called for the air wing's entire complement of the combat aircraft to be aloft at the same time. Bringing the fight to the enemy in a shock and awe display of overwhelming force was the *raison d'etre* for the existence of all of the Navy's nine air wings.

With the first wave of fighters aloft, the deck was re-spotted with Hornets to be fueled, loaded, and then launched, with all this taking place before the first flight could be recovered. It called for an intricate ballet of exquisite coordination and split-second timing on the part of sailors working in seven disciplines, each identified by their blue, purple, green, yellow, red, brown, and white shirts. A carrier flight deck during air operations is the most dangerous place on earth and is a testament to the bravery and skill of men and women whose average age is just nineteen.

* * * * *

Fleming was returning to his cabin when CAG called him into his office.

Gowdy was seated behind his metal desk, his booted feet perched on top, his helmet and oxygen mask lying nearby. He was drinking iced-tea and reading a journal about the F-35C.

"At ease, have a seat," he said, pointing with his can of tea toward the lone metal chair by his desk. "How did the day's flying go?"

"Fine, Sir. No twinges of apprehension because of the ejection," he added. "Same goes for Chuck. It was a good flight."

"Glad to hear it. I've been flying for over twenty years and I've never had to part company with my plane ... and I hope I never will," he added with a lopsided grin. "I'm now way too old for that kind of an adventure." He took another swig from his drink. "I spoke with the admiral a few minutes ago, and he informed me that you, Captain

194

Blizzard, myself, Father Caffarone, and Commander Birdwell are going on a TDY (Temporary Duty) trip."

"Can I ask where we're going, Sir?" said Fleming, showing surprise.

"Home. More precisely, Washington. It seems that the Chief of Naval Operations wants to be briefed personally by the five of us about what happened this week. "We're to fly off the *LBJ* on Saturday and grab a flight to DC later that same day."

"How long do you think we'll be gone, Sir?"

Gowdy shrugged. "No way of knowing. The ramifications of what we went through are enormous; heck, I don't have to tell you that. The Pentagon will be setting up a top secret task group to study the whole possibility of traveling into the fourth dimension now that we've actually done it. We could be there a week, or maybe a month, I really can't say."

"Two questions, Sir. Can I tell my wife I'm coming, and can I tell her that I had to bail out a couple of days ago, or is that classified?"

CAG took a moment to gather his thoughts and smiled. "Actually, that's three questions, Fleming. First, there's nothing secret about the TDY. Two, its real purpose has been classified top secret, so we're going to DC on the pretext of preparing the *LBJ* and the air wing for transitioning to the F-35C later this year. You've been included because as an Air Force officer serving with a Navy Air Wing, the CNO thinks your unique input will be invaluable. That's what you'll tell your wife and any of your buddies who ask. It's the perfect cover story. As for your third question, there's nothing to stop you from telling your wife that you had to punch out during a mission. However, the *why* is definitely classified, but the fact that you did so is going to become a part of your permanent medical record. That's in case you develop problems later in your career because of the ejection. My advice would be that if you tell her, try to do so in a matter-of-fact way, as if you don't see it as any big deal. Pilots' spouses tend to worry. A lot. You follow me?"

"Yes, Sir."

"Good. That's all," said Gowdy, returning Fleming's salute with his feet still up on his desk.

Rank sure does 'hath' its privileges, Fleming thought with an inward smile as he headed to his cabin, delighting in the prospect of seeing Susan again so soon.

* * * * *

Four Navy officers and one Air Force officer boarded a Navy C-37B aircraft, a variant of the Gulfstream 550 Executive Jet, in Naples, Italy, on Saturday evening for a night flight to Washington DC.

Fleming had called his wife that morning. "It's about a nine-hour flight," he explained, "so with all the time changes, we should be arriving about midnight, DC time. If you can catch a flight today, we can meet at your favorite hotel, the Willard. How does that sound, honey?"

"Dave, is everything OK?" she had asked, the concern he heard in her voice was real. "I've had that horrible dream again all week, and it's really frightened me. I'm worried I might be losing my mind."

"Everything's fine, I promise. I can't wait to see you tomorrow. Love you, babe."

PART TWO

CHAPTER 25

Washington Dc

Sunday Morning - June 27th

Fleming woke with a start. It him took a moment to remember where he was. *Yeah, I'm in the Willard.* He lay still and smiled into the darkness, the only sound a faint rustling coming from the room's two air conditioning ducts. He turned to gaze at his still-sleeping wife. *You really are one lucky dude*, he reminded himself for the gazillionth time since their marriage eight months earlier. The illuminated dial on his Apple smartwatch showed 7:12, which meant the sun had been up for over an hour. Time to begin a day of just hanging out together.

"You're awake," the voice beside him murmured. "Can we just stay in bed? We can order room service, watch TV, and maybe rut a time or two. How does that sound?"

Fleming laughed aloud. "Well, I like the rutting part, but I'm thinking we should at least make a pretense of doing some other things." He switched on the bedside lamp.

Susan Fleming sat up wearing a pout, maintained the charade for two seconds, then burst into laughter. She threw her arms around his neck and the two embraced. For the next half-hour they made love with exquisite tenderness.

Forty-five minutes later they were finishing a leisurely breakfast in the Café du Parc. A day of sightseeing had been planned, beginning with a bus tour of the city. Fleming had learned long ago this was a must-do when visiting a new city, or one he hadn't been to in ages.

"I've loved this town and this hotel since I was a little girl," Susan said, an index finger absently circling the rim of her empty water glass. "Daddy would take me here twice a year when he had business meetings, and we always stayed at the Willard. Once it was at Christmastime, and I'll never forget the mountains of magical decorations in all the public areas. To me it was better than Disney World!" She sighed at the memory. "Mother tried to continue the tradition after daddy passed, but it was never the same." She turned silent, lost in a memory of those days long gone.

Fleming waited a few discreet moments, then said quietly, "I wish I had met your dad; he sounds like he loved his little girl a lot. Too often fathers get wrapped up in their busy careers as the years slip away until one day the little girl or little boy is all grown up and gone. I hope I'm not that kind of a dad when we have kids."

Susan reached across the table and entwined her fingers in his. Her smile melted his heart.

"You'll be the best father in the world, David Fleming. I've known that from the moment we met; it's one of the reasons I fell head over heels for you." She squeezed his hand harder, and the smile got bigger. He was in Heaven.

"Let's go play tourist, Mrs. Fleming," he said, rising to his feet. Still holding hands, he guided her out of the dining room.

CHAPTER 26

Washington Dc

Monday Morning early- June 28th

On a sunny but steamy late June morning the five officers stepped through the door at the Mall Entrance to The Pentagon at eight o'clock, and into the air conditioned coolness of the world's largest office building totaling a staggering six and-a-half million square feet.

A waiting Navy captain stepped forward to greet them. "Good morning, Gentlemen, I'm Captain Jon Buff, senior aide to Admiral Christensen." He held his hand out to Blizzard. "Good seeing you again, Miles, it's been awhile."

Blizzard introduced his companions, and the group set off to the CNO's suite in the E Ring.

Ten minutes later they stood at attention as Admiral Christiansen entered the conference room through a connecting door from his office. He was all smiles. "At ease, gentlemen, please be seated."

Fleming studied the man, thinking, *this guy looks like an admiral.* Wayne Christensen was tall, slim, and tanned. His uniform was obviously custom-made, enhancing the dashing look of a Central Casting Agency admiral. But Fleming knew this admiral was no make-believe officer. He had studied the man's biography the night before.

Christensen had graduated first in his class at the Naval Academy forty years earlier; first in his naval aviator class, and later as a

Distinguished Graduate of the National War College. He read through the many postings culminating with this Presidential appointment two years ago.

"Let me begin by welcoming you to Washington. I realize it was on a very short notice, but I felt the circumstances required immediate action. The President was briefed on what little we know so far. He is not dismissing any part of what happened this past week, and neither am I. In fact, President Bradley has asked that you gentlemen come to the White House tomorrow at five o'clock for a meeting in the Oval Office. He had wanted you to wear civilian clothes to keep the White House Press Corp from becoming overly curious, but I suggested you be in uniform so that your cover story reflects what's on your TDY Orders: You're here to discuss the *LBJ's* air wing transition from flying Hornets to the new F-35C. I said that wouldn't raise any undue curiosity. He agreed and requested that I accompany you." He looked around the conference table, his eyes coming to rest on Fleming. "I bet you never dreamed you'd be sitting in the Pentagon with a very tall tale to tell?" He raised a questioning eyebrow, then added with a smile, "Would I have won that bet, Major Fleming?"

"Yes, Admiral, that bet would have been a sure thing."

"No adverse effects from your bailing out?"

Fleming shook his head and tapped on the gleaming mahogany table. "None so far, Admiral. It was a controlled emergency situation, so my back-seater and I had enough time to prepare."

"That's good to hear." The CNO turned and addressed the group. "For the next few days, you will be debriefed by experts in several disciplines. Your collective experience is unlike anything the U. S. Navy has ever encountered, so we'll need to get all of the facts gathered and collated in order to determine what really happened, and where to go next. So, here's how we'll proceed.

"You will each be debriefed separately. That way you'll be free to recount your own experiences in your own words. Of course, the interviews will be videorecorded for in-depth studies later." He glanced at his watch. "You'll get to meet your analysts after a short break for coffee. They will be dressed in civvies, so you will have no idea if they're military or civilian. I haven't a clue as to what questions they will ask, or even if some of their questions might be considered offensive. However, I do anticipate that at times they might try to goad you into making an angered response, so I would strongly suggest you listen carefully to each question and take the time necessary to think through your answer. But above all, just tell the truth. They come from different federal agencies; and the hope is that by working as a team we will uncover the absolute proof for what you say happened last week in the Med, and then determine if such a journey could ever be *deliberately* replicated sometime in the future. Which leads me to my final thought. Do not see these analysts as inquisitors, but as practitioners of the scientific method as they all approach the idea of time-travel with a healthy dose of skepticism." The admiral rose. "Good luck, gentlemen. I'll join up with you tomorrow when we go to the White House."

* * * * *

Fleming slumped low in his chair. He was worn out. His debriefing partner had thanked him for his candor when he had called it a day at seven o'clock.

The man had introduced himself as Eric, and encouraged Fleming to address him by that name. Eric would call him David, but only if that were OK. Otherwise, he would address him by his military rank.

Although they had covered a lot of ground in almost eleven hours, Eric seemed to concentrate on the conditions aboard the airplane immediately before, and then right after he had collided with the unknown wall. At times, Eric would unexpectedly circle back to ask Fleming about something already answered, but he did so in a very disarming manner.

"Oh, before I forget, do you remember if you felt any nausea the moment you found yourself transported back to the 15th century?"

202

"Nauseous? No, but I do remember a sensation of vertigo, but that disappeared almost immediately." Fleming frowned, then asked, "Didn't we cover this topic earlier?"

He had tried to ferret out a sense of the man during their long hours together. Eric appeared to be about his same age, and though he exuded a natural casualness, Fleming could readily see the man was a serious professional. His probative questions would be interspersed with innocuous queries regarding his homelife or his time aboard the *LBJ*. How well did he get along with his squadron partners? Did they see and treat him as an outsider, or was he fully accepted by the group? Had he any second thoughts regarding his choice of career? Fleming had answered all questions truthfully, but with an underlying wariness. He realized he was being sized up to determine if somewhere deep within his psyche lurked an unstable personality, something he saw as unnerving. Was he capable of retreating into some dark world of denial when faced with a serious problem, or worse, a life-threatening emergency? Was it possible that he had hatched the entire flying back-in-time drivel to coverup a gross "pilot error" which had caused the loss of a 75 million dollar Super Hornet? Or instead, maybe he was a true-to-life character sprung from "The Secret Life of Walter Mitty," James Thurber's classic tale of a milquetoast finding escape in a daydream of being a derring-do military pilot whom everybody admired?

They would meet again in the morning at eight sharp.

Because of the top secret classification, Fleming was careful with what he said to his wife of the day's events. She believed he was in Washington to give an Air Force officer's perspective of life flying with the Navy and was delighted to have this unexpected time together.

"Honey, I've been thinking about something," Fleming said, pushing aside a dessert plate which minutes earlier had held a huge, shared-slice of decadent Black Forest cheesecake. It was the perfect finish to a dinner at the Willard's famous Round Robin Bar. "We could be in Washington for as long as a couple of weeks. This is a pretty expensive hotel, so I'm wondering if maybe we should move to somewhere cheaper like a Hilton or a Marriott?"

Susan smiled. "That's sweet of you, Dave, but really, I can afford this. It's my treat."

"I know you can, honey, but the rest of the guys are staying at hotels they can cover with the money allotted them by the government for travel expenses. I don't want them thinking that I'm some rich kid who spends money like water. No one knows I'm married to a wealthy woman, and I would like to keep it that way. It's important to me, sweetheart, OK?"

Susan Fleming nodded. "You're right. The last thing I'd want is to embarrass you. I'll get us a different hotel tomorrow while you're at work, and I'll text you when I've moved our things."

CHAPTER 27

Washington Dc

Tuesday Evening – June 29th

After a second day of intense investigation, the group was ushered into the Oval Office at five o'clock. President John Bradley III was known for his punctuality. He stood flanked by the Vice President and his chief of staff.

"Welcome to the White House, gentlemen, I appreciate your coming on such short notice. Please, have a seat." The President waited until the officers were comfortable and asked, "So, do any of you have a change of mind about what happened last week in the Med? I guess what I'm really asking is this: Upon reflection, do you now believe it wasn't a time travel event that you experienced, but something else? That maybe there's a more fitting explanation?"

All five shook their heads, then Blizzard spoke up. "Mr. President, nothing will change our minds. Speaking for myself, I can say that before last week's experience I scoffed at the very notion spaceships could exist; that aliens are secretly being housed and studied in Area 51; that travel to distant galaxies will one day be possible, or that journeying into the future or back to the past is real. And I dismissed those folks who held such beliefs as crackpots. Well, no longer, Sir. The constant thought that we might never return from the 15th century was absolutely terrifying, and I still get goosebumps just thinking about it. No, what happened to us, and the entire crew of the *LBJ* was real, I can assure you of that."

"Which leads me to my next question, Captain. Has the rest of your crew been told?"

"No, Mr. President. They believe the *LBJ* was undergoing a special test directed by the strike group admiral, and that was the reason for a communications blackout during those few days. Now, how long will it be before that secret gets out, I can't say because keeping it from five thousand men and women is quite the tall order."

"I agree, but do try to keep a lid on it until we know the how and the why of what happened."

The President then addressed each man in turn, asking probative questions and listening intently to their answers. He was particularly interested in what Father Caffarone had to say about his time with Leonardo da Vinci, and if the President doubted for a moment what he was being told, his poker-face did not reflect it.

The meeting lasted twenty minutes, and after individual photos were taken with a smiling President Bradley, the official White House photographer promised autographed prints would be delivered to Admiral Christensen's office in the morning.

On the drive back to the Pentagon, Christenson's phone chirped loudly, interrupting the back-and-forth banter.

"Admiral Christensen," he announced, then listened as someone seemed to be giving him instructions while his fellow passengers feigned a disinterest in the conversation by staring out the windows. "We're on it, Mister Secretary, and thank you," he said, and hung up.

"That was the Secretary of State calling to say there's been a 'change of plans' to use his exact words. We've been asked—that's really a polite euphemism for ordered—to attend a meeting with none other than the Russian ambassador, and my counterpart, Admiral of the Fleet Yuri Gorshkov, who flew into DC a few hours ago. He's traveling under a diplomatic passport, which in itself is highly unusual. It seems no one at State, or Defense, knew he was coming, and he's scheduled to fly out right after the meeting with you. The Secretary claims he has no idea what it's about, but we must assume it has something to do with the submarine surfacing in the middle of the Med last week. The question being discussed was where would we meet with the Russians? The Pentagon was out of the question; the Russian Embassy was a non-starter for obvious reasons, but then the Secretary of Defense suggested using the conference room at Blair House. It's a neutral site, a residence used by foreign heads of state and other dignitaries when visiting the White House which is just across the street. The President gave it his green light moments ago, so, we'll grab a quick bite and meet with the Russians at seven." Admiral Christensen let loose a chuckle. "This should prove interesting, gentlemen. My advice is that whatever information the Russians are looking for, we play our cards close to the vest. I also have a feeling President Bradley knew about this sudden 'change of plans' well before he met with us."

* * * * *

Admiral of the Fleet Yuri Gorshkov towered over the Russian Ambassador. Both men seemed tense and wore worried looks. After everyone was seated around a magnificent black cherry conference table, Gorshkov looked to his ambassador who signaled with a slight nod that the stage was now his.

"Gentlemen, thank you for agreeing to this meeting," he began, his accent sounding more London than Leningrad. "You see, I am facing a problem that has no answer. At least none I have found yet, and yes, Captain Blizzard, I'm referring to the incident last week in the Mediterranean Sea, where one of our submarines surfaced right in the middle of your strike group. That is why I come looking for your help."

"Good evening, Admiral," Blizzard replied, "but before I answer, I'm curious to hear how it is that you knew to find me in Washington?"

The Russian's shrug was immediate, and matter of fact. "I was briefed by our naval intelligence at Fleet Headquarters that you were coming to the Pentagon for a conference about the new Navy F-35C program. It was no secret. There was a press release from your 6th Fleet Headquarters about it, and a follow-up story was written in the *Stars and Stripes* military newspaper. We monitor both because they give us a lot of good information. It was nothing more nefarious than that. I hope that answers your question, Captain Blizzard." His wry smile suggested he had delivered the perfect gotcha moment.

"It does. So, how can we be of help?"

"There is much I don't know, so I begin by asking what you remember about that day?"

Blizzard spent the next several minutes recounting what he remembered, from the moment the submarine had surfaced, until the *LBJ* and its strike group sailed away. He summed up. "By then, a Russian trawler was alongside the *Yakutsk*, and we were told that two Russian frigates were en route to render any needed assistance. We were thanked for our help and were asked not to come closer than one hundred meters to the submarine. We complied."

"Thank you, Captain. A couple of items you mentioned struck me as possibly being important. First, you said the submarine captain seemed surprised when he learned that the longitude and latitude coordinates he was given by the *Tacoma* placed him in the middle of the Mediterranean Sea?"

"No, Admiral, I said his reaction was one of genuine shock, not merely surprise. The captain of the *Tacoma* and the captain of the *Yakutsk* spoke directly to each other using loudspeakers, they were that close. Our captain definitely saw the shocked expression on the Russian's face through his binoculars the moment he learned of his exact position." A fact that Blizzard had deliberately withheld during his summary was that the *Tacoma* had also been eavesdropping and had a videorecording of the entire conversation between the submarine commander and the other Russian officer in the sail. The Americans had clearly heard the two quietly talking about how the coordinates given by the Americans had to be wrong because their last known position before losing all of their navigation aids was some fifteen miles off the coast of Southern Spain which was over a thousand nautical miles away. What they were now being told was a physical impossibility, yet the stunned looks on their faces suggested they believed the Americans were telling them the truth.

Admiral Gorshkov spent several seconds digesting this new information. He glanced at his ambassador who had remained stone-faced throughout. Finally, "I do have a question to ask regarding the health of the *Yakutsk's* crewmen. You mentioned that the captain informed *Tacoma* some of his sailors were ill, but also declined medical assistance when it was offered?"

"That's true, Admiral. Your captain was gracious in his refusal; he thanked *Tacoma* for the offer to assist, but said his crew would be taken care of by Russian medical officers when the frigates arrived. I saw his refusal for any medical aid as a matter of Russian pride; nothing more, nothing less."

Again, Blizzard had deliberately chosen not to reveal all he knew. When the captain of the *Tacoma* had briefed Admiral Taylor and the strike group commanders an hour later about the ill sailors on the submarine, he recounted how the videorecording *Tacoma* had made of the captain and the other officer with him in the sail clearly showed how they had discussed whether or not to accept medical aid from the Americans. The junior officer wanted the Americans to know that the entire submarine crew was desperately ill from some unknown cause, that several sailors were already dead, and the ones still alive needed immediate help. But the captain was adamant; he was having none of it.

The videorecording had also shown that while they waited for the *Tacoma* to confirm the coordinates of the submarine's position, the captain, still visibly shivering, had mentioned in a low voice to his colleague that based on the unique acoustical signature generated by a very large ship with four screws, it was highly probable that the *LBJ* had been the unidentified US aircraft carrier they had shadowed several days earlier in the Mid-Atlantic. After several moments of silence during which both stared at the *LBJ* through their binoculars, the captain segued into a muted recounting of how they had also tracked and identified the English cruise ship *Princess Royal* using their suite of sophisticated listening devices while submerged off the French Coast. At this juncture, the Russians still had no idea they were in the Mediterranean Sea, and Captain Blizzard had reminded Admiral Taylor that a stealthy Russian intercept of the *LBJ* while running deep and well astern, could easily have happened during their crossing from Norfolk.

"Thank you," Admiral Gorshkov said. "I appreciate that you offered to treat the sick on board our submarine. I can tell you it was not radiation sickness. The reactor on the *Yakutsk* was never in danger of a meltdown." Gorshkov turned to his ambassador and spoke rapidly in Russian. The ambassador nodded his agreement to whatever it was being said. The admiral turned back to Blizzard. "Captain, I sincerely hope you will truthfully answer me this question, and please take no offense with my asking. Were you caught off guard when our submarine suddenly appeared out of nowhere? I mean, had your escorts not been tracking it before she surfaced?"

Blizzard answered without missing a beat. "Admiral, we were very much aware of *Yakutsk's* presence and had been for quite some time, but yes, we were surprised when she actually surfaced. Every sailor knows that a submarine will never surface under such conditions unless it was in imminent danger of sinking. We assumed that was the case with the *Yakutsk*. Remember, your captain informed us almost immediately that he had lost his communications and navigational aids and admitted that all of his anti-submarine countermeasures were useless. He was down deep and sailing blind. Obviously, he had no way of knowing our strike group was on the surface directly above him, so I can only imagine the utter disbelief he must have felt when he saw us. But by then only one thought would have been on his mind: '*I must surface my boat and save my crew.*'"

The others sat silent as they listened to Blizzard's bald-faced lie.

"I agree, Captain Blizzard." Again, Admiral Gorshkov whispered something to the ambassador, who murmured a lengthy reply. The Americans sat in silence. Both Russians seemed to have reached an agreement because the ambassador shrugged, then switched to English. "Admiral, you have my approval to divulge any classified information if you think it will help us all understand what really happened to the *Yakutsk* that day."

Admiral Gorshkov gave an involuntary sigh, took out a pristine handkerchief and wiped his brow and upper lip. Fleming saw the gesture as merely a delaying tactic while he pondered his next move. Moments passed. The Russian admiral had reached a decision. He opened an attaché case that had been parked by his feet and took out a solitary sheet of paper.

"Captain Blizzard, Gentlemen, I have not been entirely candid with you," he began, "not because I was trying to deceive or mislead, but I just did not know how to broach the subject." He shook his head and held open both hands in supplication. It was a gesture of resignation.

The Americans all leaned forward in anticipation of what was about to be revealed.

"Something terrible happened aboard our submarine that day," the Russian began, "but it was only the last in a long sequence of events which had begun two days earlier. I will tell you what we do know, and what we don't. First, the entire crew is dead. All one hundred twenty-four officers and sailors have died; we don't know why and probably never will. When our medical officers boarded her, they were shocked at what they found. Those sailors who were already dead had taken on the appearance of old men. No, that is not correct. They *were* old men." He waved a polite, but silencing hand, indicating there was more. "I know that is a preposterous statement to make, but it is how

211

our doctors described the situation. Captain Gasparin was the last to die, but he was able to tell us a little about what had happened. He said the *Yakutsk* hit something that had surrounded his boat at a depth of two hundred meters. He told of an object that had no physical characteristics that his sonar could identify, yet it was most assuredly real, nonetheless. And for lack of a better word, he just called it a forcefield. The *Yakutsk* hit that forcefield twice within the same hour, and it was the second encounter that destroyed his submarine. But not right away.

"They surfaced off the coast of Southern Spain to radio the Northern Fleet Headquarters but were unable to acquire a satellite. The captain spoke of not being able to contact any other ships in the area, and said that he couldn't receive any signals from civilian AM stations in Spain. Later that night, and still sailing on the surface, they stayed close to the shoreline, but for an entire hour they saw no signs of civilization anywhere. He described it as if the entire country had turned off all of the lights. His officers concluded that there must have been a massive power outage up and down the entire Iberian Coast that night, but of course, we know that was not the case. Shortly after that, the *Yakutsk* dived to a depth of two hundred meters, and that's when the reactor shut itself down. Of course, they lost all of the boat's operating systems and could not raise it to the surface. Even the emergency surfacing procedures didn't work. They could not communicate with anyone to ask for help, and the crew had resigned themselves to dying a slow, agonizing death as their oxygen ran out. All they could now do was pray. A few hours later, sometime in the morning hours of June 20, the *Yakutsk* was unexpectedly hit again by a similar forcefield which blew the boat to the surface, right in the middle of your strike group."

Admiral Gorshkov paused to steal a quick glance at his ambassador, then continued his tale for the enthralled audience.

"But the truly unexplainable phenomenon which occurred that day was this: *Our submarine was now fifteen hundred kilometers from its last verifiably known position*, a fact that was indeed corroborated by your *Tacoma*. We know this is true because the *Yakutsk* never transited the Straits of Gibraltar, for if she had, our satellites would have tracked that movement. Our acoustical monitors would have done the same, as I'm sure yours would have too. That never happened. So how did a submarine suddenly find itself transported such a huge distance while submerged and crippled, and did so in the blink of the proverbial eye? It's just not possible, gentlemen, and that's where we need your help."

"Admiral, can we back up for just a moment?" asked Admiral Christensen, speaking for the first time. "You said the crewmembers are all dead, and they died of old age. Did I hear that part correctly?"

"You did, Admiral, but it gets worse. We now had the *Yakutsk* under tow, hoping to take her back to our Northern Command Submarine Base. But we soon had to abandon that idea because the boat had literally begun to fall apart. It was aging, and at an extremely rapid pace, just like her crew had aged. In less than six hours the *Yakutsk* was no longer seaworthy. The frigate captain called and briefed me personally on the situation. I gave the order to get the salvage crew off and to scuttle her. She went down with all hands entombed. The reactor was fully cold. A nuclear engineer from one of our frigates reported that the reactor was showing the same signs we see in all reactors that have reached the end of their useful life cycle. It was my decision. I did not want the families to know what had happened to their loved ones. How could we possibly say these young sailors had all died looking like old men? No, I want these brave mariners seen at home as the heroes they are. We will have a national day of mourning soon after our president tells the people of this tragic accident."

The Russian ambassador pointed to the paper in front of the admiral. Gorshkov nodded, and picked it up.

"Gentlemen, this is a copy of a letter emailed to me from the senior medical officer who boarded the *Yakutsk* and treated the dying as best he could. Captain Gasparin was the last to die. Here is what the doctor wrote."

TO: Admiral of the Fleet Yuri Gorshkov
Dear Admiral,
What I saw today no man should ever have to witness; a human being aging right before my eyes at a terrifying rate, and finally succumbing to the ravages of extreme old age. It happened in the space of ninety minutes.
When Captain Gasparin died, I estimate he was two hundred years old, possibly more, and the fate for anyone living so long is almost impossible to describe. The face was barely recognizable as human. All the upper and lower teeth were long gone, causing the mandible - that's the lower jaw - to shrink to an extent that the maxilla - the frontal bone of the skull that supports the upper part of the mouth and teeth - to overhang the lower jaw. That change to the maxilla caused the nose to actually lengthen and hook, so much so that it became a hideous caricature of itself. The eyes were covered by such thick cataracts that I suspect any surgical intervention would have been impossible. The man was now totally deaf, lying in bed in a vegetative state, and I had no way of knowing whether or not he was in pain. His skin had become so thin and translucent - not unlike ancient vellum - that I could actually see the blood slowly moving through the veins, while the nails on the hands had withdrawn almost all the way back to the cuticle, and were a ghoulish gray-black color. I did not disrobe the corpse because, frankly, I did not want to see more. I was that disturbed. But I did take several photos which I have transmitted to you as attachments to this email.
Respectfully,
Captain, Second Rank, Boris Soltzhenitsyn
Fleet Medical Officer

Gorshkov looked at his hushed audience and simply shook his head. After what seemed like an eternity to Fleming, he continued.

"The photo attachments did not transmit with the letter, so I asked the doctor to resend them. He replied an hour later that all of the digital photographs he had taken while aboard the *Yakutsk* no longer existed; they had disappeared from his camera. It was as though they had aged along with Gasparin to the point those particular digital images had simply vanished due to the passage of time. Yet all of his other photos remained intact. I have no idea how that's even possible, and I cannot offer you any better explanation."

Admiral Christensen replied for them all. "Admiral, I too find myself at a loss for words on how to reply to what you have just shared, so I will say nothing other than to say thank you."

Admiral Gorshkov glanced at his watch. It was almost nine. "Captain Blizzard, let me make a suggestion. Maybe a request would be the better English word. Tomorrow morning, could you and your officers go over again what we have just discussed, and search amongst yourselves to see if there was something that slipped your minds, some little thing that could help shed a revealing light on what exactly happened to the *Yakutsk*? Anything at all, no matter how insignificant? I could postpone my return trip home."

Blizzard looked to Admiral Christensen for guidance. The CNO nodded, giving tacit approval to Blizzard to reply for the group. "Admiral, that's an excellent idea, so yes, we'll go over everything again in the morning and get back to you."

Admiral Christensen spoke. "Let me wrap up by again thanking you for your candor. I know it wasn't easy, and you have our deepest sympathy for the loss of a very courageous submarine crew. I will inform President Bradley of this conversation. I am sure he will want to express his feelings of sympathy on behalf of all Americans to the Russian president and his people."

Christensen held out his hand. "Good night, Admiral."

CHAPTER 28

Washington Dc

Wednesday Morning – June 30ᵗʰ

The meeting started at eight o'clock sharp. Admiral Christensen's senior aide had made sure coffee and Danish pastries were on hand, and the admiral pressed the group to dig in and enjoy. After ten minutes of light back and forth, he called for their attention.

"We'll kick this meeting off by going around the table, and each will get a chance to tell the rest of us what you made of last evening's meeting and how you think we should respond to Admiral Gorshkov's request. Remember, there is no right or wrong answer, so feel free to say whatever's on your minds."

Fleming was the last to speak. He'd had the advantage of listening to all the other opinions, observations, and recommendations, and had jotted down bullet points on the pad before him. At the end of the meeting, all notes would be placed in a garbage bag and burned.

"So, what did you make of the Russian admiral, Major Fleming?"

Fleming unconsciously sat up a little straighter. "Admiral, I agree with the consensus opinion which is that Admiral Gorshkov's a worried man who has no idea of the consequential magnitude of the event that destroyed the *Yakutsk*. And nor could he. The crew certainly

216

never knew that they had traveled back in time, a journey that sealed their fates. Because if they had made a clean passage through the time portal as we did, they would be alive today. But they were not so lucky. Remember, the submarine captain told of colliding twice with the unknown forcefield, and I'm thinking that it was the first encounter, and not the second, that ended up killing them,. They spent way too much time hanging on the cusp, bouncing back and forth between two or more different centuries. God only knows how far apart those centuries were, and that's what destroyed their bodies down at the cellular level." He shook his head. "And I cannot begin to imagine how painful their deaths must have been. Remember, our two pilots suffered a similar fate. Do we tell the admiral what happened to those men, and how they, too, had aged before they died?"

He paused, and looked around the table at each in turn. "But I think there are bigger problems that we haven't given any thought to, such as: Which century, or centuries, did the *Yakutsk* travel back to, and what other time-space cosmic force made it possible for that boat to journey over a thousand miles underwater in a matter of milliseconds to be thrust to the surface in the middle of the Mediterranean Sea? I suggest everything points to the very real possibility that they did not go back to the fifteenth century as we did, but were transported to some other moment in time. They could have visited some prehistoric age or anything in-between. But we can be certain it was not back to a time we experienced. And how do I know this? Because had they had gone back to the seventeenth or eighteenth centuries for example, the captain would have spotted signs of civilization, even at night. In the hour that they sailed along the Spanish Coast, they would have seen at least one fire, more likely multiple fires, but definitely torchlights in any number of villages and towns. But we know they saw nothing of the kind, which suggests they never went back to the same time that we were in, but to one many centuries earlier. So how would we present such a wild hypothesis to a Russian who doesn't trust us to begin with?"

Blizzard was the first to reply, but his frown spoke volumes. "Major Fleming, you've just forced us to consider somethings we hadn't given much thought to, the possibility of traveling back to any number of waypoints along the timeline continuum. Well, if that's true, and I'm beginning to believe that it is highly probable, then our return wasn't just remarkable, it was nothing short of a miracle."

Fleming nodded his agreement. "Admiral, Captain," he said, addressing both, "that is why my recommendation is to say nothing about our travel back in time to the Russian admiral."

Admiral Christensen bolted upright. "You suggest we say nothing further to the Russians? That they don't deserve to know what really happened? An explanation only we can provide?"

Fleming firmly shook his head, wondering if maybe he had gone too far. He realized he had better explain himself and do so quickly. He stood up. "Admiral, it's not a matter of doing the morally correct thing because doing that will not alter the truth. We can tell the Russians what we *know* to be factual, but after that it's sheer speculation as to what we *think* might have happened to their submarine. And Admiral Gorshkov will return home and tell the Russian President that what he's learned from the meeting with the Americans is that the submarine traveled back in time. So, what will happen? He will immediately be relieved of his command as being mentally unfit for believing a tale no six-year-old would fall for. Instead, the Russians will think that *we* caused their submarine to surface in the middle of our strike group after crippling it with some newfound technology. They will conclude that we're sending them a warning: Don't screw with America, because *we* have developed a weapon that neither you, nor any of our other enemies will ever be able to hide from. The Russians are a paranoid people, and that goes for their leaders, in spades. They've stayed in power all this time by convincing their subjects that America has always wanted to destroy them; it's been that way since Lenin's rule, and nothing will convince them otherwise. Admiral, I recommend we say nothing."

Fleming sat down, allowing his words to find a home in the minds of the five Naval officers around the conference table.

Admiral Christensen glanced at his watch and rose without showing his hand. "I have to leave you gentlemen. The plan is to wrap up your individual debriefings today and collate the information overnight. I had mentioned when we first met on Monday that there would be experts working around the clock to come up with a definitive answer to the overarching question: did you really travel back in time, and can we prove it beyond a reasonable doubt? That's quite a tall order, but it's one we have to get right." He looked directly at Fleming. "Our young Air Force friend here makes a compelling argument, and it's one I will consider seriously. I will give you all my decision later as to what we'll tell Admiral Gorshkov."

The group stood at attention as the Chief of Naval Operations left the room.

* * * * *

Fleming was surprised to find two interrogators present for this final session; Eric, and a woman who introduced herself as a practicing parapsychologist. "Do you know what parapsychology is, Major Fleming?" she had asked.

"No, ma'am, I sure don't, but my guess is that you're here because you suspect I might be more than just a little crazy." The look on his face told her that Fleming was deadly serious.

She emphatically shook her head. "No, Major, I think nothing of the kind, so let me start by telling you exactly what it is that I do. A parapsychologist studies those anomalies of human behavior and human experiences which, when bundled together, form a grouping of a select few disciplines which are labeled as being paranormal. But what is unique to this singular scientific field is the fact that these paranormal phenomena transcend the boundaries of time, space, and force. Our government and our universities have been in a collaborative engagement for over seventy years studying these paranormal happenings. So, too, have the Russians, the Israelis, and for a while, the English. You might be surprised at just how much we have learned, yet shocked at how much we still don't know. The expression, 'I don't know what I don't know,' is a profound truth. So, when I learned of last week's incidents in the Mediterranean, I knew that just maybe we could finally get an answer to that elusive, age-old question: Is time travel possible? Well, I assure you, Major, I have an open mind as to what the answer might be. And lastly, I do not think for a moment that a group of highly intelligent military officers experienced the same unexplainable event only to be written off at some later date, and pigeon-holed as a non-medical mass hysteria simply as a matter of expediency. I can assure you, that will not happen."

Fleming sat silent and inscrutable; his demeanor telling her to continue.

"An excellent example of a non-medical mass hysteria took place in Fatima, Portugal, in October 1917, when one hundred thousand Catholic pilgrims claimed to have seen a spinning sun suddenly careen down toward them, then began to zig-zag across the sky for about ten minutes while emitting brilliant rays of multi-colored light. And all this took place while the Virgin Mary appeared before three small peasant children, as she had done for several consecutive months prior. History records it as the *Miracle of Fatima*, and a thorough recounting of the event was carried by all the major European newspapers. Yet, no other place on earth reported a similar phenomenon occurring that day. But the overarching question still remains more than a century later: Was *Fatima* a mass hysteria event, or was it truly a miracle from heaven? Well, far be it from me to say." She smiled at Fleming. "So, as with *Fatima*, we must strive to find the absolute proof for what you and your friends are claiming, which is: 'Yes, we most assuredly traveled back in time, and here is our scientific evidence to back up that claim.'"

"Then let's get started with it, shall we?" said Fleming.

* * * * *

Ian A. O'Connor

Wednesday - afternoon

It was two-fifteen in the afternoon, and the group had returned to the conference room for a lecture. Their guest's *curriculum vitae* introduced him as Alfred Champlain, Ph.D., APAA, AAMC, CAA., a man who considered himself to be *the* authority on the life, art, inventions, and interpreter of the seven thousand two hundred pages of notes penned by Leonardo Da Vinci over a busy lifetime of overachievement. Fleming found himself admitting that he was more than just a little impressed with Alfred Champion's alphabet soup *résumé*.

"Let me rush through the boring stuff," Alfred Champlain began, "then we'll delve deeper into the more pertinent details of this remarkable life. Leonardo da Vinci was born on April 15, 1452, and died on May 3, 1519, at age sixty-seven, which was considered quite old at the time. Leonardo was a bastard. His father, Pietro was a lawyer and notary, his mother, Caterina, a scullery maid. They never married. The surname name da Vinci merely tells us the town where he was born, Vinci in the district of Florence. It neither suggests, nor confers, any form of royalty or nobility. Leonardo lived with his father for the first several years of his life, attending school on and off, and oftentimes getting into mischief with a rowdy group of young friends. One interesting fact we glean from copious notes written much later in life is that he learned to speak Latin from his father while still a young child. Pietro was fluent, but that's really not surprising: Latin was the official language of both the civil and ecclesiastical courts of the time.

"When Leonardo was eleven, his father packed him off to the small fishing town of Livorno on the coast to live with his uncle Domenico, who was more of a disciplinarian. He remained there for almost two years, and writes later that he became a changed youth while in his uncle's care. It was here he developed an interest in learning and began showing an aptitude as a painter."

Champlain droned on in the same vein, taking his audience through da Vinci's formative years as an apprentice to Andrea del Verrocchio,

221

the most famous artist and sculptor in Florence at the time, and then went on to cover a boring listing of his early commissioned works.

Noticing he was losing his audience, Alfred picked up the pace. "When he was twenty, Leonardo qualified as a master in the Guild of St. Luke, a rare honor for one so young. He continued to paint until the end of his life, and among his many works are the three he's most famous for: *Virgin of the Rocks*, Louvre Museum (1484); *The Last Supper*, The Monastery of Santa Maria delle Grazie (1485); and *Mona Lisa*, Louvre Museum (1506). Regarding the *Mona Lisa* portrait, his model was presumed to have been a real person named Lisa del Giocondo, the wife of an Italian nobleman and wealthy silk merchant."

Champlain shuffled through his notes, took several swallows of water, and continued. "But I think you gentlemen are naturally more interested in Leonardo da Vinci's scientific endeavors and discoveries which are indeed legion. But before getting to that, am I correct in saying that your young guest was aboard the aircraft carrier for only twelve hours?" He was looking at Blizzard as he asked the question.

"That is correct."

"Then he was a busy boy to have taken in all that he saw in such a short time. Of course, there were airplanes and helicopters, and he even got a ride in one, is that correct?"

Blizzard nodded.

"But he spent most of his time in the hospital, where he must have seen many anatomical charts hanging on the walls of the examination rooms?"

"All true," replied Blizzard.

"Permit me to add something here," Father Caffarone interrupted. "When I took Leonardo back to the mainland in the helicopter, I spotted a medical journal in his pocket and took it from him. He only smiled, gave me a hug, jumped off, turned back to wave once, and disappeared into the night." Caffarone paused, then added in a subdued voice, "but I now think he had secreted other magazines and pictures under his clothes. There was just no time to search him."

Champlain's eyes widened. "Like what other magazines, Commander?"

"Well, I can't find a particular copy of *Popular Mechanics*. It was the *125ᵗʰ Special Anniversary Edition* which was dedicated to the most significant inventions and discoveries of the 20ᵗʰ century. Their first magazine was published back on January 11, 1902, which was more than a year before the Wright Brothers flew their first airplane in December 1903 at Kitty Hawk, and long before Igor Sikorsky flew his first helicopter in 1939. I'm an aviation buff, and it's one of the reasons I've spent most of my career on carriers. Anyway, that particular *Popular Mechanics* issue was chock full of inventions that history tells us were also found among Leonardo's many detailed sketches and copious notebook entries. In fact, there were a couple of pages in that anniversary edition dedicated to Leonard da Vinci and his influence on aviation-related inventions several centuries after his death. I kept it on my desktop, but I'm afraid I haven't been able to find it anywhere since the boy left."

Blizzard paled. "Father Caffarone is right. I remember now that Chief Petty Officer Clarke in Engineering called me on the bridge to say we had a kid stowaway on board and that he was running around holding a medical magazine and a copy of *Popular Mechanics*."

CHAPTER 29

Washington Dc

Wednesday Evening – June 30th

Admiral Christensen took his seat at the head of the conference table, arranged a sheaf of typed notes, cleared his throat, and began to speak.

"Gentlemen, it's been an intense couple of days, and I want you all to know how much I appreciate your input and cooperation with our scientific friends. What you experienced last week in the Mediterranean was a watershed event, but now I must decide where the Navy goes from here." He looked to each officer individually, then continued.

"I informed the Russian ambassador this afternoon that none of you had anything more to add to what you shared with Admiral Gorshkov yesterday evening. I conveyed your deepest sympathies to the Russian Submarine Command for the loss of their brave crew and hoped that we were able to help in some small way to add a sense of closure to the tragedy. In turn, the ambassador asked me to pass along his thanks to all of you. If he thought you were withholding vital information, he kept it hidden." Christensen chose that moment to single out Fleming. "Major, I want to thank you for your solid reasoning earlier which helped convince me that silence about time travel was our best course of action. You might well have prevented an international incident or worse. Good work."

"Thank you, Admiral."

Admiral Christensen selected a second sheet from his stack and placed it on top. "Gentlemen, here are the facts I must consider in order to reach a decision whether or not to go forward or end everything today. I intend to be the devil's advocate for the next few minutes because that's my job, but yours is to convince me I'm wrong."

He looked around the table. "Everyone ready?"

Five nodding heads gave him his answer.

"First, when the *LBJ* returned from the 15th century, for irrefutable proof that no such time-travel took place we need look no further than to her on-board atomic clock. Everyone agrees that the clock showed a loss of signal for two minutes, something that's readily explained. The radio signals beamed down from the multiple cesium and rubidium atomic clocks found aboard all of our GPS satellites get interrupted for many reasons, but are easily reacquired by the receiving stations. It takes about two minutes for a receiver to reset itself to show the current time and date, and life marches on. It happens thousands of times a day, all over the world, which translates to say, *nothing to see here folks; move along.*

"Next, all of the data inputted into the ship's logs via the eLogBook System during the *LBJ's* time back in the 15th century were never recorded. And I'm including all of her deck logs, engineering logs, combat systems logs, as well as those logs which account for daily fuel, oil, and water consumption, which means those entries were never made; ergo, they never existed." He held up his right hand. "I know, I know. Of course, they couldn't have been recorded because satellites didn't exist in the 15th century and neither did the Internet which links the eLogs to the Navy Cloud Storage System. But again, we must stick to the facts, and the facts show there was no interruption in the date-time stampings for any of the entries made by the deck officers on duty, or any of the other logs produced by the other departments on the *LBJ*. I mean, not for one single minute! Gentlemen, that's not just hard to overcome, it's impossible!"

Blizzard interrupted. "But I made contemporaneous entries in my personal daily journal, Admiral, and I referenced all the important happenings that took place during those few days we went back in time. That is hard proof, Sir, because I've added several entries to my journal since last week, which is proof of the uninterrupted continuity of my writings."

CAG raised a hand. "I have a similar written record, Admiral."

Fleming, Birdwell, and Caffarone all nodded that they too had kept individual journals.

CAG pressed ahead with his objection. "Admiral, I personally flew the recce mission up the Italian coast from Rome to Pisa and back to the *LBJ*. Those photos I took are pretty solid evidence that I was flying in the 15th century because that tower at Pisa was standing upright. Photos don't lie, Sir."

Christensen shook his head. "You're wrong, CAG, photos do lie, and that's why no one trusts them anymore. Just look at what they can do in the movies. Audiences get to see cities blown apart in seconds, then rebuilt at lightning speed with the whole thing looking chillingly real. Hollywood filmmakers are today's masters of illusions, but with the help of sophisticated gaming cards, I can create the same razzle-dazzle on my laptop in just a couple of hours. No, I'm afraid not, CAG: those photos would be used against us in a heartbeat."

Blizzard and Gowdy remained silent. They were not about to continue an argument with the admiral when all he was doing was showing them what an uphill battle they faced.

Christensen continued. "Next, let's look for a moment at the *Félicité*. Miles, you told me that the two owners were traveling with ladies who were not their wives. You said that if they were ever to speak out about their treatment in Livorno, you would counter with a telling to the press exactly what you found: a luxury yacht adrift and in distress in the middle of the Mediterranean with a drunken crew and several passengers all exhibiting symptoms of acute drug overdosing. But I tend to agree with you here. We'll never hear from them again, which means no rescue of prisoners about to be burned at the stake ever took place. *Félicité* is another non-starter."

Again, Gowdy chimed in. "What about the two pilots who overflew the town and dropped napalm on several boats in the harbor? They would tell the truth about what they saw and what they did if asked, Admiral."

"Of course they would, CAG," Christensen agreed, "but so what? They flew a mission where they were told to make a couple of low passes and drop napalm cannisters on some derelicts floating in the harbor. And that's all they knew. The mission couldn't have been too important in their eyes because they weren't even armed with air-to-air missiles, an absolute must for every jet flying off a U.S. carrier. No, the Navy would counter that argument saying they were supporting a movie company on location with the Navy's full blessings, and that would be the end that."

"Which brings us to Leonardo," said Father Caffarone. "Too many crew members on the carrier saw him, Admiral. How do we explain him away?"

"We don't. The kid was aboard the *Félicité* when you rendered aid and took the crew and passengers onto the *LBJ*. He was later dropped off at the harbor. End of story."

"So, this whole incident never happened; will that be the finding, Admiral?" Blizzard asked.

"Miles, we must follow the facts, and after a thorough examination of the facts, there's no irrefutable evidence to support your claim of what happened. I'm sorry, but those *are* the facts."

Admiral Christensen now addressed the entire group. "Gentlemen, do I believe you?" he asked. "Of course I do. But a Navy Fact Finding Board of Inquiry would see things differently simply because they would refuse to believe your story from the get-go. Their verdict would be preordained. They would find that you created those diary entries out of whole cloth and that you all colluded to advance a preposterous theory of time travel in order to coverup some serious misdeed you had to keep under wraps. Major Fleming aptly pointed out that the Russians would retaliate after being served such utter nonsense that their submarine had been destroyed in a time-travel mishap. So why would you expect a United States Navy Board to see things differently? The answer is it wouldn't. The Navy has a long history of protecting itself. For proof, you need look no further than the trumped-up charges against General Billy Mitchell in his 1925 court martial trial after accusing the Navy of gross incompetence following a string of helium-filled dirigible crashes and three seaplane losses. The Navy wanted Mitchell muzzled, and convinced the Army Brass to help them. General Mitchell was found guilty on all charges, and the Navy got its pound of flesh. I'm sure you see my point. And even though I can assure you no such intimidation would ever be tolerated under my watch as the CNO, a Navy Board would ask for you be relieved of your commands which would mean the end of your careers. So, without that irrefutable proof, this really is the end of the line, gentlemen, and I'm sorry."

The room was quiet while everyone mulled over the admiral's conclusion. It was devastating to think that this was how the most incredible journey in history would end.

Defeat was on all their faces until Fleming jumped up and rapped on the table for attention. "Admiral, we have irrefutable proof that Leonardo da Vinci was aboard the *LBJ*, and it will absolutely confirm that we did in fact travel back in time."

Everyone turned to look at this Air Force upstart who dared question a verdict from the Chief of Naval Operations. If Christensen was angered by the challenge, it did not show.

"Major, you made a persuasive argument earlier for us to say nothing more to Admiral Gorshkov, and I chose to follow that advice because it was sound. I'm also a believer in the possibility that lightning can strike twice, so, please, tell me what's on your mind. You have permission to speak freely."

"We have all of Leonardo da Vinci's clothes," Fleming replied in a subdued voice.

"What's that?" the admiral asked, looking momentarily confused. "I'm not following you."

Commander Caffarone jumped up. "Major Fleming is right, Admiral! We have Leonardo's clothes. The kid left them behind." Caffarone was now filling with excitement. "When I took him back to shore in the helicopter he was wearing hospital pajamas, a heavy sweater, and wool socks to keep his feet warm. Captain Blizzard told me there was no time to dress him in his own clothes, which means they're still in the ship's laundry. Our irrefutable proof lies in a laundry bag, Sir." He began to laugh loudly and was soon joined by the others.

Admiral Christensen leaned far back in his chair, lost in thought. He drummed his fingertips on the table, then abruptly stopped. "You sure of this?"

"One hundred percent, Admiral," Caffarone replied, the grin still on his face.

"Which means we can carbon date those clothes and prove they're from the 15th century," Christensen mused softly, as if speaking only to himself.

"Yes, Admiral. And remember, those clothes won't be old and threadbare, they'll look and feel like new. They haven't aged because when the boy was wearing them, he was on the *LBJ*, and the carrier was still in the 15th century. In fact, he never left his own century, but his clothes sure did. They were still aboard the *LBJ* when we returned to the present." Caffarone was now beside himself. "This will be as momentous a discovery as the recent report on the newest carbon dating of the *Shroud of Turin*, which proved beyond all doubt that that holy garment was woven in the Middle East sometime between 200 B.C. and 300 A.D., and that its image is that of Christ."

The CNO sat upright, a renewed sense of purpose reflected in his demeanor. "Father Caffarone, I want you to return to the *LBJ* immediately where you will gather up the boy's clothes and personally deliver them back here. And you won't let them out of your sight for even a moment."

"Aye, Aye, Admiral."

Christensen turned to his senior aide who had been buzzed into the room. "Jon, I want you to cut Father Caffarone a set of orders to include priority air travel out to the *LBJ* and to return here with all dispatch. If you have to requisition my plane for the trip, then do so. I want you to have a carbon dating team on standby at the Naval Lab to get to work immediately when those clothes arrive. And, Jon, I need all this like yesterday."

"Understood, Admiral." The aide turned to Caffarone. "Father, please come with me."

Caffarone barely had time to say goodbye to the others, but the grin on his face said it all.

Admiral Christensen rose. "All right, gentlemen, there's nothing more we can do until the good padre returns. I suspect that won't be until Saturday, or maybe Sunday at the earliest, so if any of you want to take a few days leave, do so, but drop off a phone contact number with my office in case I need you back before then. Otherwise, plan on being here first thing Tuesday morning. Enjoy the 4th of July holiday weekend, gentlemen. That will be all."

CHAPTER 30

CHICAGO

Thursday July 1ˢᵗ – Monday, July 5ᵗʰ

"Five whole days, what a wonderful surprise!" Susan had been beside herself at hearing the good news. "Could we go to Chicago and be with mom for the long weekend? She would love to see you."

Fleming had laughed. "Sure, but it might be next to impossible getting plane tickets because of the long holiday."

Susan waved off the objection. "Leave it to me. We need to pack and be ready to Uber over to either Reagan or Dulles Airports. Let's order breakfast from room service, that way we won't waste any time."

Four hours later they were seated in first-class on American Airlines and cruising at thirty-six thousand feet somewhere over Indiana. When Fleming had protested the cost, Susan had brushed aside his concern. "David, you must learn to accept the fact that I am wealthy. I appreciate you wanting to be careful with our spending, but there are times when having a little discretionary income is good. This is one of those times, so indulge me."

They were met at O'Hare Airport by the same chauffeured Bentley and whisked to the mansion on Lake Michigan. Theresa Renninger had been tied up all day with meetings, but joined them for dinner.

She now dabbed at her lips, put down her napkin, and beamed at them both. "What a wonderful surprise, I still can't believe you're actually here." She tuned to her daughter. "Why didn't you tell me? I would have changed my schedule and met you at the airport."

"Because I wanted it to be a surprise, *silly!*"

Theresa turned to her son-in-law. "Dave, I can offer you an after dinner brandy, but I draw the line at any thought of having cigars in the library."

"Neither, thank you." He sat back, contented, and laughed at the thought of the two of them puffing away in the oak-paneled library. "If I ate like this all the time I would soon weigh three hundred pounds, and my beautiful wife would divorce me for a younger model."

"I'll make sure that doesn't happen," Theresa replied, "but I must warn you, we will be hosting a special gathering on the Fourth, and there'll be tons of sinfully good food. It's been a tradition for the past fifteen years, and you'll have an opportunity to meet some interesting guests. Anyway, what have you two got planned for the next few days?"

"Absolutely nothing," they said in unison, and laughed.

"Dave's been super busy, Mom. His flying schedule has been brutal, so he wants to chill out. And *I'm* going to make every minute count just being with my man."

The days whizzed by, and before Fleming knew it, Monday was here, and their flight back to Washington was scheduled for six that evening. Theresa had been subdued during breakfast.

The gathering of guests the day before had been everything the mother had promised. Fleming had met two U.S. senators, a governor, four presidents of Fortune 500 companies, two whom he recognized on sight, and a score of other interesting people. What truly impressed him was seeing for himself how genuinely liked Theresa Henninger was by all. Theirs was not a fawning to curry favor: these people were truly her friends.

She now reached across the table and took hold of their hands. "Susan, Dave, I need to talk to you about something ..."

"Oh, God, Mom, what's wrong?" a wide-eyed Susan asked in a dread-filled whisper. *"You're dying!"*

"No, no, child. I'm sorry if I startled you. I'm as healthy as the proverbial horse, but I do need to discuss an important issue and now seemed the best time to do so."

Both waited with bated breath.

"I'll be turning sixty on my next birthday," she began, "and the time has come for me to prepare a plan for Rentran Industries to prosper under the next generation's leadership. As you know, the company currently operates three manufacturing plants: two here in the U.S., and one in Taiwan. Because of the ever-increasing demand for electric vehicles worldwide, we'll be adding a fourth soon, probably in Brazil, and a fifth, most likely in Germany. EVs are no longer a fad; they're here to stay. But let me digress for just a moment. You would think a manufacturing plant belonged in China, but I decided against doing just that several years ago, and my instinct proved right. You see, the Chinese took my transmissions, reversed engineered them, and began producing cheap knock-offs even though I had patent protection, or so I thought. I learned the hard way that China does not honor patents, or any other intellectual property rights for that matter, but I was not about to get into a protracted, costly, legal battle with a sovereign nation."

She paused for a sip of orange juice, then continued. "For a few years China dominated the markets in Asia by underpricing Rentran through massive government subsidies that is, until their Achilles heel was exposed. Their transmissions were not only unreliable, but they were also downright dangerous. Injuries and deaths became commonplace in EVs using their transmissions and, within a couple of years, no manufacturer anywhere would buy a transmission made in China. Our plant in Taiwan was soon flooded with orders, so much so, it is now our largest. Rentran employs just shy of thirteen thousand associates worldwide, and I expect to double that number within three years. But I'm very concerned that China has designs on invading Taiwan, probably sooner than later, so I'm actively looking to build a plant somewhere else in the region. Lastly, I've been mulling over the idea of taking the company public. It's a long, difficult process which requires intimate knowledge of the many SEC rules and regulations one must adhere to for an Initial Public Offering (IPO) to pass muster. All of which leads me to this."

She now looked directly at Fleming. "I know you love your life as an Air Force pilot, and the adage *the sky's the limit* was coined just for you. Chances are very good you will retire as a general officer, no small feat in today's competitive military." Theresa paused for a few moments, then said, "But I would like you to consider an alternative."

She correctly read his face. "I know, Dave, believe me I know, but please hear me out. What I'm asking is this: Would you consider coming to work for Rentran Industries? You are certainly well qualified. You have a mechanical engineering degree from the Air Force Academy and an aeronautical engineering master's from Purdue. In two years, possibly less, I could teach you everything you would need to know to run this company. But most of all, I would love to see Susan's father's dream of Rentran becoming a true family dynasty, something akin to the Ford's, a family he so admired." She paused to look at her daughter. "By then you will have started a family, giving me the grandchildren that I promise you both I'll spoil rotten."

Her ensuing chuckle broke the ice. "Dave, I'm not asking for an answer today, tomorrow, or even next month. I only ask that the two of you talk about it, weigh the pros and cons, and discuss how it would impact your chosen career path. Just think about it, all right?"

Fleming sat in silence for a long moment, then said, "Theresa, I promise we will weigh your offer with the utmost care. Your generosity and your confidence in my abilities is humbling, and so you deserve no less. We will not keep you hanging. I promise, you will have an answer much sooner than later. And all I can say is thank you."

CHAPTER 31

WASHINGTON DC

TUESDAY Morning, July 6th

The small group of officers led by Admiral Christensen welcomed back a visibly tired Commander Caffarone, whose wide grin spoke volumes. The trip had been a resounding success, but Caffarone had even better news to tell.

"Admiral, we've hit a home run."

"Really, Padre? I'm all ears, tell me more."

"When I got back on board the *LBJ* and went to collect Leonardo's clothes, I was told by a laundry technician that they hadn't been washed yet and were still sitting in a laundry bag stashed away in some corner. I found the bag, wrapped it in plastic, then sealed it good and tight. It never left my side until I handed it over to a lieutenant at the Research Lab and made sure he signed a receipt for it."

Admiral Christensen interrupted with a fist pump and a loud, "*Hallelujah!*" He understood immediately the enormity of Caffarone's revelation. "*Now* you've brought me something I can really sink my teeth into." He turned to Blizzard and asked, "Can you guess where I'm going with this, Miles?"

"Indeed I can, Admiral. You're thinking we now have the boy's DNA in those dirty clothes, plus God only knows what other nasty 15th century creepy crawlies which might be hiding in that bag as well.

Father Caffarone has returned with a treasure trove that will keep our scientists busy for years, but best of all: We now have irrefutable proof that we journeyed back in time, just as we've been saying all along. So, yeah, I'll be adding my Hallelujah to yours!"

Everyone broke out in applause.

Admiral Christensen held up a hand to signal that he wasn't quite finished. He turned again to Father Caffarone. "The radiocarbon dating process started immediately after you delivered Leonardo's clothes to the U.S. Naval Research Laboratory. The initial tests take fourteen days to complete. The lieutenant I spoke with was the same one you had sign the receipt, and he went on to explain how carbon-14 would be converted to carbon-12, or maybe it was the other way around, I'm really not sure. He also spoke about the possibility of using or producing nitrogen-13, and then he tossed around a lot of fancy words such as gas proportional counting, spectroscopy, and infrared light. I had no idea what he was talking about, but if he was just trying to impress me with his scientific mumbo-jumbo, he definitely succeeded!"

The group laughed politely.

"But on a more serious note," Christensen continued, "having the boy's clothing to carbon date and his DNA to analyze will convince even the most skeptical soul that the *LBJ* journeyed through a time-portal back to the Middle Ages. Of course, we'll also continue with the thorough examination of the damaged Hornet to determine just how much it too, had aged, but I'm told that report could take up to a year to complete. I was also informed on Saturday that each of you will be required to undergo annual medical exams at Walter Reed Hospital for the next five years, possibly longer. That's to see if there are any long-term effects of such a journey on the human body, whether or not you were officially believed. The concern that maybe something happened to you is very real because we know for a fact that those healthy young flyers died as old men within hours of landing on the *LBJ*. No one can deny that something horrific took place that day. Unfortunately, we'll never really know what happened to that Russian submarine and its crew, but I'd wager all of your money, Miles, they were doomed by a similar set of circumstances. Anyway, our work is finished here, at least for the moment. It's my intention to approach the President and National Security Council as soon as we get the DNA results back, with a recommendation to ask Congress to fund a Black Ops Department to see if your time travel excursion can be duplicated. It will remain a top secret project because we cannot tip our hand to our adversaries to show that we are taking the whole idea of time travel seriously. In terms of national security, this is now a more important undertaking than the *Project Blue Book* of the nineteen fifties, or even that underwhelming June 2021 Pentagon Report on *Unidentified Aerial Phenomenon*. And lastly, I promise to get word to each of you regarding the carbon dating, and the DNA results from Leonardo's clothes as soon as I get them. The information will come in the form of an innocuous email, but you'll easily understand its meaning. Any questions?"

The five officers shook their heads.

"Miles, Sean, Padre, you need to get back to the *LBJ*, and you too, Commander Birdwell," Christensen said, then turned to Fleming. "Do you know the word *shanghaied*?"

Fleming wondered where such a question was leading. "To force a landlubber to join a ship's crew against his will, Admiral. I don't think that practice has been in vogue for more than a century now."

Admiral Christensen laughed. "Wrong about being out of vogue because I'm about to *Shanghai* you ... but only with your approval, CAG," he quickly added.

"Aye, Admiral, he's all yours to *shanghai*, but I must warn you, the lad's not well-versed in Navy ways. However, I do believe he's trainable."

"Thank you, CAG." Christensen turned back to face Fleming, now wearing a more serious mien. "Major, I want you to come work with me on another special project I have in mind. I got a green light from my Air Force counterpart, General Adrian McFarland, to *shanghai* you, but your acceptance really must be freely made. If you decide to decline, there will be no repercussions, I can assure you of that. But I was impressed with your actions regarding the entire time-travel encounter. Both Captain Blizzard and Captain Gowdy told me of your logical and persuasive reasoning for wanting to wait until nightfall to be picked up so as not to terrify the locals with the appearance of a helicopter. And here last week, it was you who came up with the idea of bringing Leonardo da Vinci's clothes from the LBJ for analysis. Those lab results will be used as the nexus for how the Navy will proceed in studying this phenomenon. Anyway, I would like you to think it over and give me your decision by Thursday. Unfortunately, I can't tell you anything more until then. Agreed?"

"Yes, Admiral, and thank you. You will have my decision by Thursday."

CHAPTER 32

The Following December

It wouldn't be correct to say she heard it first because he never heard it at all. Bolting upright, she covered her ears to shut out the offending clamor. After what seemed like an eternity, she reached across his sleeping figure and brought a hand down on top of the alarm clock. She found the light switch and snapped it on. What noise couldn't accomplish; light did. His breathing stopped, and an arm reached up in reflex action to guard his eyes against the enemy.

"Five o'clock, Dave," she whispered. "Are you sure you've got to go?" A moment passed and she added, her voice wheedling, 'Couldn't you call in sick or something?"

"Fat chance, but nice try," he mumbled. A few seconds passed. "Why am I having a déjà vu moment? I'm pretty sure I heard that same argument somewhere before. He began laughing, then turned to face his wife. "Honey, it's just my drill weekend with the Florida Air Guard. I need two more flights to the Avon Park Gunnery Range to close out this year's flying requirements. Which means it's time for *moi* to shake the lead out. This boy must get his butt to Florida, and *pronto!*" Fleming jumped out of bed and headed for the kitchen to start the coffee maker.

Five busy months had passed since that last meeting with Admiral Christensen, and in the interim, Fleming's life had taken a 180 degree turn. He had informed the admiral of his decision not to come work for him, explaining how he had made the hard choice to leave active

239

duty in order to help in the family business. The out-processing procedure had taken three weeks, but in that short time he had secured a slot to fly the new F-15EX Eagle II with the Florida Air National Guard's 125th Wing stationed at Jacksonville International Airport. Lady Luck had been most kind and had dealt him four aces. He had snagged a rare pilot slot that had suddenly opened up, beating out a dozen other equally qualified pilots who had also cast their hats into that very small ring.

On his last day, he received a cryptic email from Admiral Christensen confirming the authenticity of Leonardo da Vinci's clothing. The DNA tests would take longer. He included a simple sentence which Fleming immediately likened to lightning in a bottle. Their guest lecturer expert, Alfred Champlain, had searched Italian genealogical records at Admiral Christensen's request and had identified thirty-five living people related to Leonardo da Vinci, including the internationally acclaimed film star, Angela Caprini.

The admiral was right. This was the gamechanger. Time travel was real.

Fleming finished his coffee, then called out to his wife. "I told the guys I won't be hanging around for the Christmas party Sunday evening, so I should be home by dinnertime."

"I'm glad you're not staying that extra day, Dave." They were expecting a baby girl in early April, and oftentimes laughed together at the thought of Theresa being more excited than they were. "Oh, I just remembered," she added, "your renewal passport came yesterday, so you're all set for the January trip to Taiwan with mother. This'll be the first time she'll have company going overseas." Susan walked into the kitchen, wrapped her arms around his waist, and squeezed. "No regrets about leaving the Air Force to go work with mom?"

Fleming squeezed back. "Absolutely none. I'm learning the ropes from the *numero uno* boss in the business, and you've got to admit, I now have the best of both worlds. I get to fly fast movers with the Florida Guard every month, and I'm married to the love of my life. What more could a guy ask for?"

"And I'm happy too." She pulled away just enough to look up at his face. "It's strange how those horrible nightmares literally stopped the day you told me you were going to accept mom's offer. I had thought it was your flying that had me nervous and upset, but I was wrong. I don't worry about your training weekends flying with the new squadron, but for some reason that I'll never understand, I was terrified every minute you were with the Navy." She flashed her most radiant smile.

Fleming hoisted a flight bag to his shoulder, winked at his wife, and Susan winked back.

EPILOGUE

Seven months later – The following July 4th

The morning of July 4th found Fleming cradling his newborn daughter in front of the large screen TV, his full attention directed to the sleeping child. The announcer's sudden change in tone made him look up.

"We now turn to our CNN correspondent in Tokyo for an update on a very bizarre story coming to us from the South China Sea. What new information do you have, Lindsey?"

"Josh, this is getting stranger by the hour, but here's what we do know. Twelve hours ago, the British luxury liner, *SS Princess Royal*, vanished with all 1800 passengers and crew. The ship was en-route from Da Nang in Vietnam to Manilla in The Philippines. The last radio contact with the *Princess Royal* was a routine ship-to-shore satellite call to the company's home office in London. She reported localized heavy fog, and said she was encountering minor intermittent failures with some of the ship's radar, navigation, and communications systems. However, the captain said he expected everything to be back to normal within a few minutes. And, now, nothing has been heard from her since."

Fleming silently handed the sleeping child to Susan and stood transfixed in front of the TV.

"Coast Guard assets from all of the countries in the region have been alerted, and a search is already underway. We've been told that Admiral Christensen, he's the Chief of Naval Operations in the U.S., has taken a personal interest in this. He has ordered the Seventh Fleet to dispatch the *Ford Strike Group* sailing in the area to render all assistance by using its very impressive resources. Let me conclude by saying there is no suspicion of foul play, at least not for the moment, but it's worth mentioning that tensions between Great Britain and China have been close to a boiling point since early June. And one final note. A Qantas Airline pilot flying at 38,000 feet in the area at the time, reported seeing an extremely bright green flash on the horizon, but no one is suggesting there is a correlation between that and the disappearance of the *Princess Royal*. Josh, I will be staying with this story and update our viewers as more information becomes available. Now, back to you in New York for the rest of the news."

"Are you OK, Dave?" Susan Fleming asked as she switched off the TV, her voice reflecting genuine concern. "You look like you've seen a ghost. Did you know anyone aboard that ship?"

Fleming shook his head. "No, no, I didn't." He stared at the darkened screen for several seconds while conjuring up a vivid picture of the *Princess Royal* sailing alongside the *LBJ* for several carefree minutes a year earlier in the Med. He now wondered if maybe some sort of a cosmic fusion of time and space had been exchanged during that encounter.

An ashen-faced Fleming turned to his wife. "I'm getting some really bad vibes about what we just saw and heard, babe. I'm afraid the *Princess Royal* is never going to be found."

THE END

Thank you for reading my book. I hope you enjoyed it as much as I did writing it. Would you please consider leaving a review at Amazon? Even just a few words would be helpful to other readers.. Warm regards, and thank you in advance. Ian A. O'Connor

About The Author

I an A. O'Connor is a retired Air Force colonel who has held several senior military leadership positions in the field of national security management. His novel, *The Twilight of the Day*, was a military-themed thriller which received high praise in the *Military Times* for its realism and chilling story line. The book was awarded a Bronze Medal by the Military Writers Society of America.

It was soon followed with the first printing of *The Seventh Seal* by Winterwolf Publishing Company, which introduced Ian's readers to retired FBI agent Justin Scott.

Both books were re-released in May 2015.

His second book in the Justin Scott thriller series, *The Barbarossa Covenant*, was first printed in August 2015.

The next novel, *The Wrong Road Home*, was published by Pegasus Publishing & Entertainment Group in March 2016.

Ian is the co-author of *SCRAPPY: A Memoir of a U.S. Fighter Pilot*, published by McFarland & Company in April 2008 to rave reviews.

Colonel O'Connor also holds an FAA commercial pilot's certificate with single engine and multi-engine ratings.

He is a member of the *Air Commando Association*, an associate member of *The Red River Valley Fighter Pilots Association*, the *Mystery Writers of America*, and lives on Florida's Treasure Coast with his wife, Candice.

Visit Ian at: www.ianaoconnor.com
Contact Ian at: ianaoconnor@ianaoconnor.com

Pegasus Publishing & Entertainment Group

CPSIA information can be obtained
at www.ICGtesting.com
Printed in the USA
LVHW020927191021
700836LV00002B/56